PRAISE FOR ROBIN PAIGE'S
VICTORIAN MYSTERIES

"I read it with enjoyment ... I found myself burning for the injustice of it, and caring what happened to the people"—*Anne Perry*

"I couldn't put it down"—*Murder & Mayhem*

"An intriguing mystery ... Skillfuly unravelled" —Jean Hager, author of *Blooming Murder*

"Absolutely riveting ... An extremely articulate, genuine mystery, with well-drawn, compelling character" —*Meritorious Mysteries*

"An absolutely charming book ... An adventure worth reading ... You're sure to enjoy it"—*Romantic Times*

THE *Victorian Mystery* SERIES
6

Death at WHITECHAPEL

ROBIN PAIGE

SOUTH
DOWNS
CRIME &
MYSTERY

First published in the UK in 2016
by South Downs CRIME & MYSTERY,
an imprint of The Crime & Mystery Club Ltd,
PO Box 394, Harpenden,
Herts, AL5 1XJ, UK
Reprinted 2107

www.crimeandmystery.club

© Susan Wittig Albert and Bill Albert, 2016

The right of Susan Wittig Albert and Bill Albert to be identified as the
author of this work has been asserted in accordance with the Copyright,
Designs and Patents Act 1988.

All rights reserved. No part of this book may be reproduced, stored in or
introduced into a retrieval system, or transmitted, in any form or by any
means (electronic, mechanical, photocopying, recording or otherwise)
without the written permission of the publishers.
Any person who does any unauthorised act in relation to this publication
may be liable to criminal prosecution and civil claims for damages. A
CIP catalogue record for this book is available from the British Library.

This is a work of fiction. Names, characters, places, and incidents either
are the product of the author's imagination or are used fictitiously,
and any resemblance to actual persons, living or dead, businesses,
companies, events or locales is entirely coincidental.

ISBN
978-0-85730-023-2 (print)
978-0-85730-024-9 (epub)

Typeset in 11.5pt Palatino
by Avocet Typeset, Somerton, Somerset TA11 6RT

Printed in Great Britain by Clays Ltd, St Ives plc

ACKNOWLEDGMENTS

We are grateful to Ruby Hild and her late husband, Ron Hild, who introduced us to Dedham, the River Stour, and the beauties of Essex. Thanks, too, to the legion of Ripperologists without whose diligent research and imaginative speculations we could not have devised this plot. And thanks, as well, to the loyal readers who have encouraged us in the creation of these historical mysteries.

Robin Paige
aka Bill and Susan Albert

CAST OF CHARACTERS

Lord Charles Sheridan, Baron of Somersworth

Lady Kathryn Ardleigh Sheridan, Baroness of
   Somersworth and mistress of Bishop's Keep

Jennie Jerome Churchill, Lady Randolph Churchill

Lieutenant Winston Churchill, Jennie's older son

George Cornwallis-West, Jennie's lover

Manfred Raeburn, managing editor of *The Anglo-Saxon
   Review*

Frederick Abberline, Detective Inspector, Scotland
   Yard (retired)

Walter Sickert, artist, Number 13 Robert Street

Bradford Marsden, master of Marsden Manor

Mr. Hodge, butler, Bishop's Keep

Sarah Pratt, cook, Bishop's Keep

Mary Plumm, kitchen maid, Bishop's Keep

Dick Pratt, Sarah's husband

1

"Dearest this is the only subject on which we ever fall out. If you only realised how little I have, & how impossible it is for me to get any more. I have raised all I can, & I assure you unless something extraordinary turns up I see ruin staring me in the face."

LADY RANDOLPH CHURCHILL
to Winston Spencer Churchill
5 March, 1897

35A Great Cumberland Place, London
3 October, 1898

JENNIE CHURCHILL OPENED the drawer of her writing desk and took out an envelope. Her mouth taut, dark brows pulled together, she counted the notes, feeling an enormous resentment, then sealed the envelope and addressed it, fiercely, to A. Byrd. She was done with it—until the next time.

The small black pug at her feet roused and looked up at her with an anxious expression, as if to ask what the matter was. The next time! Jennie picked up the little dog and held it close, rocking back and forth. "How much longer can this terrible thing go on, Caro?" she whispered. "And what in heaven's name shall I do if he asks for even more? How can I—"

There was a rap at the door, and it opened. A slender young man wearing the dress uniform of the 21st Lancers stood in the doorway, stick in one hand, helmet under his arm.

"Hello, Mama," he said.

"Darling boy!" Jennie cried. She put the pug down and leaped to her feet, holding out her arms. "What a *relief*!"

"Dearest Mama!" Winston threw aside his helmet and stick, strode across the carpet. "How wonderful to see your face at last!"

The two could scarcely have looked at each other, however, so close was their embrace. Eventually, this emotional greeting gave way to holding each other at arm's length, each exclaiming how marvelous the other looked, then returning to the embrace again, and to more exclamations and more tears. After a time—a *very* long time—they seated themselves on the sofa, still quite close together. They made a striking pair: the son not yet twenty-four years of age, pale, with thin reddish-brown hair and his father's protuberant eyes; the dark, elegant mother, astoundingly youthful at forty-four and renowned as one of the great beauties of England.

"I cannot tell you, my dear, dear Winston," Jennie said gravely, "how frightened I have been for you." She pushed her heavy dark hair away from her face with a shudder. "Omdurman—even the name conjures up fears. The news of the attack was in *The Times* on that

Friday. I waited all through the day, and the next, for your telegram, which didn't arrive until after luncheon on Sunday. Lady Grenfell sent word that the offensive against the fort had been successful and that we had suffered no casualties, but you can imagine my state." She shook her head, making a wry face. "And to think how hard I worked to get around General Kitchener and get you posted to Egypt. And then, at the last, you had to pay your own expenses! I know it was your heart's desire, but if anything had happened to you, I should have blamed myself."

"To be sure, Mama." Winston smiled. "You left no wire unpulled and no cutlet uncooked to put me into the Expeditionary Force. I shall be eternally grateful to you for giving me my chance to join a significant action. But you know my luck in these things. At Omdurman, I was under fire all day and survived without a scratch, not even a rip in my sleeve."

"Thank God for that," Jennie said.

Winston made a dramatic gesture. "I am sorry to say, however, that I shot five men, perhaps seven—although out of ten thousand dead Dervishes I don't suppose my effort signifies. We lost only five officers and sixty-five men, but Colonel Rhodes was wounded and poor Hubert Howard was killed with a friendly shell. You cannot gild war. All the raw shows through." He smiled faintly. "But I intend to settle down to writing another history—*The War for the Waterway*, I am calling it. You can read all the glorious details there."

"I can wait," Jennie said. "War is not my favorite subject—although of course, dear boy, I am all for *anything* you write, as you well know." She patted his hand with a proud smile. "Your dispatches for

11

Borthwick in the *Morning Post* have caught everyone's eye, although I daresay General Kitchener is mightily miffed at your having written them. Your story of *The Malakand Field Force* has sold six thousand copies and is still strong, especially in India, where Lady Curzon says it is read by all the officers. Your agent, Mr. Watt, has sent you an accounting—it appears that you have already earned over three hundred pounds in royalties."

"Three hundred pounds!" Winston's smile was rueful. "That's more than I would receive in four years as a subaltern, and the writing was done in a few weeks. As for Kitchener, I don't care a fig for what he thinks of the *Post* dispatches. The glorious victory at Omdurman was disgraced by the slaughter of the wounded, for which he alone must be held to account. He may be a general, but never a gentleman." The smile became a grumbling laugh. "In that direction lies my future, Mama—not in the sword, but in pen and in politics, speaking the truth as frankly and fully as is possible."

"I don't know about the truth," Jennie said, "but I have no doubt about your political future. You have heard me say many times how anxious I am to see you in the Commons, taking up where your father left off."

She paused, thinking of Randolph and what had gone into the envelope, and how much it cost her to defend him, not for his sake, certainly—she would not have lifted a finger to save her dead husband's reputation—but for Winston's. She would stop at nothing—*nothing*!—to enable Winston to fulfill the promise of leadership she knew he possessed. He knew this, but he also needed to know that she counted on him to help.

"I am very glad to see you earning something by your writing," she said quietly. "I don't suppose it's necessary to remind you that every shilling is wanted. I fear that we are in dire straits."

There was a moment's silence. Winston bit his lip, while Jennie reflected on the grim truth of her words. Randolph had died nearly three years before, leaving an estate of some seventy-five thousand pounds. After his debts were paid, the remainder was put in trust for the boys, Winston and Jack. Although Jennie had been Randolph's wife for twenty years, she had received precious little—only the horses, the household goods, and a meager five hundred pounds a year. It was all she would ever get of the Marlborough millions, for the old duchess would leave no more than a token to Jennie, whose American forthrightness she had never appreciated, or Jennie's boys, of whom she was none too fond. Randolph's slim legacy, added to the annual ten thousand dollars Jennie received from the rental of her father's Manhattan mansion, was her entire income. For a woman in upper-class British society with two sons to support, it was not nearly enough to keep up appearances, much less do the other things Jennie wanted to do.

But Jennie was determined that no one—except her solicitor Lumley, and Winston, of course—should know the extent of her financial woes. She had taken a house in Great Cumberland Place, only a few blocks from Hyde Park, a fine seven-story house of Georgian design, albeit on the wrong side of Oxford Street, which somewhat reduced the cost. She had planned to economize on the furnishings and refurbishments, but the whole thing had needed painting, and hot water and electric light, the cost of which was appalling. Equally appalling was the cost of the multitude of servants required to staff the place and manage the dinner parties for which she had always been famous. And then there had been that deplorable business with Cruikshank, the fraud who had swindled her and her sisters out of more than four thousand pounds. The miserable wretch had been sent off to jail—eight years at hard labor—but not before he had spent all the money on fine living, making recovery impossible.

Jennie's financial situation was so precarious that she had not even been able to pay Winston's allowance into the bank, and several of his checks had been dishonored. But of course he was as careless of his finances as she was of hers. In India he had lived far beyond the five hundred pounds he got from her and the fourteen shillings a day the Army paid him, and visited the native moneylenders on a quite regular basis.

Winston pushed his lips in and out. "I did hope," he said, after a long silence, "that the loan Lumley arranged should have made things more comfortable for you." He spoke carefully, not quite looking at her.

Jennie felt herself tense. At the beginning of the year, she had been forced to take out a loan for seventeen thousand pounds. Seventeen thousand! The size of the debt, and the impossibility of repaying even a small portion of it—still filled her with enormous anxiety. But equally hard was the rift the thing had caused between her and Winston. She had told him she needed the money to repay her many smaller notes and to settle some urgent dressmaker's and jeweler's bills—almost the whole truth, but not quite. He had taken the matter quite hard, for Lumley had unfortunately arranged the business so that Winston was required to guarantee seven hundred a year. The unfavorable contract wasn't

Lumley's fault, of course. Her credit with the banks was so *very* bad, and she had already borrowed what she could from her friends.

Now Winston turned his head to look directly at her, and she saw that his pale eyes were hard as marbles. They reminded her, unhappily, of his father's eyes. "I hoped," he repeated, "that the loan should have made you more comfortable, Mama."

Jennie's hands fluttered and she clasped them in her lap. "Oh, it has," she said quickly. Now was the time to tell him about the photograph and those miserable letters, before he distracted himself with the many projects he had arranged to undertake on his return. "But I am afraid that something has arisen that I could not have anticipated when I—"

"Are you speaking of *Maggie*?" Winston asked in a cautionary tone. "You should not consider the magazine *your* financial obligation, you know. You are to be the editor, not an investor. Not a penny of your money should go into it." *Maggie* was the sobriquet that one of Jennie's friends had given to her latest undertaking—a quarterly literary journal.

"No, not of *Maggie*," Jennie said. "I have hired a managing editor who is raising the necessary funds. No, there is something else." She cleared her throat nervously. "I'm afraid I must tell you that—"

"Listen to me, Mama." Winston spoke in a firm, measured tone. "You and I are both spendthrift and extravagant and neither of us pays the proper sort of attention to money. But—and I say this in all sympathy, my darling, and not at all in anger—in comparison to your follies, my own are quite trifling. I may squander a few hundred on a pony, or rare books, or a dozen bottles of fine Scotch. But you are utterly suicidal in your expenditures. You must have lost a thousand pounds or more at the races at Goodwood."

Jennie frowned. She loved her son dearly, but when he climbed onto his high horse and began to lecture her, he was really quite insufferable. "This is not the time for you to preach to me on extravagance, Winston," she replied sharply. "The current difficulty is not of my making, and it has enormous consequences for you."

Winston did not appear to have heard her. "I am sorry to be so blunt, Mama, but someone must say it. You have brought us to the brink. If this constant financial drain continues, we will surely be ruined, and our peace and contentment will be ended forever."

Then, his mouth relaxing, smiling the shy, boyish smile that always charmed Jennie, he added, "But the soldiers are home from the wars, dearest, and this should be a day of celebration! We shall put this wretched business aside and amuse ourselves. Is Jack in town? Is there a small dinner party somewhere tonight where I might pick up a few shreds of political gossip? I am speaking again at Bradford in a few days, and I should very much like to appear in the know." His smile became wistful. "How I wish, oh how I *wish*, Mama, that dear Papa could have heard me speak there in July. I was listened to with the greatest of attention for over an hour, and there was really a very great deal of enthusiasm, people mounting their chairs and applauding me. It was enormously gratifying."

Jennie sat back, thinking. Perhaps this was not the time to tell him about the bank notes in the envelope, or where they were going, or why. Perhaps it was not fair to seek her son's help in resolving this ugly business.

He was so full of political ambitions and his plans for another book, so aglow with the promise of his future. No, he was not the person to help her think how to put a stop to this dreadful affair.

But then who? Certainly not dear Jack—he was too young, and just beginning to find his feet. But the burden was so great that she could not bear it alone much longer. Perhaps, shameful as the matter was, she should share it with the Prince. The connection between Randolph and HRH had been strong to the end. Indeed, Bertie supported Winston's ambitions and had promised to help him in every way possible. The thought of it gave her a new hope. Yes, she would talk with the Prince, and save Winston the trauma of knowing her secret—at least for now.

She smiled tightly. "Your brother has gone off with Ernest Cassel on some sort of business. But the Sheridans are in town and have invited a very small group to Sibley House for dinner. Lord Charles will be glad to hear your reports. He asked me about you just the other day."

"Sheridan? Ah, that great anomaly, a liberal lord." Winston smiled a worldly smile and put his hand on his hip, his elbow jutting out in the style he had copied from his father. "I heard that he was in the Sudan in the eighties—had quite a time there, in fact—so we can exchange reminiscences. Did you know that his wife is the pen behind those pseudonymous Bardwell stories you fancy? A female Conan Doyle, or so she is being called."

"It is a well-deserved compliment," Jennie said. "Lady Charles and I are discussing the possibility of her writing something for *Maggie*'s first issue. A story from her is sure to attract readers."

"Well, then." Winston stood. "I'll just go and see if Walden has finished unpacking my gear. I have one or two little presents for you."

"And I shall send Lady Charles a note and let her know that you will be coming," Jennie said, making up her mind. "She won't object—she is delightfully informal." She glanced at Winston out of the corner of her eye. "George Cornwallis-West is escorting me, since of course I had no idea when you would manage to get home."

Winston paused on his way to the door. "George, heh?" Jennie could tell that he was making an effort, albeit not a very successful one, to screen the disapproval from his voice. "Since you hadn't mentioned him recently in your letters, I thought that perhaps the two of you were no longer..." His lips tightened.

Jennie, who did not intend to let her son tell her who she might take as a lover, let the silence lengthen. "Winston, my dear," she said at last, "you can't possibly suppose that I tell you *everything* that is happening in my life?"

2

"Our duty is to be useful, not according to our desires but according to our powers."

HENRI FREDERIC AMIEL
Journal

"England expects that every man will do his duty."

HORATIO, LORD NELSON
at the Battle of Trafalgar

Sibley House, London
3 October, 1898

KATE SHERIDAN HURRIEDLY wrote a few lines, folded and sealed the note, and handed it to the footman.

"To Lady Randolph," she said. "In Number 35 Great Cumberland Place. And ask Parsons to lay another place, please. We will be seven at dinner."

As the footman went off, Charles looked up from his newspaper. They were in the library, in Kate's opinion the only habitable room in Sibley House, the grand Mayfair mansion that was part of Charles's ancestral heritage. Kate much preferred her own home, Bishop's Keep, and spent as much time there as possible, coming to London—and to Sibley House—only when it was necessary.

"So young Churchill is back from the wars," Charles remarked. "I suppose he is already writing a new book to tell us all about Omdurman. I quite enjoyed his report on the Indian campaign, though. He is a precocious boy."

"He's hardly a boy," Kate objected. She picked up a book containing one of Wilkie Collins's mysteries and went to sit by the fire. A damp, chill fog, thick with the coal smoke of London chimney pots, had settled into the streets. She was glad they were leaving the next day for East Anglia, where the sun shone and a few roses still bloomed in her garden. She settled into her chair, thinking of Winston and of the relief Lady Randolph must feel now that her son was safely home from the Egyptian campaign. "That young man has been in some quite deadly battles."

"To hear him tell it, at least," Charles said dryly. He grinned. "But his adventures will be popular with the Tory working men, which I suppose is what he has in mind by writing those letters for the *Morning Post*. One suspects that he is already in the running for a seat in the Commons."

"Charles," Kate said, in some surprise. "I thought you admired Winston."

"So I do, more or less," Charles replied. "He has zeal and ambition and a great future—although I can't agree with his Conservative politics. But why does he have to be in such an infernal hurry to make a name for himself?" Answering his own question, he said, "It's his mother's American blood, I suppose, that gives him that indomitable spirit." He raised his paper and from behind it, added, "You have the same fire. That's what so infuriates Mama, you know. If you gave in now and then, you might win the old lady over."

"I doubt it," Kate said, with a laugh that was half a sigh. "I could give in to your mother's demands from now until the Resurrection, but that wouldn't alter the fact that *my* mother was Irish."

Charles chuckled. "Mama can think as she likes," he replied, still behind the newspaper. "It won't alter the fact that I love you—American, Irish, whatever you are."

"And I you, my dear," Kate said softly, "all that you are." Her husband rarely spoke of his feelings, and she treasured the moments when he opened his heart.

She sat back and opened her book but her glance lingered on the fire instead of the page. When she fell in love with Charles, she had been twenty-seven and a spinster, accustomed to living her own life and earning her own living. Her inheritance of her aunts' estate and manor house had strengthened her independence, as had the financial and literary success of the stories she wrote under the pen name of Beryl Bardwell. Whether it was her Irish blood, or her upbringing in a New York City working-class family, or the financial freedom she had gained with her pen, Kathryn Ardleigh Sheridan was her own woman, and her mother-in-law, the dowager Lady Somersworth, could not forgive her for it.

For a time, Lady Somersworth's stern disapproval had made Kate unhappy, for she had hoped to be close to Charles's mother. In the last eighteen months, though, this difficulty had been overshadowed by another: her loss of the child she carried and the doctor's announcement that she could never again conceive. Now, even that darkness was fading, for Charles had made it clear that he did not long for a child, that he was quite content that their marriage be exactly as it was. Anyway, Kate had satisfying work of her own to fill any empty hours. She had started a vocational school for girls, called a School for the Useful Arts, at Bishop's Keep. And her latest Bardwell book, an historical novel set in the seacoast village of Rottingdean and called *Smugglers' Village*, had just appeared. The reviews had been excellent, and she was beginning to think it was time to start another book, although she had no idea what sort of book it ought to be.

On the other side of the fire, Charles Sheridan, the fifth Baron of Somersworth, was also neglecting his reading. He was thinking, quite unhappily, about his mother and the visit he should have to pay next week to the family estate in Norwich, where the dowager Lady Somersworth lived when not in residence at Sibley House.

Until two years ago, Somersworth and Sibley House had also been home to his older brother, Robert, the fourth Baron, whose death had shifted to Charles's unwilling shoulders not only the barony but the duties and responsibilities that went with it: the management of estates in England and Ireland, the family seat in the House of Lords, and a place in Society—none of which Charles wanted. The estates presented far too many intractable problems, his liberal leanings made him unpopular with the other lords, and he didn't give a shilling for Society, which he found trivial and tedious. He had even insisted on retaining the name of Sheridan, his *own* name, which had served him well for his lifetime.

Now, after two long years of being Lord Sheridan, Charles was bored, frustrated, and ready to throw the whole damn thing over. If he had his way, he and Kate would retire to her Essex estate, where she could write her books and tend her gardens and he could indulge himself by modernizing the old house, cataloging the local flora and fauna, and pursuing the new developments in forensic technologies in which he had a strong interest.

The clock in the corner proffered a tentative whirr, wheezed twice, and began to chime the hour. If he wanted to retire to the country, why the devil didn't he retire? The answer unfortunately lay in his oppressive sense of duty. When he and Robert were children, their father had dinned into their ears the favorite British catechism: *Not what you will but what you must,* and that hoary old exhortation of Nelson's: *England expects that every man will do his duty.*

Unfortunately, Charles had learned his lesson all too well. Until his mother was dead, he would do what he must to uphold the family name, which would die with him, since Kate could not bear him any children. What he *would* not do was allow his mother to behave discourteously to his wife, and the safest way to guarantee that was to keep them apart. Hence, Kate was taking the train to Essex in the morning, and he would go off to Somersworth to discuss the year's harvest yields with his estate agent, act the beneficent landlord to his tenants, and play the role of dutiful son to his overbearing mother—all very dull, terribly boring, and unfortunately obligatory.

Charles sighed and went back to his newspaper.

3

11 April, 1898
Marlborough House

My dear Winston,

I cannot resist writing a few lines to congratulate you on the success of your book! I have read it with the greatest possible interest and I think the descriptions and the language generally excellent. Everybody is reading it, and I·only hear it spoken of with praise. Having now seen active service you will wish to see more, and have as great a chance I am sure of winning the V.C. as Fincastle had; and I hope you will not follow the example of the latter, who I regret to say intends leaving the Army in order to go into Parliament.

You have plenty of time before you, and should certainly stick to the Army before adding MP to your name.

Hoping that you are flourishing,
I am, Yours very sincerely,
A.E. [Albert Edward, Prince of Wales]

THE DINING ROOM at Sibley House was as large and as bleak as a cave, but Kate had screened off an area near the fireplace and had a table for seven arranged there. Their guests were Lady Randolph and her companion, a handsome young (very young) lieutenant of the Scots Guards named George Cornwallis-West; Manfred Raeburn, the managing editor of Jennie's magazine; Mr. Raeburn's vivacious and thoroughly modern sister, Maude, who had recently returned from a walking tour of Italy and Greece; and Winston.

The staff at Sibley House was so excellently trained that Kate gave scarcely a thought to the mechanics of dinner. Elegant dishes appeared and disappeared and fine wines were poured with a flourish, while sparkling conversation ebbed and flowed the length of the intimate table. The only difficulty that Kate could see was a marked coldness between Winston and Mr. Raeburn, a bespectacled man who had apparently been in his regiment, and a definite stiffness between Winston and Lieutenant Cornwallis-West. Kate understood perfectly well what *that* was about, because the young Guardsman, who was almost exactly Winston's age, was Lady Randolph's current *affaire du coeur*. Lady Randolph—her dark beauty emphasized by her pale green satin gown, quite *décolleté*—was a stunningly attractive woman who always had a coterie of men at her heels, usually younger men. The rumors about her relationship with the gallant and self-assured Guardsman had been flying wildly about London all summer, even finding their way into the newspapers. Kate put Winston's aloofness down to jealousy, for it was obvious from the way he looked at his mother that he was extraordinarily attached to Jennie, and not a little possessive.

The women made their usual departure after dinner, Kate leading them to the smallest of the three drawing rooms, where fresh flowers from the conservatory scented the air and coffee and liqueurs were arranged on a table in front of the fire. Miss Raeburn excused herself to freshen up, and Kate and Lady Randolph were left alone.

Kate leaned back in her chair, wishing that she were an artist and might sketch this beautiful woman with the enigmatic eyes. "I am so glad to get to know you better, Lady Randolph."

"I should like to call you Kate," Lady Randolph said decidedly, "and I wish you would call me Jennie." She returned Kate's smile and lowered her voice confidentially. "After all, we are both Americans, married into English families. We both know how difficult *that* can be." She paused. "And you already know that I am a great admirer of Beryl Bardwell. I have read *all* her work."

"Thank you," Kate said, although she doubted that Jennie Churchill knew everything she had written. Back in New York, where she had supported herself entirely with her pen, Kate had produced whatever she could sell—mostly sensational penny dreadfuls with titles like *Missing Pearl* and *The Daughter's Deadly Revenge* for Frank Leslie's monthly magazine. She wasn't ashamed of the work, for it had put food on the table and a roof over her head, and had taught her a good bit into the bargain. But the surprising inheritance that had delivered her from writing for a living now allowed her to write as she chose. While her recent work still belonged more or less to the popular genre of detective fiction, it was far more psychologically inclined, with a deeper exploration of motive and mood. Kate was especially interested in portraying strong and self-willed women who made their own way in the world, sometimes becoming victims of their own ambition, sometimes becoming villains, sometimes heroines. Strong-willed, forthright women who managed their own affairs, knew their own minds, and followed their own hearts. Women like Jennie Churchill—and hence Kate's interest in her guest.

"Perhaps," Jennie said, "you would consider writing a story for the first issue of my new literary venture. And I should very much like to have your advice and counsel on the magazine itself."

"Mine?" Kate asked in surprise. "But I thought that Mr. Raeburn—"

"Mr. Raeburn," Jennie said firmly, "is experienced in the technical and financial aspects of publishing. But I need someone who knows the literary scene and can help me make an editorial plan for the first four issues." Her dark eyes were intense, her face passionate. "I have such *dreams* for the magazine, Kate! My life has grown meaningless these last two years. I sometimes think that all I have to look forward to is an endless parade of country-house parties, dinners, and balls." She leaned forward. "The magazine can change all that. It will give my life direction. More than that, it will have an influence on the way people think."

"I quite agree," Kate said. "If I can help in any way, please do call on me."

"Wonderful!" Jennie exclaimed. "Perhaps, then, we might spend several mornings next week discussing what might be done."

"I'm sorry," Kate said. "I'm leaving for the country

tomorrow." At Jennie's crestfallen look, she added, "But I should be very pleased if you would come to stay with me at Bishop's Keep. Charles will be at Somersworth and I have only a few little projects to keep me occupied. Please come, whenever you like."

It was true that Kate had only a few projects currently in hand, but one of them was hardly "little." Her School for the Useful Arts had created quite a controversy in the neighborhood, especially among certain local churchmen who considered public education their prerogative, and she was going to have to deal with the problem. But that shouldn't occupy all her time.

"We can be quite alone," she went on, "and walk in the garden and drive to the village and talk to our hearts' content—if you wouldn't find it all too boring." She smiled. "I'm afraid there is no Society to speak of, and we are *very* quiet."

"No Society!" Jennie clapped her hands delightedly. "Oh, Kate, it sounds delightful! No parties, no balls, no silly chatter—just quiet talks and evenings before the fire. I shall come whenever it is convenient for you."

At that point, Miss Raeburn entered the room and turned the conversation to her recent, extended tour of the Mediterranean countries. It was nearly twenty minutes before she drew a breath and Kate could suggest that they join the men in the library.

"So, Winston, I hear that you're bound for India again. You'll be rejoining the Fourth, will you?"

Charles sat down in a wing chair with his snifter of brandy and crossed his legs. Raeburn and Cornwallis-West had detached themselves and were engaged in an animated discussion by the fire, the topic of which seemed to be stag shooting in Scotland. Actually, Charles thought, this was rather a relief. Though he seldom noticed such things, the tension between Winston and the two other men had been quite evident at dinner. Winston obviously resented the young Guardsman's attentions to his mother and had turned a noticeable cold shoulder to Raeburn, in spite of the fact that they'd been at Aldershot together.

"Yes, after the first of the year," Winston said, accepting a cigar from the butler and folding himself into the chair opposite. "I departed India so precipitously that I left quite a few loose ends." He grinned in boyish pleasure. "Although I must admit that it is less India that summons me than the Inter-Regimental Tournament."

"Ah, polo," Charles said, tilting his glass. "The emperor of games." The game in which so many British officers in India spent their idle hours—their *long* idle hours. "Is the tournament ground still at Meerut?"

"Indeed," Winston said. "Still stirrup-deep in red dust."

"And Sir Pertab Singh is still regent of Jodhpur?"

"To be sure. You know him, then?"

Charles nodded. "Give him my regards, will you?" He himself had returned to India after a battle, to "tie up loose ends." But that had been a long time ago. He changed the subject. "I understand that you are writing another book."

"*The War for the Waterway*," Winston replied. "It is much in my mind."

"I greatly enjoyed your last." Charles rose, went to the shelf, and selected his copy of *The Malakand Field Force*. "I must say, I am impressed by your work—and by the reviews. As I recall, the *Spectator* hailed it as a minor classic. And the Prince has been praising it to everyone who will listen." He extended the book. "Perhaps you will be good enough to autograph it for me."

"I should be delighted," Winston replied, taking out a pen. "Given your heroism in the Sudan, I consider it a great honor." He took out a pen and wrote swiftly in the book. "Your courage is spoken of in high places," he said, as he handed it back. "With high praise."

Charles's right brow went up and he regarded Winston curiously. He had not disclosed those events of his military life, not even to Kate. Where the devil had Winston Churchill heard of it? In India or Egypt, most likely, from one of his former comrades. He sighed, reflecting that the Army had always loved a rousing war story that exemplified the soldierly virtues of heroism, self-sacrifice, and all that rot. High places, eh? The remark might be merely Winston's posturing— the young man was certainly prone to dropping great names on any occasion where he thought it might earn him attention. But it was also remotely possible that the tale had come from HRH, who seemed of late to have taken an interest in Winston's career.

The relationship between the Prince and the Churchills was long and full of intrigue. It was no secret that Albert Edward had long been, and perhaps still was, one of Lady Randolph's many lovers. The late Lord Randolph—Randy, to his friends—had winked at that adultery but foolishly attempted to call the Prince's hand on another, involving Randy's brother, Blandford, and one of the Prince's former paramours, Countess Aylesford. Randy, the most self-destructive man Charles had ever known, tried to use some of HRH's indiscreet letters to force the Prince to help Blandford.

But this treachery only brought disgrace. It was a long time before Lord Randolph and his wife were allowed to rejoin the royal entourage.

Charles sat down, lit his pipe, and leaned back in his chair. "And just what," he asked dryly, "have you heard about my 'courage'?"

Winston hesitated, as if drafting a response designed not to give offense. "Well," he said carefully, "at the Battle of Abu Fahr—that would have been in '85—they say a certain lieutenant of engineers led his detachment in a forlorn hope against the Dervishes' flank after they had broken through the regiment's square. The detachment was slaughtered, except for the lieutenant, but his bravery saved the rest of the regiment." Then wonderingly, and almost as if talking to himself, he added, "They say he refused the Victoria Cross."

Charles drew on his pipe. He had heard, from acquaintances close to Kitchener, that Winston was considered a "self-advertiser" and a "publicity hound." One of the Sirdar's aides had even gone so far as to suggest to Charles that Winston, who had pulled every string he could reach for an assignment to the Expeditionary Force, had gone to the Sudan in search of campaign medals to further his political hopes back home. If that were true, Winston must ascribe Charles's refusal of a V.C. to sheer lunacy.

But the point was not to be argued. Instead, Charles said mildly: "The Sudan campaign has certainly proved popular here. Most people say that Kitchener's army put a proper end to the business we should have finished thirteen years ago." He paused. "You must have had an interesting time of it at Omdurman."

"Ah, Omdurman!" Winston lost his diffidence and

his pale eyes lit as if by electricity. "The battle entirely strengthened my faith in our race and our blood. We may have appeared to those savages as barbarous aggressors, but I am proud to raise my sword and my pen in honor of the persevering British, who, though often affronted, usually get their way in the end."

"Oh?" Charles said. Both his eyebrows went up this time.

"It's the game, you know," Winston said, leaning forward eagerly. "War is the finest, honestest work of every man. Omdurman proved to the world that the spirit which flamed in the Light Brigade at Balaclava still burns in the British cavalry of today! Such gallantry! Such deeds of distinction!"

"Indeed," Charles murmured. He cleared his throat. "Well, if you take that line in your book, I daresay it shall sell very well, and undoubtedly raise you to any pinnacle you choose."

"Thank you," Winston said. "I believe it is my duty to give readers a taste of the fury of war." He put on a grim look that was at odds with his youthfulness. "We were in a tight spot at Omdurman, you know. If it hadn't been for my Mauser pistol, my bones would be bleaching in the Sudan."

"The M96 self-loader?" Charles asked, reaching for another change of subject before they could soar to more lofty heights of rhetoric.

"Yes, that one. You've used it?"

"I have had occasion to examine it," Charles said thoughtfully. He had in fact discovered a whole crate of this particular weapon, which was manufactured in Germany, the year before. One weapon from that consignment had very nearly ended his investigation, and his life. He did not elaborate because HRH had declared the matter secret in the interests of national security and Charles doubted that Winston could keep a confidence. "It is a fine defensive weapon," he said. "It must deliver a remarkable volume of fire power."

Winston became quite animated. "Oh, yes, yes! Not only does it fire as fast as you can squeeze the trigger, but reloading is simplicity itself. The bolt locks open at the last shot and you simply ram another clip of cartridges down into the magazine." He raised his hand and pointed his finger as if it were a gun. "And there you are! Ten more dead men!"

George turned from the fireside conversation. "Is it as accurate as they claim?"

Raeburn looked up, the fire glinting on his glasses. "I understand," he said, "that the rear sight is adjustable to a hundred yards."

"Several hundred," Winston said.

"I shall consider acquiring one," George said. "Where did you get yours?"

"You might try Wesley Richards in New Bond Street." Charles rose from his chair. "Ah, here are the ladies, at last!" he said, with relief.

4

"A very independent spirit is a marked characteristic of the lower classes of servants. Even when seeking a place, after arranging with a mistress, they not unfrequently fail to appear on the specified day. They have changed their mind, thinking the work too hard, or the neighbourhood too far from their friends, or what not."

"Domestic Household Service"
Life and Labour in London
1903

Bishop's Keep
Dedham, Essex
13 November, 1898

"WELL, MY GIRL," Sarah Pratt said angrily, "it's 'igh time ye showed yer face." She shoved the copper stock-pot to the back of the iron range. "Where 'ave ye bin, Mary Plumm? It's nearly four, an' the potatoes not peeled for supper nor the tea table laid in the servants' hall."

The new kitchen maid, a pert, redheaded girl of fifteen with an ivory complexion and a tip-tilted nose, looked at her with innocent eyes, blue as the summer sky.

"Why, I've bin t' school, Mrs. Pratt. Don't you remember? Her ladyship told me I might, from two to four, wi' the village girls." She tied a clean white apron over her gray cotton dress and got out a loaf of bread. "I bin learnin' t' use Mrs. Quibbley's sewin' machine."

"School!" Sarah hissed, between clenched teeth. She took down the pudding that was meant for the servants' tea. "I thought ye were done wi' learnin' a long time ago."

Mary Plumm, whose experience as second kitchen maid at Marsden Hall made her seem eminently suitable for the kitchen at Bishop's Keep, was a replacement for Harriet, who had departed a fortnight earlier. Sarah missed Harriet sorely, though she would not have admitted it. The girl had always been willing (albeit a trifle untidy), never talked back, and had followed Sarah's instructions with diligence if not always with attention. Unfortunately, Harriet was now employed in the post office in the nearby village of Manningtree, where (she had proudly confided to Sarah in a penciled letter betraying many erasures), her hours were fewer, the work less strenuous, and she had been promised promotion after a year's satisfactory employment. Harriet's betrayal galled Sarah, all the more because her ladyship—quite inexplicably—had encouraged the girl to take the new position when it was offered to her.

"Advancement and a change of scene," Lady Charles had said approvingly. "I applaud your ambition, my dear." Whereupon she had given Harriet a sovereign for good service and promised a strong character reference should that be required in the future.

Sarah harrumphed to herself. She admired her employer but some of her schemes and notions were unfathomable. A sovereign for good service, to a servant who threw over one perfectly good post for another! But perhaps that was the way they did things in New York, where her ladyship had grown up.

Mary began to slice the bread, working rapidly and neatly. "I *am* done wi' learnin', Mrs. Pratt," she said. "Book learnin', anyway. But this is different." She raised her chin. "I'm learnin' a trade. One o' the useful arts."

"An' what is it ye're learnin' from me, I'd like t' know?" Sarah demanded. She shook her spoon at the menu slate hung on the wall beside the great cupboard, where the next day's dinner menu—carrot soup à la Creci, roast fowl, vegetables, compote of peaches, and charlotte à la vanille—was displayed. "Look at those dishes! Ye're learnin' to cook, ain't ye? That's a trade, an' a fine one! I should know—I bin doin' this for twenty-five years, in this very same kitchen!"

Mary met Mrs. Pratt's eyes. "Twenty-five years in the same kitchen," she said in a wondering tone that just missed being insolent. "Why, I don't b'lieve I could stand it."

Sarah narrowed her eyes. When she was taken on as kitchen maid, the first thing she was taught was to hold her tongue. If she had spoken with such impertinence to Mrs. Howard, who was Cook before her, she would've had her ears boxed till they rang. But like it or not, the times had changed and kitchen maids, especially experienced ones, were harder to come by—and much more independent. If Sarah boxed Mary Plumm's pretty little ears, as she felt like doing, Mary Plumm might well take off her apron and march the two miles to Stafford

Place, where Lady Stafford's cook (whose previous kitchen maid had gone off to London to work in her cousin's fish-and-chips shop) would welcome her with open arms and an extra half-holiday twice annually. Sarah would have to recruit one of the housemaids to help with the cooking until her ladyship hired another kitchen maid, who would probably have half Mary Plumm's experience and twice her impertinence. It was not an inviting prospect. Add to it the desperate personal predicament which had recently threatened Sarah Pratt's peace and tranquillity, and it might be understood that she was unusually short of patience these days.

"Not so thick wi' that bread," she snapped. "That's the last loaf till tomorrow's bakin'. An' as soon as tea is done, the potatoes is next." She paused deliberately. 'Thompson has sent in some fine large potatoes, so I b'lieve we'll make crulles for upstairs dinner." Potato crulles were potatoes cut round and round in a continuous spiraling curl before they were cooked, requiring a sharp knife wielded with careful attention. *That* should keep the saucy miss occupied. "An' mind ye wash 'em in very cold water," she added, knowing from personal experience how that chilled the fingers. "The colder the better. An' peel 'em thin as can be, but no breaks. If one breaks, throw it into the slops an' start over."

Mary Plumm's little cry of consternation was lost in the opening of the kitchen door and the entry of Mr. Hodge, the butler. He had been hired last year when the previous butler, Mudd, yielded to wanderlust and departed for New Zealand and life as a sheep farmer. Mudd had been young and inexperienced, and Sarah had ruled the roost when he was the butler. Now, she had to submit to Mr. Hodge—Frederick B. Hodge, that is—who would never, in his wildest dreams, imagine himself herding sheep in New Zealand. Experienced in the fine art of butlering, he was a reserved, formal man of indeterminate age whose coat was always brushed and tie unfailingly straight. His erect carriage and precise language reflected his insistence on professional discipline on the part of the staff.

"There has been a change of plans, Mrs. Pratt," Mr. Hodge said in his dry, correct voice. 'Tomorrow's guest has already arrived. There shall be three for dinner."

Mr. Hodge's tone did not indicate what he thought of such a breach of decorum, but Sarah was vexed. Three for dinner meant a recalculation of the fowl and the addition of another entree. But that had been the way of things ever since Miss Ardleigh married his lordship and become involved in Society, and she was resigned.

"Three for dinner, eh?" she said. "Thank'ee, Mr. 'Odge." She turned to Mary Plumm. "Ye'd best 'urry yer tea, my girl. As soon's ye're done, draw an' pluck another fowl an' peel those crulles. Mind ye now—very cold water!"

This time, Mary Plumm's dismay was clearly audible. Sarah smiled to herself. Yes, there was more than one way to handle an insolent kitchen maid.

Standing at the edge of the terrace, looking out over the gardens, Kate was pleased. The year before, she had ordered the renovation of the south gardens, which had been neglected for several generations. Her two aunts, from whom she had inherited Bishop's Keep, had been far more interested in the practical kitchen garden that provided vegetables and fruits for the table than in the extensive pleasure gardens that had once surrounded the house. Before the aunts, her grandfather had thought flower gardens frivolous, costing a great deal of money and requiring the time of men and boys who might be better employed in the fields.

But while practical Kate counted the cost of the gardens, she also respected their value—to her, to the estate, and to the boys and a few girls who were being trained in the horticultural arts by her new head gardener, Mr. Humphries. When trained, these young people would have a secure trade which would pay them far more handsomely and reliably than common field work—which, in the current agricultural situation, was not easy to come by and not very secure. A boy or girl who learned gardening was a boy or girl who would not have to go to London to find work in a factory. In Kate's view, growing young gardeners was equally as important as growing gardens—especially when it could be done with money she had earned from her books and was free to spend in any way she chose.

So it was with a great deal of satisfaction that Kate looked out over a garden reclaimed from the wilderness that had overtaken it—pruned, planted, transplanted, manured, and mulched, by a team of four boys and two girls in blue tunics, at work today trimming the yew and privet hedges so that they were straight-sided, a little narrower at the top than at the bottom.

"I congratulate you, Mr. Humphries," she said. "You have done a fine job."

Mr. Humphries grinned modestly, showing tobacco-stained teeth. "Thank you, m'lady. I'm partic'lary proud o' the old rhododendrons—there's several of the early Spanish and a yellow Siberian—and the new herbaceous border, of course. Ye won't lack flowers fer cuttin', but the border'll take less time t' tend, an' we can go on t'other things. The rose garden, fer instance."

Kate also loved the rehabilitated rose garden, which contained some lovely cultivars, including a very old L'Isle de Bourbon that had been a wedding gift to her grandmother and a moss rose called Rouge de Luxembourg that her great-grandmother was said to have planted as a young girl. Kate treasured these horticultural connections with her Ardleigh ancestors, who had lived here long before her father angrily renounced his inheritance and went off to America, where he married her Irish mother. The garden somehow made her feel more English, and while she did not want to forget who she was or the America she came from, she also cherished the English part of herself and was glad that she could help to bring the garden back to life again.

As Kate was about to ask the gardener to take her through the rose garden, she was interrupted by Sally, the parlor maid, who came through the French doors onto the terrace.

"Lady Randolph Churchill, m'lady," she said breathlessly, and curtseyed.

Kate was startled. Jennie's first visit to Bishop's Keep had been pleasant and uneventful—several days of quiet walks and relaxed country drives, sharing experiences and confidences—and the two women had become fast friends. But Jennie was an extraordinarily attractive and desirable single woman who could choose among dozens of invitations from her friends and admirers, including the Prince and Princess of Wales. So Kate had been greatly surprised when she had telegraphed two days before, inquiring as to whether she could come for another visit. And now here she was, a full day *before* her expected arrival!

'Thank you, Mr. Humphries," Kate said hastily to the gardener, and to the maid, "I'll come in, Sally. Is she in the drawing room? Oh, and do tell Mr. Hodge that there will be three for dinner."

The maid turned with a helpless gesture. "Lady Randolph, m'lady." She curtseyed again, and vanished.

"Jennie!" Kate exclaimed, as the lady came out onto the terrace. She was dressed in a blue wool traveling suit piped in darker blue velvet, her dark hair piled up under a matching blue velvet hat with white feathers and a swath of veil. She was as beautiful as always, but lacked her usual cheerful ebullience. Her cheeks were pale, her eyes heavy, and she looked exhausted. For the first time, Kate noticed the fine lines around Jennie's mouth and between her heavy dark brows that gave away her age.

"I do so hope I'm not putting you out, Kate." Jennie made a wry, self-deprecating face. "Such inexcusable rudeness—not only to invite myself but to arrive early!"

Kate took Jennie's gloved hands in hers and bent forward to kiss her cheek. "Don't be silly," she said warmly. "You've only given us more time to be together." She stepped back. "But the train has tired you. Your rooms are ready, of course, and you'll want to rest before tea. Charles returned yesterday from Somersworth. He'll be delighted to see you." She squeezed Jennie's hands and let them go. "As am I."

"You're too kind," Jennie said. She bit her lip, hesitated, then said: "I know that I owe you an explanation for imposing in this way, but I... I—" She stopped.

41

"No explanations, Jennie," Kate said. "Whatever your reasons, I know they are good ones." But she had to admit to a swift-rising curiosity. While the Jennie who had visited two weeks earlier had been calm and deliberate, the woman who stood before her now was shaken and (if Kate could trust her intuition) desperately afraid. Afraid of what? Had something happened to disrupt her love affair with George Cornwallis-West? Had Winston got himself into a scrape or some scandal? Or perhaps the difficulty had to do with money—of which, Kate knew, her guest was perpetually and dangerously short.

Jennie walked to the edge of the terrace and put her hands on the rail. "I didn't have any choice," she said in a low voice, as if Kate had not spoken. "I couldn't stay in Cumberland Place because..." She didn't finish the sentence.

Kate raised her eyebrows, saying nothing.

Jennie turned, her jaw tense, her expression enigmatic. "I asked to come because Daisy Warwick suggested that I seek Lord Charles's help with... difficult matter. I've come early—" Here, her voice broke. She swallowed, pressed the back of her gloved hand to her lips, and continued. "I've come early because the difficulty has become desperation. I fear—" She closed her eyes, then opened them wide. "I fear I am in a very serious difficulty!"

5

"I sit by selection
Upon the direction
Of several companies' bubble.
As soon as they're floated
I'm freely banknoted—
I'm pretty well paid for my trouble.
In short if you'd kindle
The spark of a swindle
Lure simpletons into your clutches,
Or hoodwink a debtor,
You cannot do better
Than trot out a duke or a duchess."

The Gondoliers
W. S. GILBERT

WHEN CHARLES HAD looked around Bishop's Keep for an appropriate site for his laboratory and darkroom, he came upon a small room, not very far from the kitchen, which had once been a game larder. The windowless room was below ground level and often damp and chilly, so he installed a gas fire to warm it, and (now that his electrical plant was working up to capacity), electric lights above his worktables. As a scientific laboratory, it was small but well-equipped, with oak cabinets filled with glassware and chemicals, two sturdy laboratory tables (one with a porcelain surface), a sink with both hot and cold water, a gas burner, a chemical balance, and other scientific equipment arranged neatly on shelves. His Lancaster achromatic microscope, fitted with rack and fine screw adjustments and a condensing lens, sat on one table. In the corner was the X-ray apparatus he had made from a Crookes tube and a Tesla coil, according to the instructions in one of Professor Roentgen's recent papers. In another corner, on its own separate stand, was his new experiment in animatography: a Prestwich Magazine Camera that stored up to 100 feet of film. With it he hoped to record simple motions for further investigation. Kate, however, had already pressed it into service to document her School for the Useful Arts, so that she could demonstrate its workings to the next meeting of the Parish Association.

The adjacent darkroom was equipped with a worktable, porcelain developing tanks, washing and drying racks, a sink, an Eastman clock, and a Knox enameler, and supply shelves, as well as a new electric safe-light. There was also a Koresco reducing and enlarging camera, and another purchased from Fallowfield in Charing Cross Road and designed exclusively to produce lantern slides, for which Charles had paid four pounds five shillings. The camera had won a silver medal at the Hackney Exhibition, and was one of his happiest purchases in spite of the cost.

Today, Charles was at work on a new cross-indexing system to keep track of his many prints and negatives.

He was updating the index when Bradford Marsden stopped in for a chat. Bradford was the master of Marsden Manor, having recently inherited his father's baronetcy. The Marsdens and the Sheridans were near neighbors, and Bradford and Charles had been friends since their days at Eton. Bradford was a strikingly handsome, fair-haired man in his early thirties, with fine, angular features, a trifle thickset but fashionably dressed in riding dress and tall polished boots.

After some desultory conversation about recent local events, Bradford tapped his boot with his riding crop and got down to the business for which he had come. "You know, old chap," he said, "times have been rather hard since Papa died."

Bradford's father had succumbed to a failing liver some eighteen months previous, leaving his son in full command of the family fortunes, such as they were. The holdings that were left included the country estate of Marsden Manor, whose lands adjoined the southern border of Bishop's Keep.

"I'm sure it's difficult," Charles murmured, trying to remember what he had done with the negative plates of the shots he had taken of Kate's roses.

But Bradford scarcely heard his friend's sympathetic words. "Damned hard," he muttered vexatiously, "and getting harder." He clasped his hands behind his back and began to pace, frowning. Where his inherited family wealth was concerned, Bradford had an uncomfortably clear understanding of the difficulties he faced, what had caused them, and what he ought to do to redeem them.

The cause, of course, had been the Old Man's refusal to face up to the challenge of the modern era and allow the family funds to be invested for the future. Instead, he insisted on living as the previous Marsden baronets had lived, following the style of life that he considered his birthright: a fully staffed mansion in Hyde Park, Marsden Manor and its extensive properties in Essex, a ruinously expensive racing stable, hunting and entertainment on a grand scale, not to mention jewels and ball gowns for Bradford's mother and sister. No wonder that Bradford's inheritance had been spent long before his father departed this earth, leaving him precious little besides debts, mortgages, jointures, and heavily encumbered, nonproductive land.

If Bradford had been able to look beyond the misery of his empty pocketbook and the irritating demands of his banks, he might not have laid such a bitter judgment upon his father, for the decline of the Marsden fortunes was symptomatic of a pervasive change in the way the world was organized. Over the last twenty years, England's agricultural markets had been devastated by the bountiful harvests in America, Australia, and the Argentine, coupled with cheap and efficient shipping, which drove prices so low that English farmers could not compete. Between this irreversible agricultural decline, falling rents, mounting death duties, burdensome interest payments, and unrenewable mortgages, the landed elite was feeling the ground shift under its feet. Their lands and trust funds no longer yielded enough to feed their avaricious desire for money and the power that went with it. Across England and the Empire, there were thousands of men like Bradford, who had inherited empty coffers and a mountain of debts.

But while Bradford was too close to the problem to see it in its entirety and not sufficiently philosophical to appreciate its long-term implications, he could at least see what he might do to redeem his own situation. While others of his class might stick their heads in the sand as his father had done, or sit in their clubs and drown their dilemmas in drink, he was of a temperament to *do* something about it. Granted, his earlier efforts had been rather ill-advised (witness Harry Lawson's automobile swindle which had swallowed up his mother's emeralds, or the failed Canadian mining scheme that had cost him so much grief), but Bradford considered that these efforts had taught him some valuable lessons. Anyway, this Rhodesian venture was different. It was a much more solid thing, based on engineering estimates and proven mineral reserves, and the men involved—well, they were gentlemen, and damned shrewd. Not your average City man, with no feel at all for the real work to be done, the profits to be gained. He couldn't keep a boastful tone from his voice when he said:

"But things are looking up, Charles. Cecil Rhodes has set up a new mining venture, the Rhodesian Mining Consortium. It will be capitalized at a hundred thousand pounds. I'm to be a director. It's a fine position, offering both interesting employment—one has to fill one's idle hours somehow—and material remuneration."

Charles grunted. "Cecil Rhodes, eh?"

His friend's tone, Bradford thought, was distinctly skeptical. He said, warily: "You have to admit that Rhodes knows what he's doing. Not one of the Rhodesian ventures has failed, and there have been several stunning successes. Cattle, land, mining—"

"I don't doubt the potential for success," Charles said. "The land is rich, and Rhodes is a brilliant opportunist who knows how to exploit its resources. It's the man

47

himself that's the problem. You may be the company's director, but he'll pull your strings." He gave Bradford a direct look. "I hate to see you going the way of Fife and Abercorn. They lent their names and reputations in return for directorships of his British South Africa Company at two thousand pounds a year. Of course, they were mere ornaments, whom Rhodes kept entirely in the dark. But that didn't stop the Committee of Inquiry into the Jameson Raid from censuring them for failing to act as responsible directors and control Rhodes. As if they could," he added wryly.

"I will be no mere ornament," Bradford said, nettled. "Rhodes has promised me a free rein."

"To ride the course he's laid out?" Charles raised a cynical eyebrow. "But I see that the deed is done. I trust you've also been promised the opportunity to buy stock at par."

"Of course," Bradford said, recalling his reason for coming. "Which reminds me of my errand."

Charles looked mildly alarmed. "If you are offering me stock in Rhodes' new venture, Bradford, I'm afraid I must decline. I—"

"No, not that," Bradford said hastily. "Of course, if you should wish to make an investment, I would be glad to assist. But to finance my own initial purchase, I intend to sell some land." He affected a carelessness he did not feel, for the fact of the matter was that he needed the money desperately—and not just to buy into the new venture. "I thought you might be interested in acquiring a thousand or so acres immediately adjoining the south boundary of Bishop's Keep—more if you like."

"You shall have to speak to Kate about that," Charles said. "This is her estate." He grinned. "She is one of the

New Women, you know. No mere ornament, she. She insists on directing her own affairs, and does a damned good job of it, I must say."

"Well, then, I shall," Bradford said, standing. He felt some relief, for he thought it would be easier to deal with Kate than with Charles. "Oh, by the way—I've been wondering if you would like to become a member of the new lodge of Freemasons which has begun meeting in Colchester. I'd be happy to support your candidacy, and I'm sure you would be accepted."

"Thank you, no," Charles said. "I was initiated into Freemasonry while I was in the Army, but no longer participate."

"If you change your mind," Bradford said, "you have only to mention it." He glanced at the clock on the wall. "I fear I must go. My mother is having company to tea, and I am expected."

"Perhaps you'd like to come to dinner tomorrow," Charles said, also rising. "Lady Randolph will be here for a few days."

"Jennie!" Bradford exclaimed, feeling the heat rise in his face. "But—"

"I know," Charles said with a little shrug. "Kate and I do not ordinarily move in Lady Randolph's social orbit. But she, too, it seems, is about to embark upon a business venture. For some weeks now, she and Kate have been tête-à-tête regarding a literary journal she is about to launch." His glance was inquiring. "So you know her?"

"We are acquainted," Bradford replied, pulling on his gloves. "But I am afraid I must refuse the invitation. I'm engaged this evening, and I shall be in the City for the next few days." He omitted to say that he had spent a weekend in Jennie's company at a house party in Kent the previous spring, and that the mere recollection of those perfect shoulders was enough to make his heart race. But Bradford was a practical man, and while Lady Randolph was, hands down, the most marvelously alluring widow he had ever met, the death of Lord Randolph had left her with two young sons and scant resources to support her extravagant habits. Had Bradford successfully wooed her—and he flattered himself that he might have done, for she preferred younger men of wit and charm—she would only have magnified his financial worries tenfold. In the event, she had turned to the arms of a young Scots Guardsman, a handsome boy whose inheritance was rumored to be as encumbered as Bradford's own. Well, young Cornwallis-West could have the lady, if he was fool enough to take her—although Bradford felt a stab of regret when he thought that he might be sitting next to Jennie at dinner the next night.

The door of the laboratory opened and Hodge, the butler, stepped in. He inclined his head with exactitude and said, "Excuse me, m'lord, but her ladyship begs me to inform you that Lady Randolph Churchill has arrived."

Charles looked confused. "She has? But I thought she was not expected until tomorrow. Have I mistaken the day?"

"No, m'lord," the butler said. "She has arrived before she was expected."

"Very well, Hodge," Charles said. He looked at Bradford. "Are you sure that we can't tempt you to stay to tea and renew your acquaintance with Lady Randolph?"

"Oh, I am tempted," Bradford replied wholeheartedly.

"But please give the lady my compliments, and tell her that if it were not for my duty to Mama, I should undoubtedly be here."

With that, he made a hasty departure, leaving Charles to reflect that this was the first time in his lengthy acquaintance with Bradford Marsden that he had seen him in a hurry to take tea with his mother.

6

"A Revolting Murder"

"A Woman Found Horribly Mutilated in
Whitechapel"

"Ghastly Crimes by a Maniac"

"A Policeman Discovers a Woman Lying in the
Gutter Her Throat Cut—After She Has Been
Removed to the Hospital She Is Found
to Be Disembowelled."

The Star,
Friday 31 August, 1888

CHARLES TOOK A cup of steaming tea from Kate and
settled back in his chair. The drawing room at
Bishop's Keep was a modest room—the Ardleighs had
apparently been given to entertaining a few intimate
friends, rather than a throng—but it was quite pleasant,
with tall, well-proportioned windows, a high ceiling,
Turkish carpets on the parquet floor, and the gas wall

sconces whose installation he himself had directed. A fire burned brightly in the large fireplace, and across from him, on the sofa, sat two very beautiful ladies, both wearing the loose and flowing tea gowns that were currently in fashion. His eyes lingered for a moment on the one with the unruly mane of auburn hair, the steady hazel-green eyes, the decisive chin, whom he loved beyond all power of expression. He smiled at her, then turned to the other. She was attempting to hide, not very successfully, a pained distress.

"I am so grateful," she said in a low voice, "that you have allowed me to come for another visit."

Kate leaned forward. "Allowed you!" she exclaimed with a little laugh, her face alight with pleasure. "We're delighted that you chose to come." Jennie Churchill was a woman of wit and charm and a sparkling zest for life, and Charles knew that Kate had enjoyed her earlier visit enormously. "I'm anxious to hear about your progress with *Maggie*," Kate added. "Does she have a proper name yet? And has Mr. Raeburn located a publisher?"

Jennie seemed to brighten. "I've been considering your proposal of *The Anglo-Saxon Review*," she said. "Winston doesn't favor it, but Mr. Raeburn agrees that it's a fine title, as does Pearl Craigie. I think you know Pearl's work—she writes under the name of John Oliver Hobbes. She has offered a short play for the second or third issue. And yes, it appears that we may have found a publisher, a Mr. John Lane. I am hoping that the first issue will appear next June, if we are successful in attracting sufficient subscribers."

"I have been thinking," Kate said, "that a French

contributor to each number might add to the international interest."

"Well, then," Jennie said, "what would you say to Paul Bourget? He is as well known in England as he is in France and America, and a friend. I think I could impose on him for a piece. I should also like to have a scientific article. I am trying to get Professor Lodge to write something on wireless telegraphy." She made a little face. "Although the good professor is not very cooperative."

"Charles," Kate said eagerly, "couldn't you ask your friend Mr. Marconi to write something for Jennie's magazine?" In explanation, she added, to Jennie, "Charles is quite well acquainted with Mr. Marconi, the inventor of the wireless. He has a laboratory at Chelmsford, which is only twenty or so miles away."

"I should be glad to inquire," Charles said. He had been listening with interest to the ladies' conversation. Jennie Churchill was no intellectual, but she was intelligent and well-informed and enormously energetic. In fact, in Charles's view, it was her energy and spirited engagement, rather than her beauty, that set her apart from the idle women of her class, most of whom watched the world go by with a remote and indifferent lassitude. However she invested that vigorous energy—whether in Winston's high-flown political aspirations or her own ambitious publishing project—she was sure to realize at least some of her goals.

"That's very kind of you, Charles," Jennie said. "Please do ask Mr. Marconi if he is interested—and if not, perhaps you would care to offer an article." She paused, and a darker look crossed her face. "But *Maggie* isn't the reason I've come." She glanced under her lashes at Charles. "As you know, the Countess of Warwick and I are friends. She didn't confide details, but I understand that you and Kate were instrumental in retrieving a certain... indiscreet letter that came to her from the Prince." Her smile was gone as quickly as it came. "I am in a similar painful situation, with a potentially ruinous outcome, not only for myself but for Winston, whose political career may hang in the balance. I've come to ask your help."

Charles maintained an untroubled expression, but inwardly he was irritated. If Jennie Churchill wanted him to recover a purloined love letter, he would have to disappoint her. He was not going to become Society's all-purpose sleuth, covering up the muck of misbegotten love affairs.

He held out his empty cup to Kate, who refilled it from the silver urn on the tea table. "If you are in need of a detective, I can recommend a man who is retired from the Yard. You will find him perfectly discreet and extremely able. If it is your letter you wish to recover—"

"You have misunderstood." Jennie met Charles's eyes with a candor and determination so fierce that it shook him. "I am speaking about a terrible *blackmail*." She looked away, toward the fire. "The blackmailer's claims are utterly ridiculous. They cannot possibly be true. But even so long after Randolph's death, many would be willing to believe anything about him. If the thing ever becomes public—" Her voice nearly broke. "The taint will damn Winston before he has had a chance to demonstrate his own merit. His political hopes for himself—and mine for him—will be ruined beyond redemption. He will never sit in Parliament."

"The blackmail has to do with Lord Randolph?"

Charles asked. Randy had never been well liked except by a small circle of friends who shared his interests in horses and gaming, or admired his audacious political maneuverings. The man had made a great many enemies in his forty-five years, in both high and low places. It wouldn't be hard to imagine some of them engaging in a spot of blackmail.

Jennie's response was measured, but her voice held such tension that it nearly vibrated. "The blackmailer claims to have proof that Randolph was Jack the Ripper."

Kate's cup rattled in its saucer. "Jack the Ripper?"

Charles felt relieved. Randolph Churchill had led an unruly life, and there were many charges against which he could not be defended. He did not think this was one of them.

Jennie picked up the reticule she had brought downstairs with her and took out a square of paper, which showed signs of much folding and unfolding. She handed the paper to Charles. "Read this."

The note was written in a scrawling, almost childish hand and adorned with several ink blots. It was neither signed nor dated. Charles read aloud:

"'Dear Lady Randolph:
 Your late husband may now be beyond the reach of the law, but the sins of the fathers are visited on the sons. I know who killed Mary Kelly and the others. My silence is worth one hundred pounds, which you will pay to the boy who calls for it tomorrow. If you don't, the world will know the true identity of Jack the Ripper.
Yrs respectfully,
A. Byrd'"

Charles folded the note and handed it back. "The Ripper, eh? Well, I don't suppose it's anything to bother yourself very much about. Anyone who knows the family will pass it off as libelous. If you hear any more from this chap, I suggest that you ask your solicitor to track him down and give his nose a good twist." He raised one eyebrow. "You said something about proof?"

Jennie put the note back into her reticule. "That is his claim," she said evasively. "But you are probably right." She composed an uneasy smile. "I fear I have been rather silly about this ridiculous business."

Kate frowned. "Jennie, I don't think—"

Jennie turned to Kate with a brittle cheer that failed to deceive. "Dear Kate," she said, "I have been *dying* to hear about Beryl Bardwell's next novel. What can you tell me?"

7

"Bloody Murder!
Man Discovered Stabbed!!

Mr. Tom Finch, a resident of Number 2 Cleveland Street, Fitzrovia, was discovered dead in his lodgings on Saturday. The dead man, who had been brutally stabbed in the back, was found by the deceased's landlady, face-down on his luncheon table. Police have learned that a veiled lady was seen entering Mr. Finch's rooms in the afternoon, before the discovery of the gruesome murder. The lady's name remains unknown to this time, although an identification is expected shortly. A police investigation is underway."

Daily Telegraph,
14 November, 1898

LIEUTENANT GEORGE CORNWALLIS-WEST stared at the item buried on the fourth page of the newspaper, his breath coming as fast as if he were running from a pack of howling dogs. Around him flowed the usual

Monday commerce of the Bachelors Club, frock-coated City men brokering business, dandies brokering the latest gossip, uniformed Regimentals discussing the Egyptian campaign, liveried footmen, lively pageboys. But George, sitting on the leather sofa with the *Telegraph* and a brandy, was oblivious to everything but the page in front of him. Jaw clenched, heart pounding, he read the short piece for the third time, trying to get control of himself.

So someone else had spotted her going into that wretched place! Damn the rotten luck! *Name unknown… although identification expected shortly.* Of course she would be identified. It was a bloody marvel she hadn't been recognized at once, on the spot, from the photographs of her that frequently appeared in shop windows—all too often, for his taste, for she had been, like his mother, one of the P.B.s, the professional beauties. But his mother had aged with time, while Jennie was ageless, like a fine painting or a precious necklace. He'd overheard a pair of old snaggletooths chattering just last week, when she'd come back from Sandringham and he'd met her at the train station.

"That angel," cooed one of them enviously. "'Oo is she?"

"Why, ye silly!" the other scoffed. "She's Lady Randolph Churchill, she is. Don't ye 'ave eyes in yer witless 'ead? 'Oo cud mistake such a beauty?"

Who indeed, George thought despairingly. No one who had ever seen Jennie Churchill could fail to remember that face—those extraordinary eyes (the eyes of a panther, someone had said), the suppressed sensuality of her mouth, the exquisitely smooth skin. Or that perfect shape, those incomparable shoulders, that generous bust, truly the form of a goddess. As long as he lived, if he lived an entire century, he would never forget their first meeting, the way she had taken his hand, the awareness in her eyes, the smile on her full, ready lips. He had fallen wholly and hopelessly in love with her at that moment, and from then until now his heart and his body—his soul, even!—had been hers alone.

It had been June, at one of those fabulous weekend parties at Warwick Castle, with around-the-clock entertainment and enormous quantities of food and drink, the guests left to as much friendly intercourse as they wished. George had been pleased to receive the countess's invitation but a trifle discomfited as well, for the First Battalion was in the midst of a musketry course and normally he'd have a devil of a time getting excused. But the Prince of Wales was to be a guest at the party, and an invitation to join His Royal Highness (who was also George's godfather) almost amounted to a command. Colonel Hamilton had given him grudging leave and he'd taken himself off to Warwick, where the countess had introduced him to Jennie—who was forty-four to his twenty-two, someone had whispered, although he'd scarcely believed it, for she didn't look a day more than thirty. She was vivacious and boldly flirtatious, and he— who had kissed only the childish cupid's-bow mouths of fragile, wide-eyed young innocents—had been utterly overwhelmed by her frank sensuality. They had drifted down the Avon in a rowboat, he leaning manfully on the oars, she lying in the shade of her white lace parasol, her fingers trailing in the water, her dark-lashed eyes never leaving his. It was an hour that George, whose deeply romantic spirit had been touched by this marvel of a woman, would forever treasure.

Two days later, back with the First, he wrote Jennie a letter decorated with hearts: "I thought about you all yesterday & built castles in the air about you & I living together." A boy's naive letter, perhaps, but conceived in a man's passion, a passion made bold by *her* passion, the merest thought of which never failed to reduce George to helpless trembling.

Their meetings—first at one country weekend, then another—continued through the summer. They took tea and listened to the military band in Burton's Court, the large green in front of the Royal Hospital at Chelsea, where the Guards played cricket. They went for pleasant walks and rode together, their time interrupted only by George's tedious military duties, such as guarding the Bank of England.

George knew that Jennie was conscious of the great difference in their ages and hesitant to make any sort of serious commitment to him, but her reluctance only fueled his growing obsession, as did his parents' opposition. His mother, who had successfully married both her daughters into wealthy families, pointed out sarcastically that Jennie's friends were known to be fast, that her lovers were too many to count, and that George was just sixteen days older than her son Winston. His father reminded him that he was meant to make himself agreeable to Mary Golet, an American heiress whose fortune could remove the family's entire burden of debt and rebuild Ruthin Castle (the family home in Denbighshire) into the bargain. In no circumstance was George to pursue an impecunious widow who had slept with half the men in the Empire.

But his parents' displeasure only strengthened George's passionate resolve. He wrote to Jennie daily, telegraphed her, begged her to see him when she seemed to respond coolly, fearing all the while that she might be romantically involved with someone else: Major Ramsden, perhaps, that Highlander with whom she had visited Egypt a few months before; or the filthy rich American, Astor. Whenever he heard her name linked with another man's—and he heard this far too often, for her romantic escapades delighted all the gossips—he became wild with an uncontrollable jealousy. She was too beautiful, too cosmopolitan, too much of the world's to be his, and yet she *must* be his and his alone, or he would go stark, staring mad!

In early September, to George's enormous relief, his battalion of Scots Guards was transferred to London. Now that he could press his demands on her, Jennie gave in. While she seemed reluctant to be seen about town with him, she began entertaining him alone at her home in Great Cumberland Place. There, in private, she wore the soft, loose kimonos that seemed to him incredibly seductive and exotic, made of the stuff of dreams, her body the stuff of yet other dreams, even more seductive, more exotic. He sighed and closed his eyes, feeling warm. Surely, where this goddess was concerned, his fierce and ungovernable jealousy could be understood and even forgiven, although it led him to do dreadful things. But surely not so dreadful, given his passion. He loved Jennie desperately, lived only for the moments he could hold her in his arms. He had sworn himself to do anything in his power to protect her from harm, from insult, from other men. Surely, then—

Two stout fellows with Havana cigars passed in front of the sofa, loudly debating the merits of the Royal Navy's shipbuilding policy, which, one insisted, had already allowed the Kaiser to get the upper hand. George's eyes snapped open, and there was the newspaper in front of him, with its story of the discovery of Finch's body, and he was once again in the depths of despair, thinking not only of the appalling sight Jennie had seen—seen with those lovely, pure eyes, which should never have looked on such bloody mayhem!—but that she *herself* had been seen and would surely be identified and hauled before some odious magistrate in some awful courtroom to explain the unexplainable: how it was that she knew the dead man, why it was that she had happened to call on him so soon after he had been visited by a murderer, who she suspected of doing the deed—

George's stomach heaved. He was not only violently jealous but wildly imaginative, and he had created that awful moment over and over again just as it must have happened, seeing the scene in his mind's eye, witness to the moment of murder. That great, horn-handled knife plunged three times hilt-deep into the wretch's back, the sound of the dying man's gurgle and gasp as he pitched face down into his shepherd's pie, the splash of ale as the jug tumbled off the table. Then the retreat down the stairs and—

George shuddered at the thought of it. For him, the worst part had been to see *her* arrive, believing as he did that she had come to visit a lover. To see *her* make the awful discovery, and flee without sounding the alarm—as surely she should have done, had she gone there on some innocent errand. He recalled it again, the moment she had stepped out of the cab. The day was cold and she was wearing a heavy woolen coat and veil of dark tulle, a perfect costume for an assignation.

But perhaps the very disguise that had sent him into a

jealous rage would be her salvation, after all. Why, if he hadn't known it was his precious Jennie, even *he* could not have said for certain it was she who climbed out of the hansom and mounted the stoop. George closed his eyes, recalling the furtive glance she had flung over her shoulder, the way she had slipped through the door without knocking, as if she were expected, as if she were accustomed to regularly calling there. And that, he acknowledged bitterly, was the root of his jealousy, the reason he had done what he did: the loathsome idea that his dearest darling Jennie had called regularly at Number Two and was intimate with Mr. Tom Finch.

But there had been no intimacy on that day. Not three minutes after she entered, while George fumed and waited and swore, the outer door had burst violently open and Jennie was fleeing down the steps and into the waiting cab and away, as if the hounds of hell were after her.

And then those hounds had turned on George and had been at his throat ever since. Their ferocity had only increased when he had discovered that Jennie had gone out of town, and that neither Winston nor the servants would tell him where she was.

8

"Never have I received a really good report of your conduct in your work from any master or tutor you had from time to time to do with. Always behind-hand, never advancing in your class, incessant complaints of total want of application... Do not think I am going to take the trouble of writing to you long letters after every failure... I no longer attach the slightest weight to anything you may say about your own acquirements and exploits."

LORD RANDOLPH CHURCHILL
to Winston Churchill,
upon Winston's acceptance into Sandhurst
August 1893

WINSTON DRUMMED HIS fingers on his desk and stared out the window that overlooked Great Cumberland Place, where a few horse-drawn carriages and one or two hansom cabs moved briskly through the gray November afternoon. It had been a trying day, the culmination of a difficult week, and Winston felt himself at the end of his tether. Even as a boy he had been given to fits of black depression, sinking into brooding spells of melancholy so dark, as he had once written to his mother, that he might have been plunged headfirst into the slough of despond. The only antidote to these dreadful depressions was company—the more flamboyant and stimulating and zestful, the better—and incessant activity. "A change is as good as a rest," he had told his brother Jack, and he whirled from one project to another as madly as a dervish, allowing himself no time to brood over the terrible evidences of his inevitable failures—evidences that, from very young days, his father had not failed to point out to him with great force and equally great regularity. No matter how hard he tried to show what he could do, no matter how much he dreamed of impressing his father with his achievements, it was all for naught. He could do nothing to make his father proud of him, and the thought had filled him with despair.

Of course, Winston knew, his father had to be right in his rebukes, for Lord Randolph was a magnificent man, a paragon, worthy of nothing other than the greatest admiration, respect, and loyalty. For his son, he had held the key to everything worth having, had known everything worth knowing. Winston had been obsessed with his father's image, clipping newspaper stories about his political career, copying his physical stance, mimicking his patterns of speech. When Lord Randolph had died three years before, in the ugly depths of a political and social disgrace that Winston was just now beginning to comprehend, the son had committed himself to the father's redemption: to lifting up his flag, to pursuing his aims to the same successful end that he should have achieved, had he lived.

And therein lay Winston's dilemma. To achieve these ends, he had to claim for himself the political success that his father had so inexplicably cast aside when he resigned his Cabinet post as Minister of the Exchequer. He had, in a phrase, to prove his infallible father wrong when he had said that his son would never, *could* never succeed. In the depths of that profound paradox lurked the true beast of Winston's depressions, a nameless black dog ready to rise out of even the most trivial of rejections and sink its furious teeth into his heart.

Today's black dog was a fierce one, perhaps the most savage yet. On the surface of it, Winston's despair arose from a relatively minor incident. At the suggestion of several rising Tories who were encouraging his political ambitions, he had gone to Conservative Party headquarters at Saint Stephen's Chambers, where Fitzroy Stewart introduced him to Richard Middleton, the "Skipper," as he was called. Mr. Middleton was held in great repute because he had steered the Party to its victory in the General Election of 1895.

Up to a point, the meeting had been successful, Stewart and the Skipper praising Winston's *Malakand Field Force* and extolling the letters he had written for the *Morning Post* as the "talk of Fleet Street." The party would certainly find a seat for such a promising candidate, who, despite his years and youthful appearance, had already shown himself a force to be reckoned with, a chip, as it were, off the Churchill block.

And then, just as Winston was about to extend his hand to seal the bargain, the question had come. If he truly wanted a constituency, the Skipper had asked, how much could he pay for it? Startled, Winston had replied that he thought he could raise the money to fund his campaign, but that was about the limit. "I'm not a rich man," he said. "I live by my earnings." (This was not quite true, for he also lived by his mother's earnings, such as they were. He did not, however, want to publicize this fact.) The Skipper, hearing the phrase "not a rich man," had grown cool. The price of a safe seat was around a thousand pounds a year; insecure seats, of course, went more cheaply, but none were free. No candidate could assume the Party's backing if he did not back the Party. Winston should return when he could afford to play the game.

Winston buried his face in his hands. If money was what it took to get into politics, it would be a very long time before he could write "MP" after the Churchill name and begin to redeem his father's memory. The only person he could ask for money was his mother, and while she was willing, she did not seem to be able to manage her money and was sometimes so short that she could not pay his allowance. Of course, she might marry again: it had been rumored the year before that she was engaged to William Waldorf Astor. But while Winston couldn't help wishing that the family coffers might be enriched with some of Mr. Astor's six-million-dollar income, he had told his mother that she should never marry anyone for money, not even Mr. Astor. And now it looked very much as if she might marry George Cornwallis-West, for love! Winston could not for the life of him imagine why a woman as enticing, as seductive as his mother should stoop to that callow boy, who was as penniless as he was profligate. Why, it was a pairing so unspeakably absurd that it made his stomach turn. But stoop she had, or rather, tumbled to it, as that sour wit in *Punch* had put it, in a remark brutal with sexual innuendo. Not even Winston's blunt warning ("Fine sentiments and empty stomachs," he had told her, "do not accord.") could keep her from doing whatever she chose.

But these—the bitter want of money and his mother's romantic follies—were not the only beasts that gnawed at Winston's vitals. No, there was something far worse, something so utterly ghastly, so abhorrent and appalling, that he could not bear to think of it. But he had to think about it, because he feared that the other man might bring it to light. He had to do *something* to keep it from being found out and ruining all his hopes for himself and for the redemption of his father's name and reputation.

But what could he do? What *could* he do? The hideous truth would sooner or later out. Worse, the other man would see that it found its ugly way into the press, always hungry for some sensation, always ready to cast the first stone, and the next, and the next. And once that happened, not even death would write *finis* to it.

9

"A Gross Cavalry Scandal

I have heard many strange stories from the British Army, but few to equal this. Here is a lad of excellent character, a crack rider, a first-class shot, and an all-around 'good sportsman'... He joins his regiment in April, and by the next January he is chucked out of the Service with ignominy; his profession lost, his long and expensive apprenticeship thrown away, and his prospects in life seriously impaired. And all for what?"

Truth,
21 May, 1896

MANFRED RAEBURN stacked the manuscripts on his desk and tied them together with a stout cord. They were the initial submissions for the first issue of Lady Randolph's *Maggie*, as she insisted on calling it—an altogether ridiculous nickname, Manfred thought with irritation, as if the journal were one of her intimate friends. He preferred to think of it as *The Anglo-Saxon*

Review, a name that had dignity and merit and should certainly command attention in the literary world.

The content of the magazine would command attention, too, if Manfred had anything to do with it. And he *would*, in spite of the fact that Lady Randolph had made it clear that she meant to have the last word with respect to the editorial decisions. He smiled to himself as he finished bundling the manuscripts. Of course, she did not go through the daily post that arrived here in the office of the *Review*, as he did. She could not know that he had already received, read, and discarded as unfit several submissions that she had invited. That silly thing from Pearl Craigie, for instance, which was so light and shallow that it would never do. He would simply tell her that the expected manuscripts had never arrived, and she would be none the wiser.

At the thought of Lady Randolph, Manfred's lip curled slightly. Of course, he had nothing against her personally, except that she was Winston's mother. And even that in itself was not a high crime, for everyone knew that it was Winston's father who had shaped his son's worst attributes: an overweening arrogance, a total lack of principle, a misconceived impression of his own importance, the lack of any compensatory quality except for compulsive industry and an astonishing ability to make things happen. At Aldershot, one of the instructors had said that Winston was nothing but a spoiled rich boy endowed by some absurd chance with the brain of a genius and the ambition of a Napoleon, and Manfred, bitterly, agreed.

Aldershot. Manfred sank down in his office chair and turned to stare out at the dirty yellow fog that rose from the tiled roofs and curled around the chimney pots on the opposite side of Fleet Street. Aldershot—where he and his brother Arthur, both of them victims of a vicious and immoral intrigue, had been stripped of their right to a military life. Aldershot—where the dearest thing in the world had been taken from him, the entire tragedy set in motion at the whim and fancy of a spoiled boy who…

Sudden tears blinded him, but Manfred blinked them away and hardened himself. The loss was immeasurable and inconsolable, but it lay in the past, and if he dwelled on it too long, he would drown in bitter rage. He did not intend that to happen. At some cost to himself, he had already taken steps to ensure that the ghastly wrong would be redressed. If that plan did not serve, he felt confident that he could think of something else.

He stood and began to pace the room, his hands behind his back, his head bent. His confidence in himself was no mere shallow conceit, or feigned, like Winston's, to cover a deep uneasiness about his merit. After all, he had managed to recover from the very worst thing that could befall an ambitious young man bent on bettering himself, had he not? The glory of a military career was forever denied him, but he had already made a name for himself in the publishing business and his present position as managing editor of Lady Randolph's *Review*—the reward for working diligently and playing his hand just right—suggested that even better and more prominent situations lay ahead.

Outside in the street, a lorry horn blared, a horse whinnied, and a man shouted. Recalled to himself, Manfred stopped in his pacing and glanced with satisfaction at the well-appointed office, with its bookshelf and filing cabinet and typewriter and leather chairs and fine walnut desk. Whatever the ambiguities and unhappinesses of his private life, he reminded himself, he was in a good place. And once the old scores were settled and the old wrongs redressed, he would be in a better.

10

> "Horror upon Horror
> Whitechapel Is Panic-Stricken
> at Another Fiendish Crime

London lies today under the spell of a great terror. A nameless reprobate—half beast, half man—is at large, who is daily gratifying his murderous instincts on the most miserable and defenceless classes of the community. There can be no shadow of a doubt now that our original theory was correct, and that the Whitechapel murderer... is one man, and that man a murderous maniac. The ghoul-like creature who stalks through the streets of London... is simply drunk with blood, and he will have more."

The Pall Mall Gazette,
8 September, 1888

KATE TOOK OFF her green velvet dressing gown and laid it across the chair. The hands on the ormolu mantel clock pointed to eleven, but she was feeling keyed up and not quite ready for sleep. The evening had given her much to think about. That odd business about blackmail that Jennie had brought up at tea seemed curiously unresolved, but at dinner, she had been as gay and witty as if she had not a care in the world, and afterward, in the library, she had entertained them with several Beethoven piano sonatas, expertly played.

Then Charles had gone off to write letters and Kate and Jennie had lingered before the fire, talking about the new magazine, and Winston's political ambitions, and the latest London gossip: Daisy Warwick, no longer the Prince's favorite, had fallen in love with the wealthy and dashing Captain Joseph Laycock. Captain Joe was hardly a handsome man but incredibly *magnetic* and of course wealthy, and five years younger than the countess.

"One really can't blame her"—Jennie sighed—"but I predict trouble ahead." Her face darkened. "Young men are so charmingly attentive and passionate—but frighteningly possessive."

Frighteningly possessive? The remark sounded as if it came out of some deep apprehension. Kate wondered if Jennie were speaking obliquely about her own relationship with the young George Cornwallis-West, but did not like to ask.

After a moment, Jennie turned the conversation back to Winston's political hopes. "You know," she said, "that when the government came to claim Randolph's robes of the Exchequer, I refused to hand them over." The firm set of her chin belied the casual tone of her voice. "I am keeping them for Winston to wear when *he* becomes a member of the Cabinet. It shan't be long now."

Kate couldn't help thinking that Jennie's confidence

was premature, for Winston had not even gotten into Parliament yet. But Jennie and her son possessed a powerful resolution that might itself shape the course of future events. "He'll campaign in the next election?" she asked.

"Of course," Jennie said. "He's been assured by the Party that a seat shall be open to him." She leaned forward, her eyes intense. "That's why this terrible blackmail must be—" She stopped, and forced a smile. "There I go again," she said lightly. "Silly me. Making a fuss over nothing."

"Is it really nothing?" Kate asked. She put her hand over Jennie's. "You can tell me, you know. I am your friend."

"I know." Jennie had looked down at their hands. "Thank you."

The door to Charles's dressing room opened, interrupting Kate's thoughts. He came out, clad in his white cotton nightshirt. "Ready for bed?" he asked.

"Very nearly," Kate said. She raised her hands and lifted her long, heavy hair so that it flowed loosely down her back, then went to stand by the window, still thinking about Jennie, still puzzling over the blackmail. She said, "I don't understand what went on at teatime, Charles."

Charles leaned over the gas lamp, the oval of golden light turning the hollows of his bearded cheeks into shadow. He turned down the mantle until the light was gone and the room fell into a pale darkness, lit only by the slender moon that hung in the branches of the copper beech outside the window. Climbing into bed, he answered Kate with a question.

"How much did you hear about the Ripper, over there

in America?" He settled his pillow into a rest for his back and leaned against it.

Kate stood beside the half-drawn drape, gazing through the window onto the wide sweep of moonlit lawn. "I read about him," she said evasively. Then, because she had fallen into the habit of telling her husband almost everything, she turned and said frankly, "I read a great deal about him, I must confess. Even as recently as three years ago, I happened across an article—a reprinting of a piece in a Chicago newspaper—about an English medium who claimed to have led the police to the killer." Actually, she had clipped the article and filed it away, thinking that it might prove to be useful material for one of Beryl Bardwell's narratives. "In that version, the Ripper was a mad doctor. He later died in a lunatic asylum."

Charles folded his arms across his chest with a chuckle. "You *are* bloodthirsty, my dear. I should have thought that a proper lady would be repulsed by so much spilled blood."

Kate tilted her head and gave him an impertinent smile. "I am hardly a proper lady, m'lord. While your Ripper was reducing the population of Whitechapel, I was earning my own living in New York City—and Beryl Bardwell was just starting to write her first stories."

Kate had begun her literary career some years before. Writing under her own name, Kathryn Ardleigh, she had intended to compose tidy domestic narratives of the sort written by Louisa May Alcott—*Little Women* and *Little Men*. But the publisher to whom she offered her work replied that, while her stories were very fine, there was no market for morality.

"Sensation is what the public wants," he had told

her, thumping on the desk. "Excitement, suspense, stimulation—and the more, the better. Heap it on!" So Kate adopted the name of Beryl Bardwell and became a writer of sensational shockers, dramatic stories that she often drew from newspaper reports of real crime. The publisher had been right. The public was hungry for sensation, and the more lurid details she included, the sharper the readers' appetites became. Her shockers had sold like hot pies on an icy street corner in winter.

"I doubt," Charles said with a crooked smile, "that you learned much of the Ripper. The newspapers were not accurate, of course. They printed what they chose to print—which was a good deal of sordid nonsense. Like that article about the clairvoyant." He beckoned. "Come to bed, Kate."

The article had stayed in Kate's mind, for it had had the ring of truth. But Charles was right. The newspapers rarely printed the truth—although that did not alter her interest in the crimes. "I suppose," she said, "that I was repulsed by the idea that a man could despise women so much that he would kill and mutilate them. How many? A dozen, was it?"

Charles shook his head ruefully. "More nonsense. Where the Ripper is concerned, there is far more fiction than fact in circulation—perhaps because the truth is so grisly that it can scarcely be imagined." He pulled the covers back. "Please come, Kate. You'll get a chill, standing by the window in that gown. Which is so thin," he added meaningfully, "that I can see right through it."

Kate left the window and climbed into bed beside her husband. "Well, then," she said, pulling the sheet up to her chin, "if not a dozen, how many *did* he kill?"

"Five," Charles said. He put his arm around Kate's shoulder and pulled her close against him. "A number of other women, all of them unfortunates, were murdered in Whitechapel during that time. But—"

"Unfortunates?"

Charles's lips tightened. "That's what such women call themselves. They are... prostitutes, Kate. But that word is not for—"

"They are prostitutes," Kate said firmly. "Go on."

Charles sighed. "Very well. Some of these other prostitutes even had their throats cut. But the *modus operandi* was not the same." He paused and added quietly, "That is, there was not the degree of mutilation that occurred with the Ripper."

Kate shuddered. "Five." Somehow—she couldn't exactly say why—that sounded more *particular*. Perhaps it was that two dozen murdered women lost all individuality. Five were more... real.

Charles's voice seemed very far away. "Yes, five. Mary Nichols died at the end of August 1888 in Buck's Row. Annie Chapman was killed in September, near her lodgings in Dorset Street. Two women—Catherine Eddowes and Elizabeth Stride—were murdered at the end of that month, on the same day. Finally, in November, Mary Kelly, also in Dorset Street."

Kate did not ask how it was that Charles remembered those names, ten years after the women who bore them were dead. Instead, she said, half to herself, "But why was the maniac never caught? To do such frightful things, he must have been totally insane." Without leaving time for him to answer, she remarked, "You don't believe that Lord Randolph could have done it, do you?"

Charles made a noise in his throat. "There are thirty million souls on this little island. I suppose he's as likely a suspect as the next man... or woman."

She turned her face toward him, surprised. "You think it might have been done by a woman?"

"So one theory goes. Or a mad Russian, or a medical student, or a Norwegian sailor. There was also a suggestion that he was a gorilla."

"You're not serious!"

His chuckle was grim. "As serious as I am about the idea that Randolph Churchill might have done it."

She frowned. "Because he was a lord?"

"Because he lacked the... skill." Charles pursed his lips, as if trying to form a distasteful reply delicately. Finally, he said, "Randolph Churchill hadn't the technical training for the job. Kate, those women were not just killed—they were butchered, in the most literal sense of the word. A butcher doesn't hack and slash at random. He cuts skillfully, with precision, to separate one part from another. That's what the Ripper did." He shuddered. "Whoever he was, he was practiced in dissection. In some of the cases, he did his work with dispatch, from capturing his victims to... cutting them up."

Kate lay very still, scarcely breathing, not wanting to picture the scene Charles's words conjured up in her mind. Given her occupation, she thought she knew something of crime, but this—

Charles cleared his throat. "This isn't a fit topic for a woman, Kate. Let's leave it, shall we?"

But Kate wasn't quite finished. "Jennie says she's being silly about the blackmail," she said, "but I think she's more frightened than she has admitted."

"Which suggests," Charles said, "that she knows more than she's told us so far."

"Can you help her?"

"I am acquainted with one of the chief investigators on the Ripper case. He's retired now, but I imagine that he still knows more about it than anyone else. I could ask him to reassure Jennie as to Randolph's innocence and suggest that she call the blackmailer's bluff. That's probably the most sensible way to handle it—if there's no more to the matter than she has said." He paused. "I hope she hasn't given the wretch any money. If she has, it will be that much harder to get rid of him."

"I doubt she has any to give, Charles," Kate replied ruefully. "From something she said during her last visit, I suspect she is deeply in debt. If that's true, it's another complication she must feel it necessary to conceal."

"Like George Cornwallis-West?" Charles chuckled. "That young man is certainly a complication—although she doesn't conceal him very cleverly. I wonder how she got out of town without his coming after her. They say he dogs her every step. If I were her, I should be a little afraid that the boy might do something unwise."

Kate thought of Jennie's comment about the passion of young men. Love—the love she felt for Charles, at least—was a wonderful thing, exciting, inspiring, vitalizing, protecting. But in the wrong proportions, or from the wrong motives, or with the wrong object, love could be dangerous. Love could be as hazardous as hate.

They lay for a while in silence. At last Charles lifted his finger to stroke her cheek. "We have said enough about unpleasantness for one night, my sweet," he whispered. The cloud slipped away, and the moon filled the room with a silvery light. "It is time for other things." He turned to kiss her.

With a sigh of pleasure, Kate brought her husband's hand to her breast, glad to be held in his strong embrace, grateful that there were no hazards here.

11

"Many felonies are committed by domestic female servants. Some of them steal tea, sugar, and other provisions, which are frequently given to acquaintances or relatives... Others occasionally abstract linens and articles of wearing-apparel..."

HENRY MAYHEW
London Labour and the London Poor,
1862

"DAMN THAT DOG," growled the whiskery man. He thumped his mug on the table and wiped his mouth with a dirty sleeve. " 'Ee'll rouse the 'ouse."

"Well, then," Sarah Pratt said, concealing her nervous eagerness, "ye'd better be off, 'adn't ye, Dick?" She glanced up at the clock that hung over the kitchen door. "It's nigh on eleven, anyway. Mr. 'Odge checks the doors at eleven."

The whiskery man leaned back in the chair, maddeningly at ease. "I'll be off when I gets wot I come fer." He tipped up his wool cap with his thumb and grinned, displaying a missing tooth. "Seein' as 'ow ye've bin blessed wi' so much, wife, an' me wi' so lit'le. Share 'n' share alike, as the Good Book sez."

Wife! Sarah felt the despair rise up in her, accompanied by a dreadful resignation so unlike her usual spirited confidence that she seemed a stranger to herself. Try as she might, she could think of no escape. Wife she had been and wife she was still, no matter how long she had lived free of the man. Twenty-two years ago, the Crown had sent Dick Pratt to Dartmoor for stealing three quid from the master mason for whom he worked, releasing Sarah from the worst mistake of her young life. With her husband gone and as good as dead, she could reasonably call herself a widow and live the life of a widow, working and earning and even saving, hiding Pratt's shameful imprisonment—her guilty secret—from all. As a young woman, and pretty, she had even allowed herself to be courted, first by one and then by another. Once she had even given in to the urgings of nature, when the first footman, so fine in his knee breeches and white stockings, had pressed his demands upon her. But once burned, twice shy. Early on, Sarah persuaded herself that an imprisoned husband was almost as good as a dead husband, and a dead husband far better than a living one. She needed no man to drink up her wages, waste her hard work, and beat her into the bargain. And so, presenting herself to the world as Mrs. Sarah Pratt, widow of the sadly deceased Dick Pratt, she had got on very well with her life...

Until a fortnight ago, when a forceful knock had rattled the kitchen door just as she was banking the fire for the night. She opened the door with a sharp reproof on her tongue, expecting the stableboy. But the words died in her throat as she recognized with horror the grizzled man before her, clad in worn boots and a shabby overcoat, the fog swirling around him as if he were an apparition. Dick Pratt, returned from Dartmoor, risen from the grave.

"Well, me pretty," he'd said with a gravelly laugh and a flash of the old insolence, "ain't ye a-goin't' let yer fond 'usband come in an' warm 'is cold bones? We got some talkin' t' do, we 'ave, aft'r all these years."

Wordlessly, Sarah had stepped aside and allowed him to enter. With the shutting of the door behind him, her freedom was ended, her widowhood over, and she was once more hostage to her husband. Lounging before the fire with a mug of ale she had fetched from the cellar, he told her that he had served out his sentence and was now a free man and anxious to pick up his life at the point where it had been so unfortunately interrupted, in the midst of the blessed and holy state of matrimony, ordained by God as the best way for man and woman to live. But Pratt had been a reasonable man in his youth and a reasonable man Pratt was still, and while it was his legal right—nay, his husbandly duty—to insist that Mrs. Pratt return to the connubial bed, he was willing to forgo those matrimonial delights in return for one or two small personal favors.

"Not much, me wife," he'd said, with a wag of his filthy hand. "Just a bit o' food from the larder an' an occasional bot'le o' the master's bubbly. Nothin' that'll be missed in a place rich as this."

Sarah was so overcome with despair that she had unthinkingly capitulated. Pratt sat by the fire for a longer time than she had liked, warming himself and admiring this and that around her well-appointed kitchen before he departed with half a cold roast chicken, a loaf of new-baked bread, a plum pudding, a cheese, and paper packets of tea and sugar. Sarah latched the door behind him and immediately fell into a violent fit of weeping.

If Sarah had hoped that she'd seen Pratt's back, or that he would get himself murdered in some tavern brawl, she was bitterly disappointed. The man returned twice, demanding more food, more drink, and a pair of the master's trousers to replace his own ragged and dirty ones. The provisions were a simple matter, for her ladyship allowed Sarah to keep her own inventory, and the key to the wine cellar hung on a hook in Mr. Hodge's butler's pantry. The trousers had proved a much greater challenge, for Sarah seldom had occasion to visit the upstairs bedrooms, and the theft had required a fair bit of conniving when the garments came to the laundry room to be cleaned. More to the point, she knew that if she were apprehended in such a felony, she could lose her place *and* her character, as well as being hauled into police-court. Her distress had become an agony of fear, and from moment to moment she imagined that the master himself would come striding into the kitchen to demand his trousers. When she handed the garment to Pratt at his last visit, she swore she would steal no more clothing for him.

Tonight, neatly trousered and well-fed, Pratt gave her an evil grin. "Well, if ye want t' be rid o' me, wife, fetch me a basket. I'll 'ave some joint t' take wi' me, as well as some fowl an' fresh bread, an' cheese too, o' course. A bit o' cake wudn't be amiss, neither, nor a bot'le o'wine." He frowned. "The last was sour, it wuz. Mind ye do better this time."

"Is that *all*?" Sarah asked sarcastically.

"That's all, me ol' dear," Pratt said in a cheerful voice. "Look sharp now."

Sarah did look sharp, for she was anxious to be rid of him. But when she had fetched the food and drink wrapped in a paper parcel, he sat in the chair, looking mournfully at his boots.

"Now that ye ask so kindly, me wife, there is somethin' else I cud do with." He held up one foot, to show the boot sole flapping loose. "As ye kin see, I'm most in need o' boots. I'm thinkin' that yer master 'as a old pair 'ee don't wear no more an' wud be glad t' give t' somebody 'oo needs 'em."

Sarah's eyes widened in utter dismay. "No!" she exclaimed. "Not boots, Pratt! I cud niver—"

Pratt sighed heavily. "No boots fer yer 'usband, fer pity's sake?" Then, quick as a flash, he grasped her arm in a clawlike grip and pulled her against him. "Yer not gettin' off wi' a few vittles an' a pair o' castoff trousers," he growled savagely. "Till death do us part, remember, me luvey? If ye ain't willin' t' provide fer yer ol' man in 'is time o' trouble, I'm sure yer mistress wud be more'n glad t' lend a 'elpin' 'and. 'Specially when she 'ears that we be yoked together these many years an' longin' to resume our married station." He gave a malevolent chortle. "Why, 'er ladyship might even be glad t' find me a bit o' light work in th' stable—nothin' too 'eavy, o' course, seein' as 'ow I 'urt me back."

Sarah swallowed. Resume their married station! She couldn't imagine anything more repulsive. But she didn't doubt that Pratt was bold enough to go to her ladyship, whose heart was easily touched. Indeed, she knew Lady Charles well enough to know that she would be glad to oblige by finding Pratt a place and finding living quarters the two of them could share, as she had done for her personal maid Amelia Quibbley and Amelia's husband, Lawrence, who worked in various capacities for Lord Charles. Sarah's heart sank. Unless she could think of some way to permanently remove Pratt from her life, she was trapped. Endlessly and eternally trapped.

"About th' boots," she said at last.

Pratt cocked his head to one side, eyeing her. "Ye don't want us t' 'ave a rose-covered bower an' me a place in th' stable?" He chuckled. "I'm good wi' the 'orses, ye know, Mrs. Pratt."

"I'll get the boots," she grated, "but it may be a few days. When will ye be back?"

"Soon." Pratt picked up the paper-wrapped parcel and dropped a gallant kiss on her cheek. "Thank 'ee, ol' girl. I'll be glad o' th' boots. Me foot's on th' ground, it is—an' th' ground's near frosted."

Sarah closed the door behind him and went to turn down the gas mantle, feeling an angry despair engulf her. But she would have been even more sick at heart had she noticed that the door leading into the passage was slightly ajar, and that Mary Plumm crouched on the other side, one ear pressed eagerly to the crack.

12

"I was... sitting next to Lord Curzon at dinner one night, when we approached a subject which, without my knowing it at the time, was fraught with great importance for me. In a despondent mood I bemoaned the empty life I was leading at that moment. Lord Curzon tried to console me by saying that a woman alone was a godsend in society, and that I might look forward to a long vista of country-house parties, dinners, and balls. Thinking over our conversation later, I found myself wondering if this indeed was all that the remainder of my life held for me. I determined to do something, and cogitating for sometime over what it should be, decided finally to start a Review."

The Reminiscences of Lady Randolph Churchill
by JENNIE JEROME CHURCHILL

THERE HAD BEEN a time in Jennie Churchill's life when she would not have thought of traveling without two lady's maids to see to her clothing and personal needs and a footman and page to manage the bags and boxes. When economizing became necessary, she had reluctantly done away with the male servants. When the situation became desperate, she had let one of the maids go and reduced the amount of baggage. But she could never in the world manage without Gentry, who had just this moment carried in her morning cup of coffee and was opening the drapes in the blue bedroom at Bishop's Keep.

"Thank you, Gentry," Jennie said, sitting up in bed. She sipped her coffee, reviewing in her mind the day ahead. "For this morning, please put out something simple—the lavender taffeta waist with the chemisette front, I think, and the gray wool skirt with the lavender velvet piping. Before tea, I shall change to the green tea-gown. And for dinner tonight, the yellow silk. The local vicar is coming, I understand."

Thinking out the several changes of costume that the day's social activities required was a habit Jennie had fallen into long ago—a useful habit, too, making for less confusion both at home and when traveling from one country house to another, as she did very often. It was *so* hard these days to find a maid like Gentry, who could manage both one's clothing and one's hair. The young women all seemed to want to go into trade, which held a greater promise of advancement.

As Gentry picked up the dress her mistress had worn the night before and went into the dressing room, Jennie reached for the telegram on the tray. It must be from Winston, for she had told no one else that she would be spending the next few days with the Sheridans. She particularly had not told George, for she was disturbed by the obsessive demands he made on her and by the frightening thought that he might have—

With an involuntary shudder, she pushed the idea away. Whatever else George might do to ensure his claim on her, he could not have gone *that* far. She must have been mistaken when she thought she saw him in the barber's doorway, across from the lodgings in Cleveland Street. In any event, it would do the boy good to cool his heels—and curb his insatiable appetite—for a few days. A tiny smile tugged at her mouth as she thought of George's appetites. It was good to know that she was still desired and desirable, at her age.

She reached for the telegram, but it was not from Winston. Manfred Raeburn had wired to say that as he was on his way to Ipswich to visit a friend, he should like to stop off for a few minutes with the samples of the leather bindings that she was considering for *Maggie*. Jennie frowned. Manfred was another one of those possessive young men—not romantically so, of course, but anxious to possess her time and jealous of her other interests. Still, it was a good thing that he was so energetic on behalf of the journal, and on her behalf, as well. For instance, persuading Winston to tell him where she had gone, interrupting his holiday with the business about the bindings, which another, less dedicated managing editor might have held over until her return. No, on balance she was glad that Manfred was making himself so useful. It gave her more time to boost Winston's political career—and in the long run, that would likely prove more important than the journal.

At the thought of Winston, Jennie's face darkened. The other terrible business had been gnawing at her ever since that awful moment in Cleveland Street when she—Her blood seemed to chill, and she shook the ugly memory out of her mind. If the affair was not resolved quickly, Winston's career would be ended before it began. She was not going to let that happen! She turned back the covers and got out of bed to begin her morning toilette. She would have to spend an hour with Charles, making sure that he understood how swiftly he needed to act and what exactly he had to do—without telling him how precarious her situation really was. She had already made two mistakes in this wretched business. She could not afford to make a third.

When Kate inherited Bishop's Keep from her aunts, she had decreed that breakfast would be a simple affair. In this insistence, she knew she was going counter to custom, but the staff had enough work to do without fretting over an elaborate breakfast. So a dish of seasonable fruit and a dish of hot porridge were set out on the sideboard, and the dining table was laid with preserves and butter, sugar, and a pitcher of fresh cream. When the diners appeared, the footman (a young man named Pocket who had been with Kate's aunts since he was a boy) brought up from the kitchen a large tray of boiled and scrambled eggs, sausages and rashers of bacon, and hot toast. Mr. Hodge, the butler, asked each person what was wanted and served it from Pocket's tray. Kate poured tea or coffee. When all were served, Mr. Hodge and Pocket placed the hot dishes over spirit-lamp warmers on the sideboard and withdrew. Guests who slept late helped themselves when they arose.

This morning, Charles had already eaten and excused himself from the table. Kate was finishing the last of her coffee and reading *The Times* when Jennie came in, carrying a large brown envelope.

Kate looked up, thinking that her guest looked a

little pale and out of sorts. "Please help yourself at the sideboard," she said with a smile. "Charles is in the library—he'll be pleased to talk with you whenever you like." She picked up a cup. "Tea or coffee?"

"Tea, please." The envelope under her arm, Jennie filled a plate at the sideboard and sat down. "I fear I must see Mr. Raeburn this morning," she said shortly. "He telegraphed to say that he would be bringing samples of the leather bindings for my approval. Each issue of the journal is going to be bound like an antique book, you know. I prevailed upon Cyril Davenport of the British Museum to show me some of the best old bindings, which we are going to copy. Mr. Raeburn's visit shouldn't take long, though. He's on his way to Ipswich."

Kate turned her head, hearing the crunch of wheels on gravel. It proved to be the pony cart from the station at Colchester, bringing their visitor. In a few moments Mr. Raeburn had joined them, refused Kate's offer of breakfast but accepted coffee, and sat down at the table.

"I apologize for the bother, your ladyships," he said humbly, inclining his head. "I should not have intruded, but I thought that Lady Randolph would like to see—"

"Oh, it's no bother," Kate said quickly.

Jennie pushed her plate away. "Show me what you've brought."

Kate watched as the young man opened a portfolio of leather engravings and placed it on the table in front of Jennie. She had not seen Manfred Raeburn since the dinner party at Sibley House some weeks before, and she thought he did not look as well as he had. He was a thin-lipped young man with an arched nose and gold-rimmed spectacles, his chin stiffly elevated over a high starched collar. Kate thought she remembered Charles saying that he had left the Fourth Hussars under some sort of cloud. He did not look the military sort—too slender, with an almost feminine grace, and nervous. His nails were bitten to the quick. Probably his work in Fleet Street had suited him better than life in a regiment. From things that Jennie had said, he certainly seemed to know how to go about publishing a journal.

Jennie did not take long to make up her mind about the bindings. "This is the one we shall have for the first number," she said, pointing. "Tell Mr. Conroy that I like the gold embossing very much and think his price quite fair."

"Very well, your ladyship," Mr. Raeburn replied, and closed the portfolio. "I stopped by Great Cumberland Place early this morning and took the liberty of collecting the post for you. I thought it might require your attention before your return." He placed five or six letters on the table and cleared his throat. "May I ask when that might be?"

"I'm not sure, Manfred," Jennie said. "I am enjoying this respite from Society." She tossed her head with a little laugh. "Perhaps I may never come back."

"Just remember that you can count on me to do whatever you want done," Mr. Raeburn said. He rose. "I must be on my way. The train for Ipswich leaves on the hour." And with that, he bowed himself out.

Jennie sorted rapidly through the envelopes. She tore one open and read it quickly, her lips tightening. "What audacity!" she exclaimed. "Why, this is nothing but blackmail!" She looked up, dark brows drawn together. "Winston writes from Manchester that the Tories have demanded a thousand pounds to guarantee him a safe seat! And after all Randolph did for the party!"

"It does seem a rather steep tariff," Kate agreed.

"I shall write to Lord Cecil at once," Jennie said, picking up another envelope and beginning to open it. "The party must understand that Randolph's son is not to be dismissed as if he were simply an ordinary—"

A clipping fell from the envelope onto the tablecloth and Jennie picked it up. Reading it, her eyes widened, the color drained from her face, and she gave an inarticulate cry.

"Jennie!" Kate exclaimed, half-rising. "What is the matter? Has someone been injured? What—?"

Jennie sat still for a moment, as if frozen. Then slowly, she drew a folded paper from the envelope, and read it. Her hand trembling, she extended both the paper and the scrap of newsprint to Kate. "Read," she whispered.

Kate sank back in her chair, looking first at the sheet of plain notepaper on which four words had been typed: "You are not free." It was unsigned. Puzzled, she turned to the clipping. "Bloody Murder," she read silently, her lips moving with the words. "Man discovered stabbed." She looked up wonderingly. "A murder? What does this have to do with *you*, Jennie?"

Jennie drew in a savage, shuddery breath. "Go on," she whispered. "Read the whole. Then tell me what you guess."

Kate scanned the newspaper story quickly. A certain Tom Finch had been found by his landlady, stabbed to death with a knife, in his lodgings at Number 2 Cleveland Street. A veiled lady had been seen entering his rooms that afternoon. Her identity was still unknown, although it was expected that she would be identified shortly.

Kate shivered, feeling suddenly cold. A chorus of questions echoed through her mind. Had Jennie simply found the dead body? Or had she wielded the knife? The idea seemed almost unthinkable, but she knew her friend to be a woman of extraordinary determination and iron will. If Mr. Tom Finch had threatened someone or something she loved, Jennie was entirely capable of killing him. And the note—*You are not free.* Who else but a blackmailer could have sent it? Was it the same person who sent the note Jennie had shown them yesterday, the note signed "A. Byrd"? Then, glancing at the clipping, she noticed something else: was A. Byrd a pseudonym for Mr. Tom Finch?

Kate did not ask these questions. She merely said: "I should guess that you were the veiled woman, and that whoever sent this note means you to know that he knows you visited the murder scene."

"You are clever," Jennie said in a thin, metallic voice. "Come. We must see Charles at once."

Carefully, Kate placed the clipping, the note, and the envelope on a small tray. "Charles will want to examine these items. But are you sure you don't want to see him alone? There may be certain things you must tell him but would rather not share with me."

Jennie's mouth softened. "I fear," she said more gently, "that I shall soon need a friend who stands beside me without judging or reservation." She picked up the large brown envelope she had brought to the table and stood, holding out her hand. "Please come, Kate. I need you."

13

"Blackmail is by common consent the blackest of the black arts, brushing with filth and an indescribable despair all whom it touches."

BERYL BARDWELL
The Smugglers' Village
1898

WITH THE DINING-ROOM breakfast sent up, a guest in the house, and the vicar expected in the evening, Sarah Pratt should have been occupied with the galantine she had planned for luncheon and the fruit jelly her ladyship had requested for dinner. But on this particular morning, Sarah's attention was distracted from her kitchen chores by Pratt's impossible demand, which hung like a sword over her head, and by the fearful dream that had visited her when she finally fell asleep the night before. In the dream, she had turned herself into a true widow and rid herself of Pratt for all eternity by the easy expedient of seasoning the man's roast chicken with rat poison. The dream, in fact, had been so real that Sarah was half-convinced that she

97

had *already* poisoned Pratt and that Constable Laken should soon appear on the kitchen doorstep to take her off to jail. With this half-real, half-imagined misdeed weighing heavily on her mind, it was no wonder that she dropped the pitcher of cream on the floor and, when she turned for the mop, knocked a jam pot into the mess.

Sarah had no more finished cleaning up when Mary Plumm tripped lightly into the room, carrying a trayful of dirty dishes from upstairs. She set the tray on the table with a rattle of crockery.

By this time, Sarah was completely out of patience. "Wash up an' be quick about it," she snapped. "We've a galantine t' make fer luncheon, an' a pot o' pea soup t' strain, an—"

But Mary Plumm was not rolling up her sleeves in preparation for the scullery chores. "I don't b'lieve," she said with a sharp sniff, "that I wishes t' do the washin' up this mornin'. I prefers t' go in the garden an' get the veg'tables instead." She adjusted her cap to a becoming angle and picked up a basket from the shelf.

"Ye *prefers* t' go t' th' garden!" Sarah Pratt cried, scarcely believing her ears. "What kind o' nonsense is that, I want t' know! Fer such sauciness, me girl, ye'll be in the scullery the 'ole blessed mornin', an' when ye're done, ye'll be scrubbin' the flagstones an' blackin' the stove. Now git on wi' it!"

But Mary Plumm did not get on with it. "I don't think so, Mrs. Pratt," she said coolly.

"Ye don't *think* so!" gasped Sarah Pratt, one hand going to her heart. In all her life, she had never heard such impertinence from a lower servant to her elder and better. Why the very thought of it was enough to make the blood boil!

But there was more. Mary Plumm narrowed her eyes, lifted her chin, and said, softly but distinctly, "Wot's sauce fer the cook is sauce fer the maid, Mrs. Pratt. If ye kin 'and over a basket o' wine an' vittles an' a pair o' the master's trousers to yer 'usband, I kin pick 'n' choose me chores. I prefers t' take the air in the garden this mornin'. An' if that don't suit ye, ye kin complain t' Mr. 'Odge." She gave a light laugh. "I'm sure both 'ee an' the mistress wud be terr'ble sad t' know about them trousers. They wud hate worse t' see ye took off t' jail. But that's as may be. Them that plays wi' fire is bound t' be burnt, as me mother allus sez."

And having triumphantly delivered this parting shot, she tossed her head and sauntered out of the kitchen, leaving Sarah Pratt, for once in her life, with absolutely nothing to say.

In the library, Charles was reading the first forty pages of *The War for the Waterway*, which Winston had sent with his mother—a better title Charles thought, was *The River War*, and he made a note to mention it to Winston. The boy had an uncanny knack for description, he thought admiringly. About the Sudan, which Charles knew well, Winston had written:

Level plains of smooth sand are interrupted only by occasional peaks of rock—black, stark, and shapeless. Rainless storms dance tirelessly over the hot, crisp surface of the ground. The fine sand, driven by the wind, gathers into deep drifts, and silts among the dark rocks of the hills, exactly as snow hangs about an Alpine summit; only it is a fiery snow, such as might fall in hell.

Charles sat for a moment with his eyes closed, smoking his pipe and thinking. Winston's words recalled to him the angry landscape that he knew very well and hoped to forget. But the past was not dead and gone, as some might wish. His own military experiences in the Sudan lived on in him, Khartoum and Gordon's defeat lived on in British souls, and now Winston's book would give an eternal life to the bitter revenge that had been exacted at Omdurman, so that it could never be forgotten, by victor or by vanquished. Even if at some future day, there might come a generation that could no longer recall why Britain was in Egypt, *The War for the Waterway*—or whatever it would come to be called—would tell them. Of course, it was good to know the past. But to know too much about it was not always a good thing.

Charles's musings were interrupted by the sound of cart wheels on gravel. He opened his eyes and went back to his reading. The cart departed a little later, and some moments after that, Kate and Jennie joined him. He put down Winston's manuscript. His smile faded at the somber looks on their faces, and a moment later, when he had read the typed note and the newspaper clipping, his expression was as somber. So there had been more—much more—to the blackmail matter than Jennie had cared to reveal last night. Unless he was mistaken, she was in a great deal of trouble.

He looked at Jennie. "You are the veiled woman seen leaving Mr. Finch's rooms?"

Her nod was barely perceptible. "I was afraid I might be seen and recognized. I wore a heavy coat and several layers of dark veil." She glanced over her shoulder, as if to assure herself that none of the servants was in the room. "I went up the stairs and knocked at the door. When there was no answer, I opened it, since I was expected. I did not want to leave and come back again." She shivered and wrapped both arms around herself. "I saw him there, dead, at his table. The knife was... still in him. I went immediately back to the cab, and home. I could not sleep that night for thinking of it, and trying to think what to do. I did not want to stay in Great Cumberland Place, for fear the police might come and question me. The next day—yesterday—I came here."

Charles opened his mouth, but Kate asked the question first. "You left from your house and returned to your house by cab?"

Jennie nodded, biting her lip. "I know now that it was foolish. The police will search out the driver, and he will surely remember me. But I only did what I was told to do—and of course, I had no idea that I would find ... a dead man!"

"What a terrible shock!" Kate exclaimed. She reached for Jennie's hand. "You must have been frightened nearly out of your wits."

Charles looked down at the address in the newspaper clipping. Cleveland Street, not far from Middlesex Hospital, in the boroughs of Marylebone and St Pancras. A rather bohemian area, frequented by artists and artisans, with salon-style coffee rooms and rather good pubs. "Why did you go to see this man?" he asked.

Jennie opened the brown envelope and took out a photograph, laying it in her lap. "I fear that I was less than forthcoming last night. I should have shown this photograph to you straightaway. But I will make amends by telling you as much as I know." She caught his glance. "As much as I know," she repeated, "and suspect."

"Thank you," Charles said dryly.

Jennie's narrative was simple. She told the story in a low voice, carefully modulated and without hesitation, as if she had rehearsed it. On the ninth of the previous November, she had received the photograph, hand delivered to Great Cumberland Place. A handwritten note signed "A. Byrd" had accompanied the photograph, threatening its release to the newspapers if Jennie did not give one hundred pounds to a boy who would call the next day. The boy had called, Jennie had given him the money, and dispatched her man Walden to follow him. But the youngster was adept at evasions and Walden lost him in the crowds at Victoria Station.

The demand was repeated in increasing amounts and with increasing regularity, a different messenger appearing each time and departing in a different direction, each note signed with the name *A. Byrd*. Jennie grew ever more desperate. She was already besieged by a great many creditors: her manner of living was excruciatingly expensive but she could not seem to control her expenditures, nor could she think of any other way to live. She sold some of her jewelry; then, to consolidate her debts, she had executed a very large loan which was guaranteed by two insurance policies Winston had been required to furnish.

Increasingly harried and desperate, increasingly short of cash, Jennie determined to tell Winston about the blackmail when he returned from the Sudan, for the publication of the photograph, if it came to that, would cause him enormous anguish. His career would be shattered—indeed, his entire life!—if his father were associated in any way with the Ripper atrocities. All Randolph's old enemies, all the newspapers, would jump onto the story like starving jackals, whipped into a frenzy of feeding.

But Winston had come home so full of plans and

dreams and hope that she could not bear to tell him. His political success depended heavily upon his confidence in himself and in the Churchill name and reputation. To others, he might seem filled with a great faith in himself. But his mother knew that Winston's self-confidence was shallow and insecure, and that beneath it lay vast, black depths of uncertainty. His self-assurance would be annihilated by the knowledge that someone had the ability to destroy him.

In despair, Jennie had thought of appealing to the Prince, who would give her a stern look and chide her for not consulting him earlier. The world might think that HRH was a flighty, frivolous man who lived only to satisfy his appetites, but his friends knew otherwise. Bertie often found ways to provide unorthodox, behind-the-scenes help, for he was acquainted with a great many men of all sorts and classes, and he always knew how to get things done.

But something had happened that convinced Jennie she need not involve the Prince. She received another communication from the blackmailer, this one by telephone. In an obviously disguised voice, the man had said he was ready to end the dirty business and that he had something to give her in return for what she had already paid. He instructed her to come to his Cleveland Street lodging immediately, alone. Full of hope and anticipation, Jennie followed the caller's instructions. But when she reached her destination, she had discovered the corpse.

"When you saw the dead man," Charles said, "did you recognize him?"

Jennie shook her head. "I didn't even know his real name until I read it in that newspaper clipping." She paused, looking distressed. "I didn't see his face, you know. He had been eating, and when he was killed, he fell face down into a dish of something on his luncheon table."

Kate said, very quietly, "You must have been very anxious to know who he was. Did you search the room? Did you perhaps... look in his pockets?"

"In his pockets?" Jennie gave her a horrified glance. "Oh, dear God, no! I was... afraid to touch him." She closed her eyes for a moment, then opened them and said, in a rush of candor, "I know it was wrong of me, but you can surely appreciate the relief I felt when I saw he was dead." She gave a bitter little laugh. "I was fool enough to hope his secret had died with him."

Charles devoutly hoped that she would not be fool enough to make that last remark to the police, should she be questioned. Lady or no, she had a very powerful motive for murder, and if she was guilty, not even the Prince could protect her. He looked down at the clipping and typed note. *You are not free.* "Do you have any idea who might have sent this to you?"

"I cannot even hazard a guess." Jennie's face had gone very pale and her large, dark eyes were brilliant with tears. "But there is one other thing you should know. When I returned to the cab, I saw someone standing in the entry to the barbershop on the other side of the street. I can't swear to it, but I thought it might be George."

"George!" Kate exclaimed.

"Yes," Jennie said. She was crying now. "It has been... hard to shake myself free of him."

Charles could not say why, but he was not surprised. George was so obviously smitten with his lady that he might have followed her all over London. What else might the boy have done? Could he have killed a man he believed to be a rival? Charles sighed. Damn it. The affair was complicated enough without having to deal with a passionate young lover unable to keep his jealousy in check.

Jennie had lost the struggle to keep her composure. She rose from her chair, giving Charles a long, imploring look. "I came here to ask you to clear Randolph's name, Charles. Now I must beg you to save *me!*"

And with a half-hysterical sob, she ran from the room.

14

"Another Murder in Whitechapel"
"Shocking Brutality"
"The Body Terribly Mutilated"
"Search for the Murderer"
"Scenes in the Neighbourhood"

The Daily Chronicle
10 September, 1888

FOR A LONG moment, neither Kate nor Charles spoke. Then Kate said, very quietly, "No wonder Jennie is so afraid. She is besieged from all directions." She could not have said, though, which element of Jennie's story held the most potential danger—the blackmail, the discovery of the murdered man, or the troublesome ambiguity of her remark about George. Obviously, Lady Randolph was a complex woman—vulnerable in many ways, dangerous in other ways, and thoroughly unpredictable.

Charles didn't answer. He had reached down to retrieve the photograph, which had fallen to the floor as

Jennie fled from the room. He took a magnifying glass from the table beside his chair and began to study the photo intently.

Kate rose to have a look. Over Charles's shoulder, she could see that the photograph was of a man and a woman engaged in intimate conversation on a city street. Behind them was visible a row of three-story buildings, with shops on the lower level. Kate had seen photographs of Lord Randolph and recognized him at once—the heavy walrus mustache that made his large head look even larger; the striking eyes, exophthalmic, giving him a look of arrogance and scorn. He was not a man whose appearance drew warmth, although from accounts she had read after his death, Kate knew that his friends had found him jaunty, witty, charming. Apparently his companion found him so, for in the photograph she was smiling flirtatiously up at him.

But the woman in the photograph was of a different class altogether from the second son of the Duke of Marlborough. She wore a dark dress with a black velvet bodice trimmed in tattered lace and a knitted crossover around her shoulders. She was quite young, but her face was lined and weary and her dark hair was a tousled, dirty-looking mane. But still, she wore a flower at her throat with a flamboyant, almost defiant gaiety, and her smile was coy. At the bottom of the photograph, under the figure of the woman, the initials M.K. & R.S.C. were inked, and a date: November, 1888.

"M.K.?" Kate asked.

"She might be Mary Kelly," Charles replied. He put down the magnifying glass and sat back. "An Irishwoman, and the last Ripper victim."

Kate stood still. Mary Kelly, in conversation with Lord

Randolph! Such a photograph, with all that it implied, was a hideous threat to the Churchill family—not just to Jennie and her sons, but to the dowager duchess and the present duke. What would *they* be willing to pay for it? The duke might not have a great deal of wealth, but he had married Consuelo Vanderbilt, whose fortune was nearly the size of the Crown's. Again, Kate wondered if Jennie had revealed everything she knew.

At last she broke the silence. "You say that the woman might be Mary Kelly. There are the initials, and the face looks clear enough. Why do you doubt?"

"Because I did not see Mary Kelly—Marie Jeannette, she often called herself—when she was alive, nor do I know of any photographs of her. When I saw her, her face was mutilated beyond recognition. She seemed scarcely... human."

Kate put her hand on Charles's shoulder to steady herself. "When *you* saw her?" she whispered.

"Yes," Charles said wearily. "Sit down, love. It is a longish story."

Kate went to the sofa and sat where she could see his face. It was somber, the eyes dark, the mouth strained, as if Charles were remembering something that gave him great pain.

"I was called on the morning of her death," he said quietly, "to photograph the poor woman's remains. As it happened, I had been dabbling for some time in the use of the camera in criminal investigation, so I had more than a passing interest in the murders. After the second killing, I wrote to Sir Charles Warren, Chief Commissioner of the Metropolitan Police, expressing my views on the case in general and the practical application of crime-scene photography in particular."

He smiled grimly. "I'm sure I was presumptuous, but I offered him my services, should the need arise. Nearly half of London must have sent him advice, but my letter apparently caught someone's attention. At the end of September, one morning before dawn, I was called to Mitre Square to photograph the scene of another killing, that of Catherine Eddowes. And on the morning of November ninth, I was summoned a second time, by a police constable who urgently required the services of my camera. The Ripper had murdered yet another woman."

Charles had been speaking in a calm, dispassionate voice, but Kate knew him well enough to know that his self-composure masked a deep agitation. He cleared his throat, not quite looking at her. "When we arrived in Dorset Street—"

"In the East End?"

"Yes. It's a hellhole. A narrow street lined with squalid lodging houses, surely the most wretched part of the whole wretched East End. Duval Street, they call it now, because of the notoriety. Millers Court, where the woman was killed, was a yard lined with houses, just off Dorset. When we arrived, we saw a crowd of police packed into the courtyard, with spectators flocking in the street outside, amid a great deal of noise and utter confusion. An officer told me that a man had gone to Number 13 that morning to collect the rent. The door was locked, but he had looked through a broken window to see a woman lying on a bloody bed. The police were summoned. Eventually, after a good bit of confusion— Warren had resigned as police commissioner the day before, and nobody was minding the shop—they went through the window, and then broke down the door.

The detective inspector in charge, Frederick Abberline, asked me to come in and make a photographic record of the scene." He grimaced. "It was as bad as anything I'd ever seen on the battlefield, Kate. Worse, in some ways. Throat cut right across, the head nearly severed from the body. Face slashed beyond recognition, abdomen ripped open, breast and arm sliced off, entrails—" He bit off the word. "It is not something you should know about, my dear."

"It must have been a ghastly sight," Kate whispered, her eyes on Charles's face. She was thinking how hard it was to imagine the brutal reality of murder; how often in her books she trivialized death, even violent death; how little she really knew of the terrors that flocked like black bats from the darkest cellars of the human heart. The sight that Charles described was one that privileged women should never have seen, should indeed be forbidden to look upon or think about. But it had been a *woman* who had been butchered in that bloody room. And even though the Ripper had disappeared a decade ago, women like Mary Kelly—an Irishwoman, like herself—still died by violence in the East End, while ladies of Society did not have to see their corpses, or know why they were killed, or try to find any meaning in it. Suddenly it seemed grossly unjust that these women had died and that other women were forbidden to ask why.

Charles's chin had sunk to his chest and his reply seemed muffled, as if he were speaking to himself. "Yes, ghastly. Unspeakably so. Artillery fire can do horrific things to a human body. But in war, the purpose is to kill the enemy, and mutilation is an unintended side effect. In Mary Kelly's case, it seemed to me almost the reverse—that death was a necessary side effect, but the real intent was mutilation. Not random mutilation either, but planned, premeditated, purposeful. Almost as if—" He stopped, frowning. "Odd thing, that. And I had not thought about it until last night." He fell silent.

Kate, captured by the flow of his thought, could not let him stop. "Almost as if what?"

He straightened, seemingly surprised that she was still there. "You don't want to know, Kate. This isn't a fit subject for you to ponder."

"But I *do* want to know!" Kate exclaimed passionately. "Those women, those victims—they've been all but forgotten. Who remembers Mary Kelly? The only name people remember is Jack the Ripper."

He looked up, studying her face. As if satisfied by something he saw there, he nodded. "Well, then. It's been generally assumed that these crimes were carried out by a lunatic who killed for the mad pleasure of killing. But suppose that the killer was as sane as you and I, and that he acted with purpose. Suppose, for instance, that he—or they—wanted to set an example, or make some sort of statement."

Kate stared at him. "They?"

"Exactly," Charles said. "Madmen are incapable of working together toward a single purpose. If we discard the insanity theory, it is just as likely that the Ripper killings were carried out by a group of men. More likely, perhaps, given the rapidity and dispatch with which the killer worked."

Kate shuddered. A madman—a man with no reason—did not need a motive, and hence was less culpable, or so it seemed to her. What motive on earth could compel a sane and reasonable man—much less a *group* of men—to butcher five women?

Charles's jaw worked for a moment. Finally, he said, "At the moment, we seem to have two tasks before us. The first, and perhaps the easier, is to learn who sent the typed note to Jennie. When we do this, we may also have found the man who killed Tom Finch, and Jennie will be cleared." He fell silent again.

"And the second?" Kate prompted, although she thought she knew what his response would be.

Charles roused himself. "The second will be considerably more difficult. In order to clear the Churchill name, it may be necessary to identify the Ripper."

"Is that possible, at this late date?" Kate asked.

"I don't know," Charles said honestly. He picked up the photograph once again and held it so that Kate could see it. "There is something odd about this photograph, Kate. Look at the shadows behind the woman." He handed her the magnifying glass. "And then here, at the highlights on Randolph's face."

Kate studied the photo with the magnifying glass. "Yes, I see. There are some very subtle differences in the lighting. It seems to be coming from different directions."

"Exactly. The shadows and highlights are inconsistent with the general lighting of the scene as a whole. I cannot know for certain without examining the negative, but I suspect that the print is a forgery. It looks to me as if it has been created from a montage of two or more carefully positioned negatives." He eyed the photo appreciatively. "A very clever effort, actually. It would fool almost anyone. Especially a wife who already has her doubts."

"Doubts?" Kate pulled in her breath. "But Jennie can't possibly suspect her husband of—"

"She might," Charles said grimly. "In the years before he died, Randolph was increasingly unbalanced."

"Mentally?"

"Yes. The truth is that he was suffering from syphilis."

"Oh, no!" Kate exclaimed. "Oh, poor Jennie!"

"Yes," Charles replied, "poor Jennie indeed. The best that could be said about Randolph's public behavior, even when he was in the Exchequer, was that he was often inexplicably eccentric. Jennie might well have seen private behavior that was much worse. She might have looked at the photograph and recalled times when Randolph seemed capable of such brutal murders."

"Then you must show her that it is a forgery, Charles," Kate said earnestly. "She will know that he was innocent, and her mind will be at rest."

"But that is not necessarily the case, Kate." Charles's voice was bleak. "In and of itself, this forged photograph is only a forged photograph. It does not provide proof of innocence. And what if the blackmailer either believed or knew that Randolph was guilty? What if he *intended* the photo to be investigated, assuming that a serious inquiry would eventually prove Randolph's guilt, in some way he could not?"

"I see," Kate said thoughtfully. "Of course, Randolph is dead and can no longer be held to account. But if the Ripper killings were committed by a group of men—" She stopped. "In that case, Charles, an investigation might endanger *them*. They might be exposed."

"Precisely," Charles said. "In fact, it is possible that *they* discovered the blackmailer and decided to silence him."

Kate shook her head wonderingly. "If all this is true, how will we ever get to the bottom of it?"

Charles put his hand over hers. "I understand your concern, Kate, and you know that I have supported your participation in other investigations. But this is not a matter in which you—or any woman—should be involved. I am going to London to visit Finch's lodgings, with the hope of locating the negative from which this photograph was printed. Then I'm on to Bournemouth to have a talk with Inspector Abberline, who is retired from Scotland Yard." He smiled gently. "And *you*, my very dear, are going to stay here at Bishop's Keep and entertain our guest."

Kate was tempted to an angry response. The five murdered women had certainly been "involved," as Charles so delicately put it! And by what right did he believe that he could restrain her activities? Did he feel that because he was her husband, he could tell her what to do? Really—these British gentlemen, thinking that they could control their wives!

But she said none of this. She bowed her head and gave him a sidelong look. "Yes, my lord," she said meekly. "Is there anything you wish done in your absence, my lord?"

Charles did not look up. "Please tell Jennie what we have talked about and what I plan to do. That might give her some respite." He spoke absently, for he had once more picked up the magnifying glass and returned to his examination of the photograph.

15

"Two More East End Atrocities"

"Horrible Murder of a Woman in Commercial
Road East"

"A Woman Murdered and Mutilated in Aldgate"

"Great Excitement"

"Latest Details"

The Daily Chronicle,
1 October, 1888

HEARING THE RUSTLE of skirts, Jennie looked up from
the desk in the morning room where she was
writing a letter of instructions to Manfred Raeburn
regarding *Maggie*'s subscription list. Kate had come into
the room, wearing a thoughtful frown.

Jennie stood. "I'm sorry I ran out so impetuously," she
said ruefully. "It really was awfully rude of me, when

both of you are trying to help. I'm sure you must think I am overdramatizing myself—and heaven only knows what Charles thinks. He probably sees me as a spoiled child."

"Please don't fret," Kate said. "You certainly are not to blame for feeling upset by all that has happened in the last few days, and before. It is quite dreadful."

Kate crossed to the tall window that looked out over the park. Her rich, handsome mane of titian hair was pulled back severely, giving her face, with its high cheekbones and firm jaw, an almost sculptured look. She stood erect, her shoulders held rigidly, her face pale. There was tension in every line of her figure, and Jennie thought at once that she and Charles must have quarreled. The thought was accompanied by a swift sadness, and a kind of guilt. They must have quarreled about *her*.

"You seem upset as well, Kate," she said contritely. "You have been of so much help to me—how may I help you?"

"I think," Kate said, "that we must be of help to one another." She turned, and Jennie saw that her hazel-green eyes held a new look, compounded of anger and firm determination, as if she would flash out. But when she spoke, her voice was quiet and controlled. "Charles says that he thinks the photograph may be a very clever forgery—an image made by placing separate images side by side. A montage, he called it."

Jennie was at once flooded by a relief so profound that it made her knees weak. "So it's a fraud!" She sank down in the chair beside the writing desk. "There is nothing to the blackmail!" Bitterly, her mouth twisting, she thought of the money she had poured into the scoundrel's pockets. He had *fleeced* her, damn it! How could she have been so weak and foolish? She should have called his hand immediately, instead of giving in to her own worst fears.

"It *appears* to be a forgery," Kate said. She went to the teapot on the sideboard and poured each of them a cup of tea. "Charles said that he could not know for certain without examining the negative. And as for there being nothing to the blackmail—that, too, is still in question, I'm afraid. The photograph may be faked and still point in the direction of a truth that you might prefer not to explore." She offered one of the cups, and Jennie saw a deep compassion in her look. "You'll think my probing impertinent, Jennie, as indeed it is. If you choose not to answer, or tell me to mind my own business, I will certainly understand."

Still in question? Jennie was not sure she wanted to know what that might mean. "Please do ask," she said. She sipped the hot tea and set the cup down on the desk. "If I can't answer, I shall at least tell you why."

"Very well." Kate sat in a nearby chair. She spoke in a steady tone, without hesitation. "When you saw the photograph for the first time, how did you feel? What did you think? Were you certain, beyond a doubt, of Lord Randolph's innocence?"

Jennie felt as if she had been slapped, and her breath caught in her throat with a quick gasp. Kate's questions went straight to the deepest heart of the fear she had carried for a full decade, a fear she scarcely admitted to herself and never, ever to another soul—not to Winston or Jack, nor her beloved sisters, nor the dowager duchess. How could she now admit it to Kate Sheridan, whom she had known for only a few months? But unless she nerved herself to speak about her terrible apprehension, it might always lurk in the depths of the shadow like the Ripper himself, waiting to disembowel her with his savage knife. She took a deep inward breath and steadied herself. If she did not speak now, she would never speak.

"How did I feel? I was terrified. The photograph was evidence that Randolph had been with that woman. And no, I could not be certain in my soul that he was not the killer."

"Dear Jennie," Kate said softly.

Jennie closed her eyes, inexorably drawn back to a time she had prayed never to revisit. "Those were terrible days, Kate. Randolph was quite... ill. He was suffering from—" Her eyes came open again. She stopped, unable to bring herself to say the word.

"I know," Kate said softly. "Charles told me. I am so dreadfully sorry."

Jennie sighed. "I was desperate to keep it private because of the boys, and for myself, of course. His family denied it—his mother insists to this day that Randolph died of a brain tumor. But I had known for some time. He confessed it when we—" Her mouth felt dry and she took another swallow of tea. "When he ceased to seek intimacy with me, and I begged him for an explanation. Later, his doctors confirmed it." She stopped, thinking of the terrible irony of appearances—that Lord Randolph, so suave and elegant, so aristocratic, should have been destroyed by a disease so shameful that she could not speak its name.

"You have a great deal of courage." Kate's tone was gravely admiring.

"Courage!" Jennie laughed bitterly. "At the end, I felt that my courage was all that was left to me, Kate. I lost my sense of wifely loyalty long before, and certainly Randolph left neither of us any dignity. He insisted on being a public spectacle to the very end, mortifying his friends and fellow party members by speaking in the Commons when he could scarcely manage to formulate a sentence. He was unreasonable and unpredictable and often driven by violent rage, especially toward women of the sort who, he said, had signed his death warrant. He hated them, and he often spoke in Parliament about the need to clean up the East End." The words so long suppressed were pushing up in a nauseating, convulsive rush and she was powerless to hold them back, even though each was an indictment of the man she had once loved. "Was he capable of killing? Yes, I fear he might have been. And once—sometime during those months, I don't know when—I found a good deal of blood on his shirt. He said he had got it at a cockfight."

Kate, who was watching her closely, said nothing.

"But could he have butchered those women in the way that the newspapers described? I cannot believe that, either." Suddenly, Jennie heard herself giggling hysterically. "Randolph could not even carve a joint. How could he possibly cut up those poor—" She stopped, pressing the back of her hand against her mouth, feeling the horror like hot bile at the back of her throat.

Kate took the cup from the desk and handed it to her. "Drink this," she commanded.

Jennie drank. She was sickened by her own ugly words, but beneath the distress was a paradoxical relief, as after a purging. For better or worse, she had at last given voice to the terrors that for a decade had rotted within her.

"Charles says that whoever mutilated those women was skilled in the craft of cutting," Kate replied, with a forced briskness. "Some have blamed the killings on a mad medical doctor, which makes a certain kind of sense."

Jennie sat for a moment. The nausea had passed, and she felt stronger, more able to be reasonable—and reason, she knew, was her only bulwark against the fear. "The chief difficulty is," she said, "that Randolph's erratic behavior was so public and notorious that it would be easy for some to believe him to have been the Ripper. The photograph deceived me. It would certainly deceive others. Unless it is *proved* to be a forgery—"

Kate nodded. "Charles agrees with you there, too. He plans to go to London to have a look at Finch's lodgings, with the idea of finding a clue to the whereabouts of the negative. Then he expects to go on to Bournemouth, to talk to a retired policeman who knows something of the Ripper case. He has instructed me to stay here with you." Her eyes glinted and her mouth took on a determined set. "But I have it in mind to do some investigating on my own, and I wondered if you might agree to accompany me. I should be glad of the company."

"Investigating?" Jennie asked, surprised.

"Yes. You may think it rather odd, but I feel a sort of special relationship to the women who were killed." Kate rose and went back to the tea urn to refill her cup. She turned, fixing her eyes steadily on Jennie's face. "You have been honest with me, and I shall be truthful with you. I grew up in New York City. My uncle O'Malley was a policeman and my aunt O'Malley took in laundry, and they lived with their little O'Malleys and me, in a tenement." Her lips twitched and her eyes held a secret, almost mocking, smile. "The rest of Manhattan regarded our Irish settlement in the same way that you Londoners regard Whitechapel."

Jennie stared at her, dumbfounded. She had known that Kate was an American with Irish blood, and from New York City—which had once been her home, too. But *her* father had built his family a magnificent mansion on Madison Square and sent his daughters to Paris to be educated. It was almost unthinkable that Kate, so cultured, so polished, so well-married, could have been brought up by a policeman and a washerwoman in the squalid poverty of a New York slum!

But of course she had lifted herself above her background by becoming a writer, Jennie reminded herself, as astonishment was swiftly replaced by admiration. The writers she knew, even the women writers, were like artists. They lived unorthodox, often daring lives, making choices that were forbidden to other people and moving across social boundaries as easily as someone else might cross a street. Perhaps it was Kate's very upbringing that made her so fearless, that gave her the ability to choose her destiny for herself, rather than allowing circumstance to choose for her.

"I... see," Jennie said at last, and then, impulsively, added, "How much I admire you, Kate! To have come so far, to have done so much, requires a spirit of extraordinary boldness and resolution." Suddenly, Jennie was wrenched by a great desire. If only *she* could be as bold as Kate, could loosen the constraints Society had bound about her like the wretched lacings of a corset! People called her free and said that she acted with daring. But that was where men were concerned— George, for instance. Perhaps, if *Maggie* were a success, she should one day be remembered for that particular boldness, for no other woman had ever founded a literary magazine. But even *Maggie* was nothing, compared to Kate's achievements.

Kate's mouth was grave but her eyes still smiled. "If you think me bold and resolute, then perhaps you won't be surprised to hear that I intend to go to Whitechapel and see what can be learned about the last Ripper victim." She paused. "Mary Kelly," she amended softly. "She was an Irishwoman, and a Kelly. As I am."

"You?" Jennie was startled.

"My mother's name was Aileen Kelly," Kate said. Her mouth curved slightly. "And all Kellys in Ireland are kin, if one goes back far enough." She gave Jennie a searching glance. "Would you care to go with me to Whitechapel, to see what can be learned about my kinswoman?"

"To Whitechapel!" Jennie exclaimed. Women she knew—Margot Asquith, for one, Daisy Warwick for another—occasionally made sorties into the East End out of some charitable motive, while men of Society went there often, for reasons that were well known although never discussed. But to go with the purpose of learning the sordid details of the life of an Irishwoman who had been murdered a full ten years before—

Suddenly feeling the weight of Kate's quiet gaze, Jennie sat quite still. The Ripper had killed Mary Kelly, and despite what she had said, she knew in her heart that it was possible that Randolph had been somehow involved. Did she dare—

"I also aim to search out a certain Mr. Lees," Kate went on. "I read of him in a newspaper article some time ago.

He is a clairvoyant—quite well known, it appears—who claims to have led the police to the killer, a lunatic physician. The article did not name this person, but perhaps Mr. Lees will tell Mary Kelly's cousin who it was."

"Mr. Robert Lees?" Jennie regarded her with some interest. She herself was fascinated with spiritualism and had attended several séances. "I am not personally acquainted with the man, but he is highly respected as a medium. It is said that when he was just nineteen, he was called before Queen Victoria to make contact with Prince Albert, who had died some while before. Presently, he heads up a spiritualist group in Boswell Street, not far from the British Museum. My sisters have seen him once or twice."

"Then you know where to find him," Kate said. "It is a slim chance, a *very* slim chance—but a place to begin. After that, who knows where the trail might lead us." She straightened her shoulders and met Jennie's eyes with a level, challenging gaze. "Of course, the inquiry might not be to your liking, Jennie. In the East End, we will no doubt see sights we would rather not see, and smell terrible smells, and hear of terrible things. There might even be danger. I have no fear for myself, since there was a time in my life when I was accustomed to living in such a place. However, I shall certainly understand if you choose not to come with me."

It was the challenge in Kate's hazel eyes that decided her. "I don't know what you are looking for or what you hope to learn about this woman," Jennie said, "but of course I shall come with you."

"I am looking for the truth about her killer," Kate said very quietly, "and it is possible that I shall learn it. Are you *sure* you are willing to join me, or would you rather not know?"

Jennie sat, scarcely breathing. Did she dare to join Kate's search? Was she willing to accept whatever truth they might learn? And if that truth involved Randolph, would it get out to the rest of the world? What then would become of Winston and his ambitions?

And with this thought, a small, hard resolve began to form inside of her. She would go to London with Kate, not just to learn the truth, if it could be learned, but also to stake a claim to it, on Winston's behalf. For if she were involved in discovering the truth, she would be in a stronger position to suppress it, if that proved necessary.

"I'll go," she said.

16

"Ladies of the Manor often undertook charitable work among the less fortunate. Upon these occasions, they abandoned their expensive finery, borrowing from the servants to garb themselves in less obtrusive, more serviceable garments."

PRISCILLA PRIDEWELL
Social Conventions and Clothing
of the 1890s

"A WORD, PLEASE, Mrs. Pratt," Lady Charles said.
Sarah Pratt, caught up in her troubled musings, turned from the kitchen range, where she was pressing cooked peas through a colander for the luncheon soup—not as good as straining through a cloth, but that required four hands, and Mary Plumm was still in the garden. "O' course, m'lady," Sarah said. Her attempt at self-possession was destroyed when the spoon dropped into the hot soup.

Her ladyship, whose pretty mouth wore an unusually firm look, glanced around the kitchen. "Where is the new maid?"

Now, Sarah was even more flustered. Where was Mary Plumm? Under the grapevines, probably, in the arms of the stableboy. Under ordinary circumstances, Sarah would have stormed after her long ago and dragged her back by her ear, but the circumstances were not ordinary. Mary Plumm had the upper hand, and Sarah knew it.

"Well, no matter where she is," her ladyship said decidedly, "as long as she isn't here. I prefer this conversation to be between the two of us." She paused and gave Sarah a thoughtful look. "I've come to inquire about some boots, Mrs. Pratt, and a few pieces of clothing."

Sarah Pratt's knees were suddenly weak and her belly filled with a sick apprehension. Oh, sweet Jesus. Mary Plumm had betrayed her! Her heart gave way and the tears began to start to her eyes. She was ruined forever, her character destroyed. She would never find another place as nice as Bishop's Keep, with her own dear kitchen and her own private quarters with a window over the garden, and a pretty little plot of flowers she had planted beside the kitchen door. Indeed, she was likely never to find another place at all, except of the very worst sort. If she were fortunate enough to escape prison, she would likely be forced to join Pratt under the bridge or the nearest haystack. And at this last, most terrible thought, Sarah Pratt's shoulders shook and she began to cry in great, gulping sobs.

Lady Charles put her hand on Sarah's arm. "My dear Mrs. Pratt, I have no idea what I have said to make you cry. Whatever it is, I am sorry, and I shall try to make it up to you. But what I want is a simple matter, really. Lady Randolph and I are off to London tomorrow, and we need to borrow some apparel."

Sarah gasped for breath. "A-a-apparel?" she asked faintly.

"Amelia has fitted us up with suitable skirts and waists," Lady Charles went on, "and I hoped that you might have a woolen jacket or a cape. A hat, too, if you please, and I should be grateful if you have a pair of boots that Lady Randolph might try on for a fit. I promise that no harm shall come to them, other than a little wet."

"Boots," Sarah said, now incredulous. "And a 'at? *My* 'at?"

"Yes, please." Frowning, her ladyship focused on her face. "Is there something wrong, Mrs. Pratt? You are very pale. I hope you are not unwell."

"N-n-n-no, mum," Sarah managed. "It's just that—" The relief she felt was so great that she thought it would sink her. "I was just tryin' t' think about the 'at, yer ladyship. I've got a green one, wi' a cabbage rose on the crown. I made it fer the last Girls Friendly Society meetin'. It's quite 'andsome, it is, or so I wuz told by the vicar, 'oo 'as a special likin' fer pretty 'ats." She knew she was babbling, but she couldn't seem to stop. "An' as fer a cape, I've got a green plaid that matches the 'at, an' me green wool jacket wi' braid trim, which is very nice, an' a black coat that sheds the rain like a duck. Yer welcome t' wotever ye want."

"Thank you, I do indeed want as many pieces as you are willing to lend us," Lady Charles declared, a sudden smile lighting her face. "I'll send Amelia to bring the clothes to my room." She looked around the kitchen with a puzzled air. Sarah knew why, for there was no evidence of preparations for tonight's dinner party, let alone luncheon. "I hope you've remembered that we are four for dinner tonight. The vicar is joining us."

"Oh, yes, m'lady," Sarah said hastily. "I'm just a bit behind, is all." She placed herself in front of the table, hiding from her ladyship's view the tray of breakfast dishes that still sat where Mary Plumm had left it.

"Does the new maid suit you?" her ladyship said. "She seemed very eager to get on, but if you have any complaints about her work, don't hesitate to speak to Mr. Hodge or myself."

"Oh, no complaints, m'lady," Sarah exclaimed— rather too heartily, it seemed, for her ladyship gave her a questioning look.

But all she said was, "Very well, then." And with a final "thank you" she was gone.

Sarah stood for a long time over the soup pot, fishing with a fork for the spoon that had gone to the bottom. She felt as if she had been reprieved from a death sentence, but her troubles weren't over, not by a long shot. In fact, they had just begun. Little Miss Telltale could take it into her head to spill her vicious secret at any moment, and even if she did not, the price of her silence was exorbitant—and bound to go higher. There were the breakfast dishes waiting to be washed and luncheon not started, nor a thought given to the dinner preparations. If Mr. Hodge came in to inquire after the progress of the day's work, as he usually did around eleven, he would see the disorder and know that something was afoot. What could she tell him if he asked after Mary Plumm's whereabouts? And of course, there was still that dreadful task to be done, the fetching of Pratt's boots. It had been difficult before—how could she manage it now, under Mary Plumm's scrutiny?

Having found the spoon, Sarah picked up the tray of dishes and took it to the scullery. As if she didn't have enough to worry about, into the midst of the snarl of personal troubles had come this silly business about borrowing her clothes! It sounded very much as if their ladyships intended to *wear* them. But they had quite beautiful clothes—silks and satins and fine wools, trimmed with lace and jet beads and lavish braids! Why did they want her ordinary hat and jacket and cape and boots? Had they been invited to a masquerade?

Sarah shook her head, sighing. The ways of Quality always seemed mysterious to the people who did their work. But this borrowing of clothing was utterly absurd—almost as preposterous as a cook being bullied by her kitchen maid.

17

"In the early days of his career... Walter Sickert
rented rooms in a great red-brick terrace house at
15 Cleveland Street, the centre of an area that had
become the Montmartre of London. Cleveland
Street ran parallel with Tottenham Court Road.
Its surrounding by-ways formed a little Bohemian
village, a self-contained community of artists,
writers and shopkeepers... The area attracted the
young, the creative and the revolutionary."

STEPHEN KNIGHT
The Final Solution: Jack the Ripper

CHARLES HAD CONSIDERED driving the Panhard to
Bournemouth by way of London, but decided
against it. The motorcar offered more freedom and
flexibility than public transportation, but its average
speed of fifteen miles an hour was only a third of that of
the train and while the automobile's engine was reliable
enough, one had to consider the time spent repairing
the inevitable flat tires. In the current circumstance,

the Panhard had one additional drawback: it tended to attract public attention—the last thing an investigator making discreet inquiries desired. So he took the early-morning train from Colchester up to London, a pleasant trip through the November countryside, with charming views of thatched cottages and black-and-white cows grazing stubbled fields.

The journey permitted Charles to arrange his thoughts. He considered his endeavors in London to be secondary to his meeting with Fred Abberline. After an exchange of telegrams, it had been agreed that they would meet in Bournemouth where the former Metropolitan Police inspector had retired half a dozen years before. Still, there was the possibility that the London detour might yield some worthwhile information. He planned to take a cab to Finch's lodgings in Cleveland Street, where he would, if possible, undertake a search for the negative. He would also take the opportunity to identify any inconsistencies in Jennie's report and to determine whether an observer (George Cornwallis-West, for instance) might have been able to conceal himself across the street and observe her entry and exit. At some point, too—perhaps on his return from Bournemouth—it would be a good idea to have a talk with George.

And there was one additional matter, a very important one, that Charles hoped to clarify while he was in London. Yesterday afternoon, in his darkroom, he had photographed the print Jennie had given him, editing out the portion that included Randolph's image and enlarging the other so that the woman's face was clearer and the background more discernible. When he did so, two clues had become more prominent: a portion of a storefront and a shop sign—the word "Tobacco"—and the street number 22.

Of course, the unnamed street might be anywhere in London, or even in some other city. But after he had studied the enlargement for some minutes, Charles had the strong feeling that he knew where the picture had been taken, and that the scene was on the very same street as Finch's lodgings—Cleveland Street. Several years before, on an errand for the Princess of Wales, he had visited the painter Walter Sickert at his studio in Cleveland Street. Princess Alexandra had wanted Sickert to paint a small portrait of the Duke of Clarence, her eldest son and one-time heir to the throne, who had died of pneumonia in '92. Charles occasionally served as unofficial photographer for the royal family and was often invited to Sandringham, where he had taken the photograph the Princess wished to have copied. For his part, Sickert had been a close friend of Eddy, the young duke. Charles and Sickert had met several times before and since, through their association with the Royal Society of British Artists and several mutual acquaintances, including H. G. Wells and the Edens.

Jennie's blackmailer—Tom Finch—had also lived in Cleveland Street, toward the south end. Was it possible that Finch himself had taken the original photo of Mary Kelly, standing in front of a tobacconist's shop at Number 22? The forged photograph had been created with a skill that suggested an experienced photographer. Also Finch, perhaps? If so, the man might have a darkroom in his lodgings, and a file of negatives. It was a long shot, but Charles had no other good place to begin.

At Liverpool Street Station, Charles hailed a hansom cab and climbed aboard. The driver, whose seat was mounted above and behind his fare, cracked his whip and they moved off—but not very far. There was more angry whip-cracking and a voluble stream of unholy oaths as an overloaded omnibus pulled into the crossing in front of the hansom and stopped. It was only the first of a dozen delays. The route from Liverpool Street to Cleveland Street was less than three miles as the crow flies, but it was getting on for ten o'clock and the London streets were a congested labyrinth. The earlier clear weather had given way to a gray overcast, and Charles pulled up his collar against the chill wind that flung a spray of pavement grit into his face and lifted loose newspaper bills like kites into the air. He hoped very much that it was not going to rain, for he had forgotten his umbrella and should have to buy another.

Cleveland Street was a narrow road angling toward the northwest between Oxford Street to the south and Euston to the north, in an area known as Fitzrovia, and as Charles's hansom finally turned off Oxford and passed Middlesex Hospital, he began to feel excited. This was a bohemian area, a favorite place for young artists at the beginning of their careers. The street was or had been the residence of associates of the Pre-Raphaelite brotherhood—Millais, the Rosettis, and Holman Hunt—and the shops reflected the artistic interests of the residents. There were bookbinders, engravers, framers, woodcarvers, and purveyors of painting and crafting supplies. There were coffee rooms as well, and several pubs—the George and Dragon, the City of Hereford, and the Crown—where a hard-working artist could find respite from the day's labors and companionable conversation over a late-night glass of ale.

Charles took the photograph out of his pocket and

directed the driver to slow his horse to a walk so that he could keep an eye on the numbers. There was Number 2, the house where Finch had been killed, and across from it a barbershop with a deep doorway where an observer might indeed have watched while Jennie made her fruitless trip to a dead man's lodgings. But Charles did not stop, not yet—he could come back later. The horse plodded on, pulling the cab past a linen-draper at Number 10, a greengrocer with a rack of vegetables and fruits displayed in front of Number 14, Matthew Endersby's Rare Books two doors down, and—

And there it was! Number 22, a tobacconist and confectioner's shop, bearing the very sign that could be seen in the photograph Charles held in his hand. "This will do," he said to the driver. "I'll get out here."

Inside, the shop was clean and bright, with a black-and-white tiled floor, crisp curtains at the front window, and a potted ivy plant on the windowsill. One glass display counter was filled with decorated sweets, another with fine pipes and cigarette and cigar holders. Shelves on one side of the shop held jars of various candies and boxes of biscuits, while those on the other wall were filled with tins and cases of tobacco products, neatly arranged to show them off to best advantage.

A bell had tinkled when he entered, and in a moment, a stout, middle-aged woman in a black dress and white apron emerged from the rear of the shop, adjusting her ruffled cap and putting a smile on her face.

"G'mornin', sir," she said, in a voice that was colored with an Irish brogue. "Ye're lookin' fer somethin' t' smoke? Or do ye prefer a sweet t'day?"

Charles reached into his coat pocket and took out a nearly empty muslin bag of pipe tobacco. "A friend purchased this tobacco for me," he said, "and I have enjoyed it greatly. Can you find me its like?"

The woman pulled the bag open, stuck her nose into it, and inhaled. "That'ud be Turkish," she said, and reached up to take a tin from a shelf. "This is wot ye're after, sir," she said with a proprietary air, pushing it across the counter. "The very thing."

Charles opened the tin and sniffed. "The very thing, indeed!" he exclaimed, although it wasn't. "You have a most experienced nose, ma'am."

The woman's pleased smile showed tobacco-stained teeth. "I should—I bin helping Mrs. Horton at this very counter for these last fifteen years. O'Reilly died 'bout that time, leavin' me t' earn me daily bread by the sweat o' me brow an' the labor o' me own 'ands. Two shillings, sir."

Charles reached for his purse. The tobacco was dear, but that was not what he was paying for. "Fifteen years!" he said in an admiring tone, handing over the coins. "Well, then, Mrs. O'Reilly. You have seen many comings and goings in this neighborhood while you've been employed here, I'll warrant."

"T'be sure," Mrs. O'Reilly said importantly. She wrote a receipt for his purchase and gave it to him. "Most ever'one 'oo lives in Cleveland Street drops in now an' again."

"Including poor Mr. Finch, I suppose," Charles sighed. "The man who was murdered last week, I mean."

Mrs. O'Reilly pulled a long face. "Yes, poor man. The p'lice 'aven't a clue, I've 'eard. But that's the way of it. The p'lice don't allus do wot they're s'posed to."

"Since you know everyone," Charles said thoughtfully, "I wonder if you might happen to remember someone who may have lived in Cleveland Street ten years or so ago." He took the photograph out of his pocket and placed it on the counter. "I believe that her name is Mary Kelly, but you may have known her as Marie Jeannette."

As if drawn by a magnet, the woman's eyes went to the photograph. Charles knew by the sudden tension in her shoulders that she recognized the face, but she shook her head violently and pushed the photograph back toward him.

"Niver seen 'er," she declared emphatically. "Niver in me 'ole life."

"Are you certain, Mrs. O'Reilly?" Charles pressed. He opened his purse again. "It is important that I—"

"Put yer money away," the woman cried, with a flutter of her fat hands. Her eyes were opened wide and her face had gone pale. "I don't know nothin', I tell ye! Ye'll git nothin' o' me, by Gawd!"

Whatever information Mrs. O'Reilly might possess, he could see that she was so genuinely terrified by his questions that she was unlikely to tell him anything. Still, this part of his inquiry had not been entirely unsuccessful. He could surmise from the woman's response that Mary Kelly had been known in this neighborhood, and he had learned where part of the blackmail photograph had been taken. What these things might mean, though, he had no idea.

Perhaps he would have better luck at Number 2.

18

"The Theory of the Mad Doctor

Robert James Lees is the person entitled to the credit of tracking down Jack the Ripper. In his early years Mr. Lees developed an extraordinary clairvoyant power. One day he was writing in his study when he became convinced that the Ripper was about to commit another murder. The whole scene arose before him. He seemed to see two persons, a man and a woman, walking down the length of a main street..."

The Sunday Times-Herald,
Chicago IL, 1895

KATE AND JENNIE ate a leisurely breakfast and then dressed for their trip. Pocket, trying not to show his bemusement at their ladyships' unusual appearance, drove them in the pony cart to Colchester, where they boarded the nine o'clock train. They disembarked at the Liverpool Street Station, the terminus of the Great Eastern and North London lines, and joined the noisy river of passengers that poured up the steps and spilled out onto the street. There the stream divided, one top-hatted and frock-coated tributary surging toward Broad Street and the Stock Exchange and banks and insurance companies, another capped and billycocked, flowing rather more sluggishly in the direction of Spitalfields and the East End. There were young mothers burdened with babies and brown paper parcels, working women hurrying off to an office, smartly dressed ladies trailed by uniformed porters pushing heavily laden baggage carts, and the ubiquitous traffic policemen whose job it was to direct the disorderly procession of cabs and omnibuses eager to claim passengers. Now that it had started to drizzle, everyone was in a great hurry to get in out of the wet.

As they moved along with the crowd, Kate thought with some satisfaction that she and Jennie were not in any way remarkable. They were both dressed in plain dark skirts, white cotton waists, and thick boots, and held black umbrellas over their heads. Jennie was wearing Mrs. Pratt's green jacket and green plaid cape, and her dark hair was topped by Mrs. Pratt's cabbage-rose hat, now swathed with additional veiling. Kate was decked out in her cook's black coat and her maid's red-trimmed bonnet and matching red-and-white checked scarf, looped against her shoulder and fastened with a gaudy brass brooch. They looked, Kate hoped, like two respectable housekeepers on holiday—except that Lady Randolph was rather more regal in her bearing than any housekeeper Kate had ever seen.

There had been some discussion when it came time to board the train, but Jennie was finally persuaded to forgo the first-class carriage and climb into the third, which should have seated ten but was being made to serve half again that many. A similar discussion took place when they reached Broad Street and Jennie raised a commanding arm to hail a hansom. At Kate's whispered objection, they boarded instead a crowded mustard-yellow omnibus with a red Lipton's Tea advertisement on the side panel. For sixpence, they were on their way to Bloomsbury, along with ten other passengers whose furled umbrellas dripped on their neighbors' skirts and boots. They disembarked at Theobalds Road and Southampton Row, put up their umbrellas again, and made in the direction of Boswell Street.

"What are we going to say when we locate Mr. Lees?" Jennie asked as they hurried along, taking care to avoid the puddles.

Kate stepped aside so that a nursemaid might pass with her green wicker pram. "If you don't mind," she said, "I should prefer to talk to him." She gave Jennie a sideways look. "Unless you can pretend to be Irish."

"Irish?" Jennie said with a trill. She tossed her head gaily. "I need not pretend t' be Irish, ye silly. Randolph's father was Viceroy, and Randolph was his secretary, and we lived in Dublin for three years. In all that time, I can remember naught but blue waters an' green hills, an' days full o' Irish sunshine and song." She tipped her umbrella and lifted her face to the falling rain. "Wi' only a wee frolic of a raindrop dancin' out of a cloud every now an' then."

Kate laughed out loud. "Well done!" she exclaimed. "Then you shall be my sister Charlotte Kelly and I shall be Kathryn Kelly, and we have come from Dublin to ask after our kinswoman."

"But if this man is indeed clairvoyant," Jennie asked, lapsing into her ordinary speech, "won't he be sure to see through our deception?"

Kate had been thinking about that very question. "If he does," she said, "then we shall confess. But perhaps he will see past our deception to our sincere search for the truth. Either way, we have nothing to lose."

"I agree," Jennie said. She pointed. "We have come to the place."

They stood in front of a red-brick house set back a few yards from the street behind an iron fence. The scrolled gate bore a brass plaque announcing that this was the home of the Bloomsbury Spiritualist Society. As they came through the gate, the front door of the house opened. The prosperous-looking gray-bearded man who came out was dressed in a dark morning coat, gray trousers, and felt hat, with an ivory-headed walking stick under one arm and an umbrella in his hand. He was just putting it up when he saw them.

"May I assist you, ladies?" he asked.

"We're lookin' for Mr. Robert Lees, if ye please, sir," Kate said, slipping easily into the thick brogue she remembered so well from her childhood with Uncle and Aunt O'Malley.

"Robert J. Lees, at your service," the man said, and took off his hat with a courteous gesture. "And you—"

"My name is Kathryn Kelly," Kate said gravely. "An' this is my sister Charlotte. We've come t' ask some questions, sir, about a cousin o' ours, in hopes ye might tell us what really happened to her, and why. Her name was Mary Kelly."

The man stood very still for a moment, his glance resting first on Kate, then on Jennie. He stepped back and pushed the door open. "I think you had better come inside out of the wet," he said. "Our conversation may take some time."

19

"We are now in a position to inform our readers of the men who are involved in the West End brothel scandal... The guilty parties include a number of well-known aristocrats, among them Lord Arthur Somerset and Lord Euston, who, it is believed, has departed from this country and gone to Peru. It is scandalous that men of position are allowed to leave the country and defeat the ends of justice because their prosecution would inculpate even more highly placed and distinguished personages..."

North London Press,
16 November, 1889

CHARLES LEARNED EVEN less at Number 2 than at Number 22. The landlady, a truculent woman with eyes like black currants, a face like a pudding, and a mole on her chin that sprouted three coarse black hairs, would not allow him into Finch's lodging.

"The rooms won't be ready to rent till Mr. Finch's brother comes to claim his belongings," she said in a proprietary tone. "He was all packed up when he was killed, for going to Paris, so it won't take his brother long to collect his things. But it'll be another few days before the carpet is cleaned and the rooms is ready. Come back next week. Monday will do." She started to close the door.

"But I don't want to rent Mr. Finch's rooms," Charles said. "I just want to have a look around. I'd like to see if he—"

The landlady's black eyes snapped. "Oh, you don't want to rent, do you? And why not, I'd like to know." Her voice rose defensively. "They're fine rooms, large and convenient, and only a little blood spilled on the carpet, which will be entirely gone as soon as it's been cleaned. You won't find any better lodging in Cleveland Street."

"But I don't intend to lodge in Cleveland Street," Charles said, already sensing the futility of his effort. "Actually, my interest in this matter is of a professional nature. I should like to see Mr. Finch's darkroom." The existence of the darkroom was a matter of speculation, but Charles felt he had nothing to lose.

"Dark rooms? Dark rooms, you say?" The landlady became scornful. "Look here, sir! The windows in those rooms is the envy of every lodging-house proprietor in Cleveland Street. A painter lived there before Finch, and he never once complained about the rooms being dark! In fact, he was quite complimentary about the light. North, it is. That's the best, they always says."

"I fear that I have not made myself clear," Charles said humbly. "I understand that Mr. Finch was a skilled photographer. He needed a small room without light—a closet, perhaps—in which to develop his photographs

143

and prepare and store his chemicals. I should like to see it. What's more, I am prepared to make his brother a handsome offer for his equipment, as well as for his collection of negatives."

The landlady snorted. "Well! If you've come round looking for foul-smelling chemicals that are liable to go off like a bomb, you're going to be disappointed, that's all I've got to say. This is a clean, *safe* house, I'll have you know." She wrinkled her nose distastefully. "If I ever got a whiff of any chemical goings-on, Mr. Finch would have been out on the pavement in one minute flat, bag and baggage! What do you think this is? A haven for anarchists?"

Charles wanted to protest that most photographic chemicals were quite odorless and generally non-combustible, but he restrained himself, feeling that the landlady would not welcome instruction in the matter. "Perhaps," he said, "Mr. Finch performed his professional work elsewhere."

"If he did," she retorted snappishly, "it wouldn't be any business of mine, now, would it?"

Charles sighed and reached into his pocket. "Here is my card. Perhaps you will be good enough to give it to Mr. Finch's brother when he calls to retrieve the belongings, and to convey my offer, as well."

The landlady studied the card as if she were scrutinizing it for evidence of chemical contamination, then pocketed it with a suspicious harrumph.

Murmuring his thanks, Charles took his leave. As he was going down the steps, he heard the door slam behind him.

But while Number 2 had yielded very little in the way of information, Number 3, across the way, produced rather more. It was a barbershop, with the deep doorway Charles had remarked earlier, where an observer might have stationed himself. The barber was a voluble little fellow named Osborn, with a shiny bald head, a remarkable pair of waxed black mustaches, and a finely honed sense of curiosity. He had, as it turned out, observed the observer, a fact that emerged after Charles sat down in the barber chair and requested a trim for his beard.

"O'course I saw the man, now, didn't I?" Osborn said, bending close for a few critical snips of his scissors. " 'Ee stood for the longest time right in that doorway there, like 'ee wuz goin' to come in and get shaved."

"Can you tell me what he looked like?"

Osborn snipped again, twice here, once there. "Blond, 'andsome, a gentleman. Admir'ble mustaches." He pursed his lips, considering. "Might've been a milit'ry man, from 'is bearin'."

Blond, handsome, mustached, military—George Cornwallis-West, to the life, Charles thought. So Jennie had been right. George had hidden himself in the doorway and watched her come and go. But how long had he been there? Long enough to run upstairs and kill the man who was waiting for Jennie?

"I don't suppose you happened to notice the time," he remarked.

"No, I didn't." Osborn plied his comb regretfully, then returned to snipping. " 'Twas before the coppers was called to the lodging across the way, though—I can tell you that much. When I went out to see wot the trouble wuz, 'ee was gone."

"Oh?" Charles asked, feigning ignorance. "There was some trouble that afternoon, then?"

'Trouble!" Osborn exclaimed. He turned Charles's chin for a better view, snipped several times, then turned it the other way.

"I'd say 'twas trouble! Tom Finch, 'oo lived in Number 2, 'ee got 'imself stabbed to death, poor man. There wuz folks buzzin' 'bout, coppers in droves, the mortuary wagon parked by the door till goin' on teatime—and the landlady 'avin' a fine fit of 'ysterics, o'course." His eyes glinted. "Most excitement we've had since that unsav'ry business at Number 19."

"Number 19?" Charles asked, and then, with a start, remembered. "Oh, yes, of course. Number 19."

The year after the Ripper killings, in the autumn of 1889, a scandal had erupted regarding a male brothel that had enjoyed a thriving business at Number 19 Cleveland Street. In fact, the affair had reached to high places, to the Royals, even, for it was widely rumored about London that Eddy, the Duke of Clarence, frequented the place in pursuit of its forbidden pleasures. After two initial arrests, however, the thing had been quickly hushed up. The brothel's owner had taken himself off to France, and the two men charged in the case received suspiciously light sentences—in return for their silence, some said. The *North London Press* had charged that men of title, Lord Euston and Lord Arthur Somerset, a close friend of Prince Eddy—had been allowed to escape justice in order to protect more highly placed persons, but the editor, a man named Ernest Parke, paid dearly for his freedom of speech: he was convicted of libel and dispatched to prison. Gossip about Eddy's part in the affair had raged until his death, some two and a half years later. And the whole thing had begun at Number 19 Cleveland

Street, Charles mused—just a few doors down from Walter Sickert's studio and across the street from the tobacconist's and confectioner's shop he had visited this morning.

"Funny thing, come t' think of it," the barber said, stepping back to admire his handiwork. "The man 'oo was killed, 'ee wuz involved in that business." He paused solicitously. "Wot d'ye think, sir? Short 'nough for ye?"

"I think you have done a first-rate job," Charles said, allowing the striped cotton cape to be removed. He stood. "So Tom Finch was part of the affair at Number 19, was he?"

" 'Deed 'ee wuz," Osborn replied, shaking the cape with a snap. "In fact, 'im an' Charles 'Ammond—'ee was the owner o' the place—went off t' France together, so's they wouldn't get arrested. Not that many did," he added significantly, "if ye take my point. There wuz 'igher-ups involved, so they say. Far as the coppers wuz concerned, it wuz 'ands off."

"Indeed," Charles said. He reached into his pocket. "I understand that Mr. Finch was something of a photographer. Is that true?"

"Oh, yessir," Osborn said, his eyes following Charles's hand. "Used t' take photos up an' down the street. Not buildings or 'orses, though, just people. Said 'ee specialized in faces." In a meaningful tone, he went on: "I've 'eard as 'ow 'ee might 'ave took a few photos at Number 19. Not just faces, neither, if ye take my meanin'."

"Oh?" Charles said. He took out a silver coin.

"An' used 'is photos to put a bit o' the black on one or two," Osborn went on. He rubbed his bald head. "Some say that Lord Euston paid Tom Finch quite a few pounds for a good picture o' hisself."

"Ah," Charles said. Lord Euston, eh? So Mr. Finch's blackmail of Jennie Churchill was not a novice's lucky first effort. Who knows how many extortion attempts the man had made? "Well, then," he said reflectively, "I suppose you have wondered whether Mr. Finch's employment might have contributed to his death."

"So I 'ave." Osborn gave an emphatic nod. "So I 'ave, indeed. I 'eard that some fine lady come to see 'im before 'ee died. I shouldn't be much surprised if she wuz tired o' the black an' decided to 'andle the matter 'erself."

"Hmmm," Charles said. He took out the photograph of Mary Kelly and handed it to the barber. "I am curious as to whether this might be an example of Mr. Finch's work. Do you recognize the woman?"

Osborn gave the photo his careful attention. After a long moment, he said, "I believe I recognize 'er, sir, but I couldn't give ye 'er name. Seems to me she lived 'ere-abouts, some while ago."

"It would have been more than ten years ago," Charles said. Still studying the photograph, the barber rubbed his hand over his bald head again. "Seems to me she was a nursemaid," he said thoughtfully. "I seem to recall 'er pushin' a pram. But ten years is a long time." He handed the photo back.

"It is indeed," Charles said, pressing two silver coins into the barber's hand. "A good trim," he said, "and more. I thank you."

"Ye're more than welcome, sir," Osborn said. He looked down at the coins, then squinted at Charles. "Ye're not from the p'lice, are ye?"

"No," Charles said, "I'm not. This is a private inquiry."

"A private inquiry?" A light broke across the barber's face. "T' be sure! Like Sherlock Holmes, eh?"

"Something like," Charles said, and took his leave.

20

From Newspaper Account of
Catherine Eddowes' Inquest

"Crawford (solicitor representing City Police):
Would you consider that the person who inflicted
the wounds possessed anatomical skill?

Brown (police surgeon): He must have had a good
deal of knowledge as to the position of the abdominal
organs and the way to remove them. The way in
which the kidney was cut out showed that it was
done by somebody who knew what he was about."

The Times,
12 October, 1888

THE DRIZZLE HAD changed to rain by the time Kate and
Jennie walked through the gate of the Bloomsbury
Spiritualist Society and out into Boswell Street. Without
speaking, they put up their umbrellas and splashed
through the puddles in the direction of the British
Museum, where they found a small tea shop with a

green awning. They took a table in a darkened corner, away from the window and the noise of traffic from the street, and ordered cress sandwiches, vegetable soup, and cups of strong, steaming tea poured from a china pot.

Kate wiggled her toes inside her damp boots and sipped her tea gratefully, glad for its warmth and for the quiet shelter of the tea shop. Mr. Lees had been far more willing to talk with them than she had anticipated, and their conversation had yielded an unexpected treasure trove of information. At the same time, it had been distinctly unsettling, not only because Mr. Lees' story was so extraordinary but because the conclusion of his tale had had such a devastating impact on Jennie, who sat across from her now, pale and silent, her eyes cast down.

Kate was accustomed to crafting fictions with a startling psychic twist. In fact, some of Beryl Bardwell's most popular early stories had involved a medium named Mrs. Leona Travis, who frequently helped the New York Police Department solve some very grisly crimes by calling on the spirits of the departed to tell what they knew. But the story that Robert Lees had related—in a reprise of the *Sunday Times-Herald* article that Kate had read and clipped—was much more amazing and far more *real* than any of Beryl Bardwell's fictions. It had, Kate thought, the ring of truth.

Over cups of coffee and a plate of biscuits brought in by a young parlor maid, Lees said that he had been working at his desk one morning in September '88, when he had a strong premonition that the Ripper was about to kill again.

"I saw the whole scene," he said. "The woman, half-

151

drunk, the man, drawing a knife from his inside pocket to slash her throat." He went immediately to Scotland Yard but found that the C.I.D., already overwhelmed with crank reports, had no patience for this latest lunatic. The following night, however, just such a murder took place. Lees was so deeply affected by his failure to prevent the death that he became ill and was advised by his doctor to go abroad for a few weeks with his wife, to distract himself from the horror of the killings. It didn't work.

"I believed," he said gravely, "that some sort of mysterious link—a magnetic wave, if you will—had been formed between me and the man who was butchering those poor women. I became obsessed. I read about the murders, thought about them, even dreamed about them." His voice became intense. "I knew—yes, I *knew*—that if I could identify the man whose intentions I sensed, the killings would stop."

A few weeks later, Lees was riding in an omnibus with his wife when he became aware that the killer was nearby. At the top of Notting Hill, a man boarded and Lees bent over to tell his wife, "That is Jack the Ripper." She tried to laugh him out of it, but Lees was firm in his conviction. When the bus turned off Edgware Road at the Marble Arch and the man got out, Lees followed him up Oxford Street in the direction of Apsley House. As they went, the man became increasingly agitated and nervous, and at last hailed a cab and made off down Piccadilly.

Some time later, dining with friends, Lees suddenly knew that the Ripper had struck again. He went immediately to Scotland Yard, arriving even before the telegram about Mary Kelly's murder arrived. Convinced that Lees' powers were genuine, one of the inspectors encouraged him to submit himself to the killer's strange magnetic connection. Trailed by the inspector and his men, Lees walked through the West End, stopping finally in front of a mansion that was the home of one of the most celebrated physicians in London. Inside, the inspector spoke to the doctor's wife, who confessed that she feared that her husband was losing his mind. His behavior had become frighteningly erratic and she had realized with horror that he was absent from home whenever a murder occurred in Whitechapel. She had been too fearful to inquire about his whereabouts.

Under questioning by doctors, the physician himself acknowledged that his mind had been unbalanced for the past year and that there were intervals when he could not recall where he had been or what he had done. On one occasion, he confessed that he had awakened as if from a dream and discovered blood on his clothing, the source of which he could not identify. Some weeks later, the physician was certified as insane and committed, under the name of Thomas Mason, to a private asylum in Islington. To conceal the truth, the family announced that he had died. His coffin was filled with stones, and his funeral was celebrated with appropriate solemnity and attended by many of Society's greats. His real death came later, in the asylum.

Kate leaned forward. "What was the doctor's name?" she asked.

Mr. Lees studied her with a sober attention. "I trust you will forgive me for being blunt, Miss Kelly—or whoever you are. I am fully aware that you have uses for this information other than the one you have told me. Even so, I offer it freely, because I feel that you have

153

lied to me out of a genuine desire to find the truth."
He turned from Kate to Jennie. "The physician whom I
identified was Sir William Gull."

Kate could see that Jennie recognized the name. At
Mr. Lees' pronouncement, her face went white. Her
large dark eyes were fixed unwaveringly upon his face
and she sat stiffly erect, gripping the arms of her chair
with both hands as if to keep from fainting. She did not
utter a sound.

Lees cleared his throat. "However, Sir William was not
the only man involved in the crimes." He paused, still
looking at Jennie, as if he were waiting for a question
from her. When she said nothing, he went on. "There
were others. The police—one inspector, anyway—knew
who they were." He held up his hand as if to forestall a
question. "I cannot tell you their names, nor even share
my suspicions. I can say only that Sir William did not
act alone, nor on his own behalf. He was, as he thought,
acting upon the commission of a greater authority." He
stood. "I see that this is terribly upsetting, so I shall
leave you to gather your thoughts before you go on your
way. Please help yourselves to more coffee."

Then he had turned, his strong face lined with the
deepest compassion, to Jennie. "I do wish you well, my
lady," he said softly. "Your path is a steep and difficult
one." He looked down at the muddy black boot showing
under her dark skirt and added, inexplicably, "Pray do
mind your step." And then he was gone.

*

The waitress placed their soup and sandwiches on the
table before them and brought another pot of tea, and

the two women began to eat without speaking. Jennie, however, ate only a little of her lunch, and that without enthusiasm. At last, she leaned back in her chair and said, in a voice that was tinged with a bitter sadness, "I suppose you want to hear about it."

"I want to hear what you are ready to tell me," Kate said quietly.

Jennie raised her chin. "Very well, then. You have probably already guessed that I knew Sir William. He was the Prince of Wales's regular physician—as well as Physician-in-Ordinary to the Queen—and he treated me when I was ill with typhoid. He treated Randolph for his disease as well, with mercury." Her jaw was set and her dark eyes were unfathomable. "Randolph and I attended his funeral. He was buried in a churchyard at Thorpe-le-Soken, and so many went that a special train had to be laid on." She pulled a deep breath. "Sir William was a very good friend of Randolph's. They were both Freemasons, you see. I once heard him say that anything Randolph asked of him, he would do. And now I'm to understand that Sir William was the Ripper, and that he did not work alone?" She shook her head. "Can you blame me for feeling... distraught?"

"Of course not," Kate said sympathetically. "If it is not too disturbing, can you tell me something of Sir William? What sort of a man was he?"

"What sort?" Jennie leaned her chin in her hand, frowning. "A man of two natures, I should say. On the one hand, he could be very kind and tender—he was to me, at least, in my illness. On the other, he could be almost inhumanly cold." She looked across the room. "After he died, a friend of his wrote that Sir William once performed a postmortem examination and took away the dead man's heart in his pocket—even though he had promised the grieving sister that he would remove none of the organs." She closed her eyes for a moment, then opened them. "He was a talented surgeon, you know." Her voice dropped. "And an ardent vivisectionist."

Kate did not have to point out that those facts made Lees' remarkable story only more plausible, for Jennie seemed fully aware of the significance of what she had said. She waited, and when it appeared that her companion had nothing more to add, said, "If you have finished your lunch, I think we should be going. It is still raining, so if you should like to take a cab to the East End, we might go so far as Bishopsgate before we disembark."

Jennie stood and arranged the green plaid cape across her shoulders. "Yes, let's take a cab." She eyed Kate warily. "Are we to stumble across any more surprising discoveries in the East End, do you think?"

"Heaven only knows what we shall stumble across," Kate said, taking up her wet umbrella. "But I do hope that we will eventually encounter the truth."

21

"Inspector Abberline was brought into the Ripper enquiry... because of his invaluable experience gained over thirteen years in the East End. At the time of the murders he was with the Central Office of Scotland Yard, but having previously been the head of Whitechapel CID he had an intimate knowledge of the East End and its criminals. According to Melville Macnaghten, writing in 1914, Abberline 'knew the East End of London as few men have known it'."

MELVYN FAIRCLOUGH
The Ripper and the Royals
1992

CHARLES TOOK A cab from Cleveland Street across the river to Waterloo Station. The afternoon was cold and damp, which one should have thought might discourage trippers, but there was a large group of them at the station, ladies dressed in tweeds, woolen capes, and stout boots, with portmanteaus at their feet, walking sticks under their arms, and birding glasses around their necks. They were clattering like a hundred magpies about their intended seaside birding expedition near Poole and along the Dorset coast.

Charles queued up at a vendor's stall, purchased a greasy parcel of fish and chips and a bottle of beer, and escaped to an empty first-class carriage. He'd not taken time for lunch, so he ate hungrily, then settled himself. With a change of trains at Portsmouth, the London and Southwestern Railway would take three hours or thereabouts to deliver him to Bournemouth, so he had plenty of time to consider his interview with Frederick Abberline—former Inspector Abberline, C.I.D.—in light of the information he had gleaned in Cleveland Street in the previous two hours.

In his telegram to Abberline requesting a meeting, Charles had been deliberately vague. Post Office claims to the contrary, telegrams were not quite as private as might be hoped or even expected, and he did not intend to share the real purpose of his journey with the Bournemouth telegraph operator. He had said only that he should like to discuss a current aspect of the "affair in Millers Court," knowing that Abberline would recognize the site of the final Ripper murder.

Abberline replied in the same vague way. To Charles's surprise, he seemed less than eager to meet, intimating that his past work was no longer important or relevant. He was aware of Charles's recent investigations, however, and would be interested in discussing matters of "mutual professional interest." He thought it might be expedient to meet on the Bournemouth public pier, a suggestion that struck Charles as singularly remarkable.

Charles had originally decided to consult Abberline because he thought the former inspector might be able to shed some light on the current status of the Ripper investigation. There had been a great many rumors over the intervening years that the Ripper—who appeared to have gone out of business after the death of Mary Kelly—had been killed, imprisoned, or committed to a lunatic asylum, and the facts concealed from the public. Some of the reports Charles had heard actually seemed quite credible, like the theory of the mad doctor from the West End who had been secretly committed to an asylum in Islington, his role in the Ripper killings concealed for the sake of his family. If anyone knew that Jack the Ripper had actually been identified—and hence could *not* have been Randolph Churchill—that man was Fred Abberline. Perhaps that was the reason for the former inspector's lack of enthusiasm for a meeting and his suggestion that his work was no longer relevant. If this were true, Charles's endeavors would be radically simplified. The authorities might be persuaded to make some sort of statement that would protect Jennie and her sons from any more of these cruel blackmail attempts, and that would be that.

But his discoveries in Cleveland Street had given Charles something more to think about. For one thing, he had learned from the talkative barber that Jennie's blackmailer was an experienced photographer. If the landlady was to be believed, Finch did not have a darkroom where he could have created the forgery, the sophistication of which strongly suggested that it had *not* been produced in his broom closet. He must, therefore, have a studio somewhere else. But where? And where were the original negatives for the forged photograph?

Charles frowned. There was no actual evidence that

Finch himself had devised the photo; as a matter of fact, someone else could just as easily have produced it and given it to Finch. But why Finch? Randolph Churchill had had any number of powerful enemies who would have been delighted to pay a great deal for the privilege of exploiting such an incriminating photograph. What was more, the barber had said that Finch had been involved in other extortion attempts in connection with the Cleveland Street brothel incident, so he was no stranger to the criminal arts. It was that suggestion, more than anything else, which now made it seem likely that Tom Finch had indeed produced the blackmail photograph, and that it was time to undertake a serious search for the studio he might have used, which was probably located in Cleveland Street or nearby. If Charles could find that studio, he might be able to find the negatives— and the person who wrote the note Jennie had received yesterday.

The conductor tapped on the door, opened it, and Charles handed him his ticket. Then he picked up *The Times* and was just settling back to read the day's news when he thought of something else. Wasn't it Abberline who had been put in charge of the inquiry into the Cleveland Street brothel affair—and who had taken most of the criticism when the police handling of the case came under fire? Perhaps he would have some information about Tom Finch. And perhaps, come to think of it, while Abberline had been investigating the Ripper killings, he might also have happened onto some information about Mary Kelly's residency in Cleveland Street.

Charles opened *The Times*, frowning slightly. It was beginning to seem that all roads led to Cleveland Street.

The Bournemouth Central station was built as a monument to the grandeur of the London and Southwestern Railway, its high roof spanned by latticed girders that were supported by buttressed red-brick side walls. The chill drizzle that plagued London was only a mist here on the South Coast, but the sky was still overcast and the waters of Poole Bay were gray and choppy. Charles walked the mile or so from the railway station to the pier, which was deserted when he arrived. In fact, the only person in sight was a lone fisherman, sitting on a folding stool at the far end of the pier. Charles strolled slowly down the pier, and in a few moments the fisherman casually pulled in his line, packed up his stool and tackle, and walked toward Charles.

It was Abberline. The former inspector's hairline had receded even farther since Charles had seen him last and his heavy mutton-chop whiskers had turned decidedly gray, but the wary look had not left his eyes and his mouth was still hard and shrewd. He had spent over thirty years in the service of the Metropolitan Police, and the work had marked him.

"Hello, Abberline," Charles said. "How's the fishing?"

"Some days it's good, some days not," Abberline replied. His voice was gruff, and Charles heard suspicion in it. "Do you fish, Lord Somersworth?"

"You can dispense with the title, if you don't mind," Charles said easily. "I've retained the name of Sheridan. And no, I don't fish. Don't go in for hunting, either. I've never been much of a sportsman." He paused. "I trust you're enjoying your retirement."

Abberline put down his gear and leaned his elbows against the railing of the pier, looking westward across the bay, where the curve of the shoreline marked the Isle of Purbeck.

"I can't complain," he said. "Bournemouth's a bit dull, after London, but the air is fresh and it's nice to be able to sleep at night." He turned his head and drew his dark brows together, studying Charles, as if reassessing him. "You seem to be making quite a name for yourself in forensics. I was impressed by your article on crime-scene photography in the *British Journal Photographic Almanac*." The corner of his mouth turned up. "If you don't mind my saying so, Sheridan, you've come a long way since that impertinent letter you wrote to Warren, complaining about those wretched photographs of the Ripper victims."

Sensing a slight thaw in Abberline's manner, Charles grinned. "You know about that? I suppose, then, that you're the one who had me drafted to record the carnage."

"Afraid so. You made some good points in your letter, and even Warren, fool that he was, had to admit that the job our man was doing was barely adequate." A pair of gulls wheeled overhead, crying lustily, and somewhere in the town, a tower clock struck the third quarter-hour. "Warren said no at first, but the word came down that you were reliable." He paused. "The right sort, I mean," he added in a level tone. "The right background. You could be counted on."

"The right background? I'm not sure I understand."

Abberline gave a short laugh. "Neither did I, at the time. Later, though, it became clearer." He gave Charles a slantwise look that held a grudging admiration. "Be that as it may, you did good work, Sheridan. Much more professional than I expected from a toff. And you've continued to do good work since, in spite of your elevation. So I've decided to be straight with you." He hesitated. "But only as far as I can."

"Thank you," Charles said.

"You have little to thank me for. And I have little to tell. A few weeks after Kelly's murder, I was ordered to close the investigation."

"*Close* it?" Charles exclaimed, surprised. "But why? The case was unsolved and the murders were only a few months old!"

Abberline watched the swooping gulls for a long moment and then turned, scanning the pier in each direction. A woman and a child were walking toward them, the woman bending her head into the wind, the child dancing along with both arms outstretched as if to fly. Abberline lowered his voice.

"What makes you think the case was unsolved?"

Charles pursed his lips. So the rumors *had* been true. "No one was ever brought to trial," he said, "and there was never an official explanation. Like everyone else, I assumed that the authorities wanted to bring the Ripper to a public justice."

Abberline's voice was edged. "That would be the wrong assumption, now, wouldn't it? The 'authorities,' as you call them, wanted to close the investigation, that's all. They made it clear that I was not to pursue it, either officially or unofficially, and that I am never to discuss what I know with anyone." His mouth took on a wry, half-mocking twist. "Not even with someone who can be counted on. Not even with someone like you, Sheridan."

Now Charles was beginning to understand. Abberline was speaking, obliquely to be sure, about some sort of police cover-up—or perhaps even higher, in the Home Office. "These authorities," he said. "They still have some influence over you, I take it, even though you are retired from the force?"

"Some influence? Well, that's one way of putting it." Abberline laughed, his mockery now turned on himself. "I've been given a fine house and a generous pension, twice what I should be getting otherwise." He lowered his head to his arms. "I don't know why I'm telling you this, except to explain why I can't do what any reputable law enforcement officer ought to be able to do." His voice was muffled, but Charles could hear the humiliation in it, and guilt, and a wretched self-pity. "And don't blame the Yard, for God's sake. Their hands are tied, as are mine."

Don't blame the Yard? To Charles, the words clearly implied that the order to close the case had come from the Home Office, which suggested that the matter had been taken as far up the line as the Cabinet. The Cabinet! What the devil had he got into?

Now it was Charles's turn to fall silent. The wind had dropped and a fog was closing fast around them, swathing the distant shoreline and the end of the pier. It was probably pointless to attempt to persuade the man, given his situation, but he had to make one more try.

"I understand your position, Abberline, but there's more here at stake than I've said so far. I've been asked to help a certain lady who is being blackmailed with a forged photograph that poses her husband with one of the Ripper victims. I don't need details. But if I can show that the case has been solved—"

Abberline's head came up. "You can't," he said. "Aren't you *listening* to me, man? It's a damn shame about the blackmail. I'm sorry for it, and sorrier for the lady. But the case is closed, and there's nothing I can tell you."

Abberline's helpless, angry frustration was contagious, and despite his resolve for calm, Charles found the passion rising in him. "But an innocent woman's future is at stake, I tell you!" he said fiercely. "And it's not just a matter of blackmail, either. The extortionist was murdered, and the police are looking for her. She could go to prison if I can't sort this out."

Abberline's face was impassive. He looked away into the distance, saying nothing.

Charles pulled in his breath. "All right, then," he said, trying to make himself speak more quietly. "If you can't talk to me about the Ripper, talk to me about Cleveland Street."

Abberline came suddenly to life. "Cleveland Street!" He pounded the railing with a sudden savage vehemence. "Sheridan, do you have any idea what you're dealing with, or the danger you're in?"

"Murder," Charles said. "And blackmail. That's what I'm dealing with. And as for danger, it's the lady who—"

"You have no idea," Abberline said quietly. "None at all." He turned to fix his gaze on Charles's face. His eyes were narrowed and his jaw was working, and when he spoke again his voice was taut, as if he were suppressing wretchedness or rage, or both. "You may think that your social position guarantees you a certain safety, but it does not. The authority that sentenced four women to death because they threatened to reveal a secret marriage surely has the power to restrain one renegade lord. I advise you to watch your step."

"A secret marriage?" Charles asked, astonished.

Resolutely, Abberline turned his face toward the water.

"I need to know, damn it, man!" Charles exclaimed. "Tell me!"

Abberline shook his head from side to side like a dog. "No more," he growled. "No more! I've already said too much."

Charles stood for a moment, hesitating. "Then say no more." He put his hand on Abberline's arm. "Except for yes or no. One word only. Or not even a word. Just a nod or a shake of the head."

Abberline frowned. "What do you mean?"

"If I tell you what I have learned from other sources, will you confirm or contradict it?"

Conflicting emotions crossed the other man's face. "Possibly," he said. "It will depend."

Charles reached into his coat pocket and drew out the photograph. "This is Mary Kelly."

Abberline glanced at it. If he was surprised, his face didn't show it. "Yes."

"The photograph was taken in Cleveland Street, in front of Number 22, by a man named Tom Finch. Did he have anything to do with the Ripper killings?"

"Finch?" Abberline seemed surprised. "No."

"Did Mary Kelly live at Number 22?"

Abberline shook his head.

"Did she live nearby?"

Abberline did not respond.

"Was the secret marriage hers?"

The town clock began to strike the hour. Abberline straightened. "The last train to London is due to leave in thirty minutes. If you hurry, you can just catch it."

Charles felt close to despair. "Is there nothing you can tell me that might help?"

The fog was swirling thick. Abberline bent over to pick up his fishing gear. "You might talk to Walter Sickert," he said. "Number 13 Robert Street, Cumberland Square. Near Regent's Park."

And with that, he turned to walk up the pier toward the shore. He did not look back.

22

"When we first came to the East End—to St. Jude's in Whitechapel, my husband was told by the bishop that it was the worst parish in the district. There were some six thousand people crowded into a maze of insanitary courts and alleys. To get into the courts you often had to walk through the stench of evil-smelling gases rising from sewage and refuse scattered in all directions. The sun never penetrates into them and they are never visited by a breath of fresh air."

DAME HENRIETTA BARNETT
wife of the founder of
Toynbee Hall Settlement

KATE EXPECTED THAT her early years in New York would have prepared her for the streets of Whitechapel, but she was wrong. For one thing, her memories of sights and sounds and smells had been blessedly dulled by the passage of time. For another, the New York in which she had lived had seemed somehow hopeful, and if lives were bleak and possibilities limited, the dream of a brighter future was compelling, the desire to change station was strong.

But there was nothing hopeful about the streets of Whitechapel. The spiritless faces Kate saw as she and Jennie trudged down Commercial Street were marked by the desolate, dreary, hopeless business of surviving the present day, with no energy or will to dream of a future. The figures seemed to move as if through a fog, slow and sad.

Commercial Street slashed a long diagonal through Spitalfields from Shoreditch High Street to Whitechapel High Street. Christ Church loomed on the left, its massive bulk of Portland stone rising through the thickening mist like some monument to a forgotten god who offered only scant comfort to his followers. Attached to the church was a patch of bare dirt under a few trees, known locally as Itchy Park, owing to the many lice-infected, homeless people who passed their time there. Now, Kate saw, its benches were filled with sleeping figures clothed in rags, huddled under newspapers or pieces of cardboard, taking refuge from the ravages of the day in the solace of sleep.

"This is the street where Mary Kelly lived," Kate said, pointing at a dirty sign that read Duval Street, directly across from the park, beside the Britannia Pub. "It was called Dorset Street then, but the notoriety was so great that the name was changed."

A raucous group of factory girls in dark stuff dresses and white aprons charged past them, pushing and shoving and calling out insults to one another. Behind them sauntered a pair of women rather more gaily dressed—prostitutes, Kate surmised—their eyes boldly searching out men's faces, their lips suggestively pursed.

Jennie had pulled her veil across her face, and behind it her eyes were deeply shadowed. She fixed them on Kate, as if to avoid seeing anything else. "I still don't understand what you hope to learn in this awful place," she said. "It all seems so grim and hopeless."

Kate, her own spirit failing her, did not answer. What *could* she hope to learn, ten years after the murders? Even if there was information to be had, some truth to be discovered, why would anyone be willing to share it with *her*? And how could this effort throw any light on the more immediate and urgent question: who was blackmailing Jennie and how could he be made to stop?

But Kate had committed herself to this search, futile and perhaps purposeless as it might seem, and she was determined to go on with it. Without a word to Jennie, she turned into Duval Street, a mean, inhospitable, evil-looking place of lodging-houses and pubs, their grimy signboards thrusting out over the narrow thoroughfare, which was ankle-deep in dirt and mud. It was, Kate thought despairingly, like a street in hell.

Millers Court lay at the end of an arched, tunnel-like passage between Numbers 26 and 27 Dorset Street. Walking through the passageway was like walking through a sewer, Kate thought, as she held a handkerchief to her nose to filter the terrible stench. The court itself was a narrow paved yard littered with blowing papers and old rags, surrounded by six houses, their walls whitewashed up to the second story. The windows had once been painted green, and from one to another was stretched a clothesline, from which were hung a wet shirt and a pair of tar-smeared canvas trousers. A mangy dog lay sleeping in one corner, a half-naked runny-nosed child played with a pile of stones in another, and a pretty young woman, barely out of her teens, sat hunched in a doorway, her feet tucked under her ragged woolen skirt, her long black hair dirty and unkempt. A broken gin bottle lay in shards on the pavement beside her. She looked up at Kate. There was a large purple bruise on one cheekbone and her jaw looked swollen.

"We should like to speak to the landlady," Kate said. "Can you tell us where to find her?"

"That would be Mrs. McCarthy," the girl said shortly. She took a broken comb out of her pocket and began to tug it through her hair. "In the chandler's shop around the corner in Dorset Street."

Kate looked at the girl in some surprise, for it was evident by her speech that she had been educated. "Thank you," she said. She paused. "Have you lived here long? Do you live alone?"

"Long enough," the girl said. She jumped up, and her dullness turned to an active hostility. "And I live with whomever I please," she snapped. She looked Kate up and down, from her respectable bonnet to her respectable boots. "I don't need any missionaries telling me that I'm a sinner. I know what I am, and it's my business."

Jennie drew herself up. "We're not missionaries," she protested. "We're—"

"—looking for our cousin," Kate interrupted hastily. "Her name was Mary Kelly. She died here ten years ago. We're hoping that someone will remember her."

The girl leaned against the doorjamb, whatever energy the anger had sparked in her seeping away. "Well, it won't be me," she said, sullenly lethargic. "Ten years ago, I was a schoolgirl in Stratford-Upon-Avon."

She turned her head to hide the bright glint of tears. "The shop is at Number 27. Back down the passageway and turn right."

The chandler's shop was lined with shelves on which were displayed a variety of cheap wares—dishes and crockery, lamps, a few bolts of coarsely woven calico, flatirons, some ragged straw hats that looked as if they had been chewed by mice, an assortment of used bottles. A gray-haired, apple-cheeked woman sat in a rocking chair near the door, her lap filled with a piece of black woolen knitting to which she was energetically plying a pair of large steel needles. She wore men's brown boots, and a mammoth orange cat lay curled between her feet.

At the sight of Kate and Jennie, the woman put on a broad gap-toothed smile. "Arternoon, ladies," she chirped. "An wot're ye lookin' fer t'day? Sheets? Pillers? Got two new goosedown pillers, niver a 'ead laid on 'em." Her eyes glinted at the prospect of some fresh customer with a full purse. "Er maybe ye're arter a nice bit o' calico. I 'ave some fine Turkey red that's sure t' suit th' daintiest taste."

The woman's voice was harsh with Cockney accents, but to Kate's ear, there was some Irish in it. She slipped into her own Irish brogue, with an inflection a bit broader than that she had used to speak with Mr. Lees.

"Faith, Mrs. McCarthy, it's yer help we've come fer, if ye'd be so kind. Me name is Kathryn Kelly an' this is me sister Charlotte. We're from—" She hesitated. Where might Mary Kelly's people have lived? She took a breath and named her own mother's home. "From Limerick, in the west o' Ireland."

"From Limerick, 'ey?" A brightness lit in the depths of Mrs. McCarthy's eyes, and she gave a sentimental sigh.

"Ah, sweet Limerick." She sat rocking for a moment, reflectively, then shook herself and shifted her feet. "But that wuz a long time ago, when I wuz a wee girl, an' I ain't laid eyes on Limerick fer years. Wot kind o' 'elp?" The orange cat, deposed from his place between the boots, blinked, sat up, and yawned.

Kate dropped her voice. "Our cousin Mary Kelly was murdered in Millers Court ten years ago, almost to the day. We're lookin' fer someone who might've known her. Her mother is dyin', ye see, an' we've been asked to find out, if we can, why she was killed."

The rocking stopped. The ball of black worsted rolled out of Mrs. McCarthy's lap and bounced on the floor. The orange cat pounced swiftly upon it and began to bat it back and forth. With a muttered exclamation, the landlady retrieved the ball, kicked the cat, and resumed her chair. Her round face, which had before been blandly cheerful, was now dark with anger.

"Why she wuz killed?" she asked grimly. Her eyes narrowed. "Wot makes ye think there was a reason to it? The Ripper wuz mad, din't ye know? 'Ee 'ad no reason, 'cept th' pore girl wuz a Unfortunate. Ye knew that, din't ye?"

Jennie leaned forward and said, with a soft lilt, "Mary's mother trusts that God in His infinite wisdom had a reason to take her dear daughter, but she longs to know what it was. Can't ye help her?"

"God in 'Is wisdom?" cried the landlady. The phrase seemed to set her off, and she gave a wild, scornful laugh that sent the cat scurrying. "God in 'Is wisdom 'lowed that girl an' the others t' be murdered, all fer th' sake of a secret marriage an' a babe!" She began to knit furiously, the needles clacking like a gaggle of geese.

"Don't talk t' me 'bout God in 'Is wisdom, er I'll kick ye out with th' cat."

"A marriage?" Kate asked, frowning. "A babe?"

Click click. "Aye, a babe!" Mrs. McCarthy snapped. "Ain't that wot I said?" Click click. "A lit'le girl. Mary Kelly was 'er nanny."

Her nanny? "Mrs. McCarthy," Kate said, by now completely confused, "are we talking about the Mary Kelly who died in Millers Court?"

" 'Oo else?" Mrs. McCarthy's anger seemed to fuel her speech, for it came in short, hard bursts, punctuated by the clicking of her needles. "I've kept th' secret all these years becuz I knew 'twas dangerous t' tell it an' I was afeerd. But I woke up this very mornin' thinkin' on Mary an' Annie Chapman an' Elizabeth an' th' others, an' thinkin' how it wuz ten years gone an' time their story wuz told."

Annie Chapman? She was the second of the Ripper's victims, Kate thought in surprise. And Elizabeth must be Elizabeth Stride, yet another. This woman had known them? Had known them *all*?

"Time their story wuz told," Mrs. McCarthy said again. Her hands had stopped, the needles had fallen silent, and she gazed straight before her, not as if she were looking out, but rather looking in, inside herself. "An' now 'ere ye are," she said in a quieter voice, "askin' 'bout Mary. So mebbee it's you I'm meant t' tell."

"P'rhaps that's the way of it, Mrs. McCarthy," Kate said in an encouraging tone. "P'rhaps we were sent to hear it."

So for the next few minutes, the two women listened as Mrs. McCarthy told what she knew. Mary Kelly was born in Limerick and moved to Wales as a child. She was the daughter of a collier; at sixteen, she was the wife of a collier; at eighteen, she was a collier's widow. Two years later she moved to London, and while searching for work in the East End, began sleeping in the Providence Row Night Refuge for Women. One of the Refuge's committee members, seeing that Mary was intelligent and ambitious for herself, found employment for her in a confectionery and tobacconist's shop in Cleveland Street. There, she was friendly with a young Roman Catholic woman named Annie Crook, who had become romantically involved with a certain man of title and high position.

In the natural course of the affair, Annie became pregnant. Within a few months, sometime in early 1885, Mary witnessed a wedding, held in Saint Saviour's chapel in Osnaburgh Street. The marriage was followed shortly by the birth of a little girl who was named Alice, after Annie's sister. Mary had no training as a nanny but she had helped to raise her younger brothers and sisters, so a friend of the baby's father arranged for her to move into the basement of Number 6 Cleveland Street with Annie, to assume the care of little Alice. Mrs. McCarthy herself had seen the child often, for Mary was encouraged to take the baby along to Dorset Street when she came to visit her friends there—visits that apparently took place when the child's father wished to stay with Annie. And Mrs. McCarthy had even accompanied Mary back to Cleveland Street several times, since she had a sister who kept a lodging house in Fitzroy Street, a block over.

This comfortable arrangement continued for some time, until one day, Mary returned with the child from an airing in Regent's Park to discover that Annie, upon the order of her husband's father, had been carried away and locked up for mad—and mad she was, indeed, when she was finally released. Mary, frightened out of her wits by what had happened, left Alice in the care of the man who had arranged her employment and fled to the anonymity of the East End. There she unhappily fell into the profession that so many other East End women came to, soliciting for customers in Leman Street or outside The Ten Bells in Commercial Street. But she was angry and very bitter about what had happened and could not keep from telling others about it, especially when (as it often occurred) she was drunk. Some time later, Mary and three of her friends—Mary Ann Nichols, Annie Chapman, and Elizabeth Stride—devised a blackmail scheme. They wrote to the friend who had paid Mary's salary, threatening to reveal everything they knew about Annie, Alice, and Alice's father, unless they were paid for their silence.

"An' that wuz why they wuz killed," Mrs. McCarthy said sadly, "one arter t'other. T' shut their mouths. T' make certain sure that th' marriage an' th' babe would stay a secret."

"And what of Catherine Eddowes?" Kate asked.

Mrs. McCarthy sighed. "Poor Catherine was mistook for your cousin," she said. " 'Twas a sad error."

Kate stared at her. "What an amazing story!" she said at last. "To think that all those lives were destroyed, and all for a secret marriage!"

Mrs. McCarthy gave a harsh, ironic laugh. "But 't'ain't no secret, not in the East End. Ever'body knows why, an' wud like t' see the bloody coppers dangle at the end of a rope fer makin' out that Mary an' the others wuz killed becuz they wuz Unfortunates, or killed 'it-or-miss-like, by some crazy. But nobody'll talk, fer fear that somethin' bad'll 'appen to themselfs, like t' the women."

Jennie let out a long-held breath. "So Jack the Ripper was no lunatic!"

"As lunatic as you 'n' me," Mrs. McCarthy replied. She picked up her knitting again. "I' fact, 'ee wuz more than one. 'Ee wuz a 'ole gang o' Rippers."

From the back of the shop came the slam of a door and a man's loud voice, shouting.

"Ol' woman, ol' woman! Where th' divil are ye?" Glass smashed, and there was the sound of cursing.

Suddenly anxious, Mrs. McCarthy screwed up her face. "That's McCarthy. 'Ee'd beat me if 'ee knew I told. Ye won't go tellin' wot I said, now, will ye?" she added in a whimper. "Only t' Mary's mother?"

"Only to Mary's mother," Kate lied. She reached into her purse. "I think I should like two yards o' that Turkey red now, if ye please, Mrs. McCarthy."

"And I should like to have that shawl," Jennie said, pointing to a blue woolen shawl draped over a wooden rack. "And those tortoiseshell combs, please."

A few moments later they were outside, with their bundles. "Whatever shall I do with this shawl?" Jennie asked, frowning. "And these combs."

"I know," Kate said, turning back toward Millers Court. When they departed Dorset Street a little later, they had left their purchases behind in the possession of a young girl with long black hair and a purple bruise on one cheek.

23

A Communication from the Queen
to Her Ministers

"This new most ghastly murder shows the absolute
necessity for some very decided action. All these
courts and alleys must be lit, and our detectives
improved. They are not what they should be."

Victoria Regina
11 November, 1888

TWILIGHT WAS FALLING by the time Kate and Jennie
arrived at Sibley House, having decided that
they were far too tired and footsore to take the train
back to Colchester that evening. They could not go
to Great Cumberland Place, since Jennie feared that
the police might come there to inquire after her, and
Kate suggested that they spend the night at Sibley
House, where a reduced staff was maintained while
the family were not in residence. She and Jennie were
not expected, but Charles was, so the cook (while she
would complain bitterly about the lack of notice) could

surely think of something for their dinners.

The butler did not blink at the sight of his mistress and her illustrious friend, garbed like ordinary servants. "Good evening, Lady Charles, Lady Randolph. You are very wet, I fear. May I take your wraps?"

Jennie began to unwind the veiling from Mrs. Pratt's green hat and Kate wearily yielded up her mud-speckled coat and Amelia's red-trimmed bonnet, much the worse for having been thoroughly dampened.

"Thank you, Richards," she said, clasping her arms around herself with a shiver. "Lady Randolph is staying the night, in the blue bedroom. She and I will take tea upstairs in our rooms and then have a rest. What time is Lord Charles expected?"

"Not until about nine-thirty, I believe, m'lady." As Richards took Mrs. Pratt's hat from Jennie, the green silk cabbage rose, now wet and bedraggled, fell off. He picked it up from the floor. "With permission, m'lady," he said gravely, "I shall see to the repair of Lady Randolph's hat."

"Thank you," Kate replied. "And please tell Cook that we shall be three at dinner. We shall eat in the library, I believe. Be sure that there is a good fire. Lord Charles will be cold and wet. Oh, and do send Rose upstairs."

Neither Richards' face nor his voice revealed what he thought of the heresy of dining in the library. "Yes, m'lady. Is there anything else, m'lady?"

Jennie handed him Mrs. Pratt's green cape. "Perhaps a footman could be sent round to Great Cumberland Place with a message for Winston," she told Kate. "I left Bishop's Keep without telling him where I could be found."

Kate was struck by how wretched Jennie looked. Well, it was no wonder, given their long, wet trek around

London, and what they had learned along the way. "Is there a telephone at your house?" she asked. "If not, you can use the telephone in Charles's study. He had it installed just a few months ago."

"There is indeed," Jennie said with alacrity. So Richards retired to the kitchen to break the news to Cook, Jennie went off to telephone Winston, and Kate went upstairs to her bedroom. She kept a wardrobe in London, and she took a change of clothing and the necessary toilette articles to the blue bedroom. Rose, the upstairs maid, appeared, and Kate requested fires and hot baths. There was much for her and Jennie to talk about and a great deal of new information to be weighed and considered, but there was no point in any discussion until they were rested, and until Charles had arrived and could hear what they had learned.

In the meantime, she looked forward to a cup of hot tea, a hot scented bath to wash away the dirt of the East End, and a nap—although she knew that her sleep would be troubled by many things, among them the poignant memory of a pretty young girl with a bruised face and the glint of tears in her eyes.

It was nearly ten by the time Charles arrived, cold and wet indeed. At Richards' direction, he went straight to the library, where he was greeted by a heartening domestic scene: a bright fire, a glass of fine, dry sherry, his slippers toasting on the fender, and the sight of his dear wife wearing his favorite blue dress, her face rosy in the firelight.

"Kate!" he exclaimed in surprise, bending to kiss her. "What the devil are *you* doing in London?" He turned, to see Jennie seated on the sofa. *"Both* of you! I thought—"

"You thought," Kate said demurely, "that we would do

as we were told and stay in the country, out of trouble." She handed him a glass of sherry and poured one for herself. "Isn't that right?"

"Well, something like that," Charles admitted. He turned to see a table laid for three, with a white damask cloth, fresh flowers, and candles. "But I see you have come to town to keep me company at dinner." How very sweet of Kate, not wanting to be parted from him for a single night.

"Something like that," Jennie said. She sighed heavily, and Charles noticed how worn and sad she looked. "But there is a great deal more. I fear you shall be very angry when you hear what we have got up to, Charles."

"No, he won't," Kate replied. "He shall be far too interested in what we have to tell him to be angry." She smiled and put her hand through Charles's arm. "But Cook has made your favorite partridge pie, my love, and nothing at all shall be said of the day's doings until you have warmed yourself, finished your sherry and dinner has been eaten."

An hour later, after they had progressed from their sherries through dinner and dessert to the port, they were once again seated in front of the fire, Charles and Kate on the sofa, Jennie in the chair opposite. Charles half-turned so that he could see his wife's face.

"Now, Kate," he said fondly, lifting a lock of her russet hair, "let me hear what you have done today. You have been shopping, I suppose?" He smiled at Jennie. "Is that why I should be angry with her, Jennie? Has she been spending a great deal of money?"

Kate pulled her hair out of his grasp. "You can stop being patronizing, Charles," she said tartly. "It is not becoming to either of us."

Charles frowned. He never meant to patronize Kate, but sometimes he didn't entirely think through the implications of his words. "I'm sorry for offending, Kate," he said, genuinely regretful. "You can spend whatever you like, of course." He paused. Should he have said that, or was it patronizing, too?

Kate stirred impatiently but did not reply to his remark. Instead, she said, "Jennie and I should like to discuss what has been learned today. What discoveries have you made?"

"I don't really think—" Charles began.

"Charles," Kate remonstrated quietly.

Charles thought for a moment. Kate had certainly proved helpful on other occasions, when there were complex issues to be untangled and difficult relationships to be sorted out. Perhaps, since she was removed from this case and knew so little about its various dimensions, she could bring a fresh view to it. And certainly Jennie had a right to know what he had attempted to do on her behalf today.

"Of course, my dear," he said, and began a recital of the discoveries of the day, however minor, in the order that they had occurred. He described the confectioner's clerk's denial that she had ever known Mary Kelly and reported the landlady's assertion that Finch had not kept a darkroom at his lodgings. He recited the barber's claim that the dead man was an expert photographer with a history of blackmail, going back to the notorious episode of the male brothel on Cleveland Street, and his recollection that Mary Kelly might have been a nursemaid. Then he recounted Abberline's stunning statement that the Ripper case had been solved long ago, and the inspector's refusal to be involved with the investigation except by—perhaps—confirming or denying what Charles might learn from other sources. He concluded with Abberline's remark that the Ripper killings had been motivated by a secret marriage, and his intimation that there had been a cover-up, at senior police levels or even higher, in the Home Office.

"In the Home Office!" Jennie exclaimed, and Kate said, "Do you suppose the police knew, all along, who was responsible?"

"It's possible," Charles said, "which makes it very unlikely that anyone, at this late date, will get at the truth. There have been too many opportunities to destroy the evidence." He sat back, feeling weary and defeated. Although he had managed to gather an impressive array of odd bits of information, he could not for the life of him put them together in any meaningful pattern.

And worse, he had kept two important things back, out of concern for Jennie's feelings. First, he had not revealed that George Cornwallis-West had indeed been stationed where he could see Jennie go up and down the stairs to Finch's lodgings, and second, that he was beginning to harbor the definite suspicion that George, in the heat of a jealous passion, might have stabbed Tom Finch to death.

24

"He [Dr. William Gull] had been attending a poor patient with heart disease, and after his death was extremely anxious for a post-mortem examination. With great difficulty this was granted, but with the proviso that nothing was to be taken away, and the sister of the diseased patient, a strong-minded old maid, was present to watch proceedings. Gull saw that it was hopeless to conceal anything from her, or to persuade her to leave the room. He therefore deliberately took out the heart, put it in his pocket and looking steadily at her, said, "I trust to your honour not to betray me." The heart is now in Guy's museum."

THOMAS ACLAND,
son-in-law of Sir William Gull
In Memoriam: Sir William Gull

KATE AND JENNIE had sat quietly through Charles's recital, alternatively glancing from him to each other and to the fire. When he came at last to the end, they sat for some moments, not speaking. Finally, Kate broke the silence.

"Well," she said, "I suppose we had better tell you about our day."

Charles got up to pour himself a second glass of port and to put another log on the fire. "Tell away, dear," he said. "I promise to be amused." He sat down, put his feet on the ottoman, and prepared himself for the gay account of the hours that his wife and her friend had spent flitting frivolously in and out of the Regent Street shops and the difficulties they had experienced in finding exactly the right hat or shoes or ribbon.

But instead, Charles found himself listening in shocked amazement and growing incredulity as Kate narrated the journey she and Jennie had made in their disguises as Mary Kelly's Irish kinswomen, first to a clairvoyant in Bloomsbury who had told them that Dr. William Gull was the man who had carried out the Ripper's butchery—and then, even more unbelievably, to Duval Street, in the most dangerous depths of the East End, where they had somehow managed to locate Mary Kelly's former landlady and hear her astonishing claim that Kelly and her three friends, attempting blackmail, had been murdered to ensure their silence, while Catherine Eddowes had been killed in error.

"So Jack the Ripper was no lunatic," Kate said, concluding. "And if Mrs. McCarthy is telling the truth, Dr. Gull—if indeed he was the one who dissected the women—did not act alone. He was only one member of a group of men who singled out these women because they had information that jeopardized the well-being of a certain highly placed individual or family. It was more expedient and more effective to murder them than to buy their silence. Besides, no matter how much the women were paid, they couldn't be trusted to hold their tongues. Sooner or later, word about the secret marriage and the baby would get out."

All through Kate's recital, Jennie had sat silent and stricken, her face quite pale, her fingers tightly laced together in her lap. It was clear to Charles that the idea of Sir William Gull's involvement distressed her deeply—and with good cause. Throughout the late eighties, Sir William and Randolph Churchill were known to have been the best of friends. If Gull had taken part in the Ripper murders, might not Randolph have done so, as well?

Charles let out his breath. "Unbelievable," he muttered. "Absolutely incredible."

"It's all true, Charles," Kate protested. "I've accurately reported every word we heard!" She appealed to Jennie. "Isn't that so, Jennie?"

"I wish I could say otherwise, but I cannot," Jennie said with a long sigh.

"I am not at all questioning your veracity," Charles said hastily. What Kate said tallied with Abberline's reluctant assertion that the Ripper killings took place because some highly placed authority found it necessary to cover up the traces of a secret marriage. He gave her a wry grin. "I suppose it's your good fortune I'm questioning—that the two of you could manage to locate and question not one but *two* people out of the whole of London who have important facts about these murders."

"I grant you that we were fortunate, Charles. However, people who know of this are not as uncommon as one might expect," Kate replied. "According to Mrs. McCarthy, the real reason for the murders is well known throughout the East End, where there's a great deal of bitterness toward the police for pretending that the women were killed because they were prostitutes, or that they were the random victims of a lunatic. Their tongues are held in check only by fear. And Mr. Lees made it very clear that Scotland Yard believed that Sir William Gull was involved with the murders, and that it was known that he did not act alone. He also said that at least one policeman—perhaps your Inspector Abberline—could identify the other members of the group."

Charles could not dispute her words. What she and Jennie had learned was corroborated by what Abberline had been willing to tell him, and all of it pointed in the direction of a massive official concealment of the truth, as high as the Home Office, perhaps even the entire Cabinet. And who was the highly placed person whose son's secret marriage and child so threatened—

"I'm afraid there's more, Charles," Kate said quietly. She rose and went to the desk, where she took out an envelope. She opened it carefully, took out a sheet of cheap white paper, and handed it to him. Charles squinted at the penciled script:

November 11, 1898

Dear Lady Randolph,

This is the last correspondence you shall receive from me, for I am quitting the country. If you go to my studio at Number 24 Cleveland Street, third floor, at ten tomorrow morning, you shall be able to retrieve the negative of the photograph I sent you earlier. I regret any distress you have suffered regarding our communications over the last year.

Yrs respectfully,
A. Byrd

Charles had to suppress a small smile. Whatever his other faults and failings, Tom Finch had had a sense of humor, at least when it came to choosing a pseudonym. But there was more than that to cheer him, for it looked very much as if he now had a lead on the whereabouts of the negative. First thing tomorrow, he would visit Number 24 and see what could be learned.

"The letter was dated and posted on the day Mr. Finch was murdered," Jennie said in a low voice, "but somehow delayed in the post. I found it with the rest of my letters, which Winston sent over at my request earlier this evening."

"Jennie and I talked about it while we were waiting for you," Kate said, "and this is what we have concluded. For whatever reason, Mr. Finch decided that it was time to end the extortion. So he wrote and posted the note to Jennie, giving her directions to the place where he kept the negative—perhaps a rented or borrowed studio. Immediately thereafter, someone else discovered what Finch planned to do and killed him—without learning that he had written this letter. Then that man telephoned Jennie and summoned her to the scene of the murder, hoping, perhaps, that she might be seen and implicated. If we can find that man, we shall have found Finch's killer *and* the man who wrote the typed blackmail note. And if we can locate the negative at this address"—she pointed to the letter—"there will be no more blackmail!"

Charles frowned. Kate's postulate of a second blackmailer sounded plausible enough, and he possessed no facts with which to contradict it. But George Cornwallis-West was also a suspect. He had a powerful motive—he was passionately jealous of Jennie and would do anything to keep her to himself—and he had been at the scene of the crime. What's more, the typed note that had accompanied the clipping might not have been a blackmail note after all. "You are not yet free" might simply be George's way of binding Jennie more closely to him. It might all seem a bit irrational, but what lover—especially a young and passionate lover—behaved rationally?

And then, as though the thought had summoned the devil, the library door flew open and George himself burst in, with Winston at his heels, ineffectually remonstrating, and Richards following after, wringing his hands in dismay at such an ill-mannered display.

"Jennie!" George cried ardently. "Jennie, my dearest, my *only* love, at last I have found you!"

Jennie straightened her shoulders and gathered a dark dignity. "Winston," she said with a frown, turning on her son, "what is the meaning of this?"

"I'm dreadfully sorry, Mama," Winston said. "I tried to stop him, but once your footman let it slip that you were here, he absolutely would not listen to reason." He cast a disgusted look at George. "I thought it best to come with him, for I feared he might create a scene."

"A scene!" George was irate. "Well, I certainly *hope* so! A scene is exactly what I mean to create." Half-recollecting himself, he bowed in Kate's direction. "Do please forgive my impetuosity, Lady Charles. I realize that I am behaving boorishly. But I must beg a word

189

with Lady Randolph alone. She and I have a great deal to—"

Winston put both hands on George's arm. "George, Mama does not want to see you. You must come away with me, now!"

George shrugged off Winston's hands. "I have nothing to say to you, Winston. I intend to talk to your mother, and I will not go away until—"

"I am utterly ashamed of you, George." Jennie had risen and fixed a haughty eye upon her lover. "What *can* you be thinking of—intruding on the Sheridans in this unconscionable way!"

"Jennie!" George all but wailed her name. "We *must* speak! I can save you! I can tell the police—"

Now it was Charles's turn to grasp George's arm, with far greater authority than had Winston. "Whatever you have to tell the police must needs be said to me first, George."

"And to me," Winston said determinedly.

Charles shook his head. "Not now, Winston." He pulled at George's arm. "Come along to the billiards room, where we can have privacy."

"Jennie!" George's cry was anguished. "Jennie, please!" But Jennie had turned her back on him, and George was left to choose between following Charles of his own volition, or being dragged.

25

"When murderers shut deeds close, this curse does seal them: If none disclose them, they themselves reveal them!"

CYRIL TOURNEUR
The Revenger's Tragedy
1607

IT WAS DREADFULLY late, gone half-past eleven, but Sarah Pratt was not yet in bed. Still fully dressed, she sat half-dozing in front of the kitchen fire, her feet on the fender and the calico cat on her lap. Sarah had not yet gone to bed because Mary Plumm had not yet returned from walking out with the stableboy, and because she worried that Dick Pratt might come drunk from the pub and bang on the kitchen door and rouse the household—and because she feared that if she went to bed, she should dream that horrible dream again, the dream where she put rat poison in Pratt's roast chicken.

Except that willy-nilly, she *had* fallen asleep, there in the chair, and dreamed it again, real as life itself. Only this time, the poison was not in the roast chicken. It was in the cup of fresh horseradish sauce she'd made to go with the slices of cold joint that had gone into the basket Pratt picked up late that afternoon, when he came for the boots.

The boots. At the thought of the boots, Sarah's eyes popped open and the sleepiness fled from her brain, to be replaced by a bone-chilling fear. And this time, her fear was not just for herself, but for her niece Amelia Quibbley, who worked as housekeeper and her ladyship's maid. Frantic with the impossibility of meeting Pratt's demand for boots and unable to think of anywhere else to turn, Sarah had gone to the housekeeper's closet, where Amelia was counting the linen sheets, and tearfully told her the whole story. About Pratt's release from prison and his sudden appearance, his ominous threats and demands, which every day grew more oppressive. About the food and the wine and the trousers. About the boots.

"Boots!" Amelia had exclaimed. Her mouth was a round, horrified O. "Yer sayin' as how ye want me t' steal a pair o' the master's *boots*?"

"Well, not steal, 'xactly," Sarah said, in a small voice.

Amelia put her hands on her hips—rounder and softer hips, now that her baby had been born. "If it's not stealin', I don't know wot it is," she said indignantly. "Ye sart'nly don't mean t' put the boots back after Pratt's done wi' 'em, d'ye?"

Faced with this question, Sarah could only shake her head numbly. "F'rgit wot I asked," she said. "'Tis not fair fer me t' drag ye into this mess. I'll think o' some other way."

Amelia put out a hand. "Don't fret," she said more

softly. "There's a old pair o' 'is lordship's ridin' boots on the top shelf in 'is dressin' room. I've niver seen 'im wear 'em. 'Ee prob'bly don't even know they're there. Will ridin' boots do fer Pratt?"

Sarah had no idea whether riding boots would do for Pratt or not, but she was so eager to put the business behind her that she nodded vigorously. So, within the hour, Amelia had brought the boots to the kitchen, where Sarah hid them behind the vegetable bin. She had not expected Pratt before nightfall, but the brazen man had appeared just before teatime, demanding not only the boots but a basket of food. He had spied the cold joint she was slicing for the servants' tea and ordered her to put it in the basket, with bread and butter and beer—a half-dozen bottles of beer—and some of the fresh-made horseradish sauce he saw on the table.

And now the dream, so real that it made Sarah Pratt break out in a cold sweat. The poison was ready to hand, just where it always was, on the shelf just inside Mr. Humphries's garden shed. She had gone in there many times to fetch poison for use in the pantry or the scullery. She could see her hand reaching for the package, see herself shaking it into a cup and carrying it into the kitchen, where she—

There was a noise at the back door, and the cat sprang from Sarah's lap. It was Mary Plumm, most like, back from her carryings-on. If it had been Harriet who'd gone out without asking, Sarah should have known what to do: her half-day holiday cut, her kitchen duties extended, and a smart dressing-down in front of Mr. Hodge. But Sarah could not discipline Mary Plumm, because to do so would invite revelations too horrible to imagine. It was an impossible situation.

But the noise at the back door was not Mary Plumm. The door shook under a heavy knock, and Sarah knew with a sinking heart that it was Pratt, back for more food and drink. But that was wrong too, for when she opened the door, she saw Constable Laken standing on the stone step. "May I come in, Mrs. Pratt?" he asked.

Sarah stared at him, cold fear striking into her heart. She was acquainted with the constable, who had visited Bishop's Keep on the deaths of her ladyship's aunts, and was a friend of his lordship. She knew him as a kind man and a good police officer, not given to rapping on people's doors near midnight just to annoy them. And from his ordinary clothing, she guessed that he, too, had been summoned from his fireside.

"May I come in?" Constable Laken asked again.

"Why?" she replied apprehensively. "Wot's wrong?"

"I have bad news for you, Sarah," the constable said. "It concerns a certain Dick Pratt."

Sarah's thoughts flew to the rat poison in the horseradish sauce, and her legs nearly failed her. "Wot about Dick Pratt?" she whispered.

But instead of Constable Laken's reply came Mr. Hodge's irritated question: "What's all the noise, Mrs. Pratt? Who's knocking at the door at this hour of the night?" He came to stand beside Sarah, wearing his night-robe and slippers. "I am Mr. Hodge, the butler," he said to the constable, in a tone of great dignity. "Who, sir, are you?"

Sarah tried to speak, but the words came out in a mouse-like squeak. The constable answered for her.

"Constable Laken, sir," he said courteously. He turned to Sarah. "Dick Pratt told Ralph Martingale, at The Lamb, that you and he are married. Is it true?"

"Married?" Mr. Hodge, both eyebrows arched, turned incredulous eyes on Sarah. *"Our* Mrs. Pratt? *Married?"*

To Sarah's credit, it did not occur to her to lie. " 'Tis true," she said wretchedly. "Pratt 'n' me 'ave bin married these twenty-five years, more's the pity."

Constable Laken put out his hand. "Then it is my duty to tell you, Sarah, that your husband is dead."

Sarah stared at him. His words seemed to come from far away, and his face loomed before her, a harbinger of doom. "Dead?" she whispered. "Pratt's... dead?"

"Yes," the constable said. "I know it's late, but I'm afraid you'll have to come with me to the jail."

But Sarah was not going anywhere for the next few minutes. She had fainted dead away on the kitchen floor.

26

"There are some frauds so well conducted that it would be stupidity not to be deceived by them."

CHARLES CALEB COLTON
Lacon, 1825

KATE WOKE EARLY, but Charles was up before her, already dressed and standing by the bed with her cup of tea on a tray. He put the tray down and bent to kiss her, then went to the window to stare out at the gray morning, his hands in his pockets. Kate pulled herself up against the pillow and gratefully sipped the tea.

"I'm sorry for what happened last night," Charles said. "I looked in on you after George left, but it was around midnight and you were sleeping so soundly that I bedded down across the hall." He paused. "I do hope Jennie is all right."

"She was angry and shaken," Kate said, "and terribly embarrassed by George's behavior. I think, though, that she was more disturbed by the scene that followed, with Winston. He insisted on hearing everything and took it all badly, of course—especially the idea that his father's photograph was associated, even though fraudulently, with that of a victim of the Ripper. As far as Winston is concerned, his father was perfect in every way." She grimaced, thinking how devastating it should be for Winston if it were discovered that Lord Randolph had anything to do with the Ripper killings. She put down her cup. "What did you learn from George?"

Charles sighed. "Not a great deal," he said, turning from the window. "I didn't tell you last night because I was trying to spare Jennie's feelings, but the barber who owns the shop across the street from Finch's lodgings confirmed that George was there the afternoon of the murder. When I confronted George with this testimony, he hemmed and hawed and finally said that he had been visiting Jennie when she received the telephone call summoning her to Cleveland Street. He overheard her part of the conversation; then, thinking that she was meeting another lover, rushed to Cleveland Street as fast as he could, to be there before her. He says that he watched her enter and leave Finch's lodgings, then ran up the stairs and found the man face down in his shepherd's pie, dead."

Kate raised an eyebrow. Charles had spoken without inflection. "Do you believe him?"

Charles sat down on the edge of the bed. "I don't know what to believe, Kate. George lives from impulse to impulse. He's passionately in love with Jennie, and he's certainly jealous enough to have killed a man he suspected of being her lover. It also occurred to me last night that, although he might not have killed Finch, he might have sent Jennie that clipping about the murder, with the typed note. The phrase 'You are not yet free' might easily have come from him. Perhaps it is not another blackmail note at all, but merely George's misguided attempt to tie Jennie to him."

"I suppose that's possible," Kate said, although it didn't seem to her that George would have gone that far. "If he did anything like that," she added, "it will ruin his chances at any long-term relationship with her. Jennie would positively run from any such connection."

Charles nodded in agreement. "He was a bit overwrought last night, but he said that he feared that Jennie killed Finch—or that the police might think so. He wanted the two of them to concoct some sort of mutual alibi that would let her off the hook." He looked rueful. "And him too, of course. But for the moment, there is certainly not enough evidence to convict him if he should be charged with Finch's murder. It's an entirely circumstantial case."

Changing the subject, Kate said, "It was a bit of luck that Finch's letter finally arrived yesterday." She put her hand over his. "I assume that you are going to Cleveland Street this morning to have a look for the negative."

"Yes," he said. He hesitated. "I thought perhaps—that is, I wondered if you—"

"If I would go with you?" Kate asked. It was the invitation she had been waiting for. "I should be very glad to, Charles."

He pointed to the window. "It's raining again," he said in a cautioning tone. "The expedition will be damp." He paused. "I hope that doesn't sound patronizing."

Kate smiled. "It does, but you are forgiven." She paused and slipped into her Irish brogue, playfully exaggerated. "I was thinkin' p'rhaps I might stop at the confectioner's shop ye visited yesterday an' have a wee bit of a word with Mrs. O'Reilly. She might be more willin' t' tell Mary's cousin what she was afeerd t' tell a strange gentleman."

"Would you, Kate?" Charles asked eagerly. "That was exactly what I was thinking!"

"And I thought that perhaps I might make a visit to Saint Saviour's, in Osnaburgh Street," Kate went on. "Mrs. McCarthy said that the wedding took place in the chapel there." She made a little face. "I somehow have the feeling that the more we can find out about the marriage and the baby, the more we will know about the Ripper murders."

"It's not likely that you'll be able to discover much," Charles said. "If there was no civil service, it's very likely that the marriage wasn't registered—and that it could even have been a sham."

"Not a real marriage at all, you mean?" Kate asked.

"Indeed," Charles said. "It wouldn't be the first time a man went through the form of a marriage ceremony in order to achieve the object of his physical desires."

Kate frowned. "But Mrs. McCarthy said that the child was born shortly after the wedding. So the man, whoever he was, would seem to have been motivated by a desire to protect the woman and her child. And if the marriage was fraudulent, why would the man's family go to the trouble of abducting the woman and locking her up—even, as Mrs. McCarthy claims, driving her mad. In that event, the woman was no wife and the child was a bastard, and no threat."

"I take your point," Charles said. "We shall go together to the studio, and then you shall drop in on Mrs. O'Reilly at the confectioner's shop—"

"And then at Saint Saviour's," Kate said determinedly.

"I want to know the name of the man who is responsible for all this trouble."

"Very well, then," Charles said, and stood. "We shall be off as soon as you have breakfasted."

Kate followed Charles up the narrow wooden stairway to the third-floor studio that had, according to the landlord, been let for the past two years to a certain Alastair Byrd, a photographer of some local repute. The landlord added rather bitterly, however, that Mr. Byrd had neglected to pay his previous month's rent. He had said he was planning to vacate the premises, but he had never appeared to clear out his belongings. What was to be done with all of his furnishings? Who was to pay the outstanding rent? It was only after Charles had supplied the ten shillings deficit that he was willing to admit them to the stairway.

"Ten shillings a month for this?" Charles muttered as they climbed.

The stairway was so steep that it was more like a ladder, Kate thought. "Perhaps the rent went up when the landlord saw how eager you were to gain admittance," she said, holding her skirts away from the walls to avoid catching cobwebs or snagging on splinters.

"Most likely." Charles unlocked a door with the key the landlord had given him and they stepped into the gloom of a small studio. One dusty window in the opposite gabled wall afforded a modicum of pale light. Overhead, the sharply pitched roof angled downward to rough-finished brick walls at either end of the room, the exposed rafters supporting laths which in turn supported the roof tiles. At some time long past, several of the laths had been cut, the tiles removed, and a frame of nine mullioned window panes set into their place, with the object of turning the dusky space below into an artist's studio. Kate shivered. It was chilly enough now; in the dead of winter, the place must be frigid. How could any artist endure the cold? Wouldn't his—or her—fingers be so stiff they would refuse to work?

She turned to study the room. Located directly below the skylight was a high worktable with a slanted wooden top, before which a stool was placed. On the walls hung photographic enlargements—studio portraits of serious-looking women and men, dressed in their finest; casual shots of East End street scenes featuring shopkeepers, laborers, and weary-looking women; and several photographs of a strikingly pretty young woman in a ragged dress, her dark hair tousled, striking a series of dramatic poses. Beneath these was a single caption: "Ellie, in the Courtyard."

"Charles," Kate said, "this looks very much like the girl I spoke with yesterday, in Millers Court!"

Charles glanced at it, then at the other East End photographs. "I don't suppose I'm surprised," he said. "Finch apparently knew the East End."

Kate continued her survey of the room. Sturdy wooden shelves along one wall held several cameras, camera bags, and an array of lenses, all arranged in an orderly fashion. A large wooden studio camera, over which had been flung a black hood, was affixed to a heavy mahogany stand and placed before a paper backdrop painted to resemble a parlor wall with an elaborately carved fireplace and mirror. On the right were a chair, a curved-back red velvet sofa, and a small table displaying a variety of parlor props, and on the left a limelight apparatus and cylinders of gas. The only other pieces of furniture in the room were a dirty sofa piled with several ragged blankets and a battered wooden file cabinet which looked as if it had seen service in the Crimean War. One corner of the room had been walled off into a sort of closet, with entry through an insubstantial panel door, its edges trimmed with flaps of black felt—the darkroom, Kate thought.

She said the obvious. "I don't see any negatives lying around." But then, what they were looking for was probably hidden somewhere—or had already been taken. There was no reason to suppose that the man who killed Finch hadn't already made off with it.

Charles applied a match to the gaslight on the wall and pulled a pair of cotton gloves out of his pocket. "I'll check the darkroom first," he said, opening the felt-edged door.

Finch had made use of every inch of the narrow cubicle. On the walls were shelves filled with large brown glass bottles and racks of shallow enameled trays. He had used a wider shelf, waist-high, as a working surface, and it was filled with a variety of developing equipment that Kate recognized from Charles's own darkroom: a plate washer, a burnisher, a print trimmer. A darkroom lamp hung from the ceiling and a great portion of the floor space was occupied by what looked like two large bellows cameras joined in the center and mounted on a long wooden base with rails.

"His enlarger," Charles said, when Kate asked what it was. "A nice piece of equipment, that. I shouldn't mind having it myself." As Kate watched, he searched the shelves, lifting the trays and other flat objects to be sure that nothing was concealed beneath. But the search was fruitless, and they returned to the larger room.

"I suppose that leaves only the file cabinet," Kate said.

She went to stand beside Charles as he pulled open the top drawer, revealing a long row of glass negatives and prints separated by cardboard dividers, the tabs of which bore cryptic notes.

"Ah," Charles said. "This looks promising. But before we start a serious search, let's see what else we have." He pulled out the second drawer, and the third, which were organized like the first. The bottom drawer was stuffed with papers—letters, invoices, newspaper clippings—and a pair of worn felt boots and a woolen cap. Kate couldn't help but wonder whether Finch had worn them to keep warm while he worked.

"The negative is probably in here somewhere," Charles said, "*if* it's here at all." He reopened the top drawer. "I suppose I shall have to look at every one of these plates." He took out the first and held it toward the skylight, scanning the image. "This could take all day," he muttered, replacing the first plate and lifting out the second.

"I shouldn't have thought he would leave it with the other negatives," Kate said, wandering to a shelf. "If someone else came here looking for it, the cabinet is the most likely place to be searched."

"It's also possible that he had it with him at his lodgings," Charles said, "meaning to bring it here before Jennie's arrival. In that case, the killer may indeed have it now."

"I suppose," Kate said. Curiously, she picked up a small pocket camera, obviously designed for concealment. Beside it was a long-focus lens. She paused to look at it, wondering how often Finch had stooped to using his photographic talents for blackmail. She turned to say something about this to Charles, but as she did so, she noticed that the slant-top table under the skylight appeared to have some sort of drawer beneath it, although she could not see how it was to be opened.

Curious, she went to the table and ran her fingers under the front edge, tentatively pulling upward. The tabletop, which she now saw was hinged along the back, lifted up and became a kind of lid. Underneath was a drawer containing pens and pencils, scraps of paper of different sizes, and a large brown envelope. She opened it carefully. Peering inside, she saw several glass negative plates and a familiar photograph.

"Charles," she said sharply, "come here, please."

"What is it?" Charles asked, holding up yet another negative. "Damn it," he muttered. "At this rate, it will be noon before we're finished."

"I don't think so," Kate said. She motioned him to the table. "Isn't this what you're looking for?"

Out of the envelope, Charles took the print and three plate glass negatives and placed them on the slant-top table. Heavy black paper masked all but a small irregular portion of the first. The piece of paper which had been cut from the black masking was fixed to the second negative. The third negative was unmasked.

One after the other, Charles held the two masked images up to the light. Then, more carefully, he examined the third, turning the plate so that the light reflected across the surface. "A very clever fraud," he said thoughtfully. "See here? This is where the emulsion has been scraped away." He pointed. "And this is where penciling has been added."

"And the photo?" Kate asked, looking at it. It was very similar to the one Jennie had given Charles, but she could clearly see that the image of the man—Lord

Randolph—was superimposed upon the background and the image of the woman. She could even see the overexposed edges.

"The photo is a contact print," Charles said. "It has been made by exposing the photographic paper to light, first with this negative—the woman and the background—placed on it, then the negative of the man. The contact print was then developed and photographed again, and that negative retouched so that the two images are blended together. From this final negative, the forger can make as many copies as he wishes."

"So we can prove that the photograph is a counterfeit," Kate said excitedly, "and if any other copies appear, they can quickly be shown to be fraudulent." She paused, frowning. "How difficult would it be to establish that it was Finch who created the forgery?"

"Not difficult at all," Charles said. "As a rule, photographers don't wear gloves. It's very likely that the negatives have Finch's fingerprints all over them." His grin was ironic. "It would be rather a bother to dig him up to get confirmation, but I can try matching the prints against those on the glassware in the darkroom." He replaced the negatives and the photograph in the envelope. "I should say that we've got what we came for," he said with satisfaction. "Bless those sharp eyes of yours, Kate. And thank you."

"You're welcome, my lord," Kate said. As Charles turned off the gaslight and they left the studio, she glanced back one last time at the photograph of the pretty dark-haired girl in the ragged dress.

27

"Oh! how many torments lie in the small circle of a wedding-ring!"

COLLEY CIBBER
The Double Gallant,
1702

THE RAIN HAD temporarily halted, but the sky had grown so dark and gloomy that the gas lamps inside the confectionery and tobacconist shop had been lit. It was a homey-looking place, Kate thought, with a scrubbed tiled floor, ruffled curtains in the window, and shelves and polished glass display cabinets filled with the shop's wares. A heady odor of rich tobacco and sweet chocolate filled the air, and from the rear of the shop came a woman's voice, singing something in Gaelic, with a high, light melody.

"A good mornin't' ye, Mrs. O'Reilly," Kate called.

The singing stopped and a stout, middle-aged woman in a navy blue dress and white ruffled apron and cap came around the partition, wiping her hands on a red-and-white checked towel. "An' a good mornin' to ye, m'dear," the woman said with a cheerful smile that showed tobacco-stained teeth. "What'll ye be 'avin' today? Some chocolates, p'raps?"

"I'll have a pound o' yer finest chocolate," Kate said. "It's t' carry home with me t' Ireland, t' the mother of someone ye used t' know."

"Someone I knew, miss?" the woman asked, opening a case in which were displayed several large bars of dark chocolate. She took one out and tipped it onto a silver scale. It weighed slightly over a pound. " 'Ow's this?"

"That'll do nicely," Kate said. "It's fer Mary Kelly's mother, ye see. She's dyin'." She paused, watching Mrs. O'Reilly's face, and added, gently, "I'm Mary's cousin, Kathryn Kelly, and I've come t' ask yer help."

Mrs. O'Reilly's eyes grew large and one fat hand went to her mouth. "Oh, but I couldn't!" she exclaimed. "I—"

"I understand that this is hard fer ye, Mrs. O'Reilly, but 'tis harder yet fer Mary's mother, who longs t' know why her daughter died." Kate held the other woman's eyes with her own. "How would *ye* feel if yer dear daughter was dead, an' people said terr'ble things about her, an' ye knew the things weren't true?"

There was a long, painful silence. Mrs. O'Reilly blinked rapidly. "Why didn't ye come *then?*" she whispered. "All those years ago?"

"I did," Kate lied. "But I din't know t' come t' Cleveland Street. I din't know that part of it until I talked t' Mary's landlady, Mrs. McCarthy, just yesterday, in Dorset Street. Duval, they call it now."

"Mrs. McCarthy talks too much, she does," Mrs. O'Reilly said bitterly. "I always told Mary t' watch out fer that woman. 'McCarthy's too free with 'er tongue,'

I allus said. 'She'll cause ye a deal o' trouble some day, she will,' I said." There was a silence. "An' what did Mrs. McCarthy tell ye?"

"About Annie an' Mary workin' in this shop an' bein' good friends, an' Annie marryin' an' lit'le Alice bein' born, an' Mary livin' with them as nursery maid, in the basement o' Number 6. Then poor Annie bein' taken away t' the madhouse." Kate took a deep breath and let it out. "An' Mary an' the others bein' murdered by the Ripper, just because they knew who Annie was married to."

"Well, then," Mrs. O'Reilly said, partially recovered. "Ye know it all a'ready. There's nothin' I can tell ye, more than that." She eyed Kate suspiciously. " 'Oo wuz th' gentleman 'oo wuz 'ere yesterday, showin' that pitcher?"

"I don't know anything about any gentleman," Kate lied again. "But I hope ye can tell me where Annie is, an' the child." She sighed. "I'd like t' tell Mary's mother that I've laid me eyes on 'em, an' that they're all right."

"All right!" Mrs. O'Reilly snorted contemptuously. "Annie's mind's gone, poor girl. They locked her up for six months an' cut something out o' 'er brain, an' when she came back, she couldn't scarcely remember 'er name. She 'ad fits, too." Her voice took on a deep sadness. "She wuz such a pretty girl, an' always so chipper-like. 'Twasn't right, wot wuz done to 'er. An' all becuz of marryin' 'oo she shouldna'."

Cut something out of her brain! Kate shuddered. Who would have done such a ghastly thing? To whom could Annie Crook's secret marriage pose such a terrible danger that she had to be treated in such a way?

"Where is she now?" Kate asked.

Mrs. O'Reilly gave a despairing shrug. " 'Ere an' there.

Saint Pancras Work'ouse, most likely. Or Saint Giles, in Endell Street. I 'aven't seen 'er for a year or more. Last time, she didn't know me, though we wuz good friends once."

"And the child? Alice?"

"Ye'd 'ave t' ask Mr. Walter Sickert 'bout 'er," Mrs. O'Reilly said. " 'Ee's the man 'oo paid Mary t' take care o' the child. When Annie was stolen away, 'ee took the babe an' gave 'er a 'ome, out of respect for 'is friend." She twisted her mouth. "Mr. Sickert, 'ee's 'ad nothing but trouble in this. But it's wot 'ee gets for 'ob-nobbin' wi' the 'igh an' mighty." She snorted contemptuously. "A. V. Sickert, 'ee called 'is friend, like 'ee wuz 'is brother."

"You mean," Kate said, trying to get it straight, "that Alice's father called himself Sickert, but that he was really someone else?"

Another snort. "That were th' name 'ee *went* by, all right. But we all knew 'oo 'ee wuz."

"Well, then," Kate said, "who was he?"

Mrs. O'Reilly's face turned stony. "Now *that,*" she said firmly, "ye're not gettin' out o' me, miss. Not arter wot 'appened to Annie. 'F ye take my advice, ye won't try t' learn it. An' if ye do, ye'd best forget it." She stuck out her hand. "Three shillings fer th' chocolate, if ye please."

And when Kate handed the money over, Mrs. O'Reilly thrust it into her apron pocket and disappeared behind the partition.

Saint Saviour's chapel was an annex to Saint Saviour's Infirmary in Osnaburgh Street, scarcely a stone's throw from the top of Cleveland Street. The building, delicately proportioned and built of gray stone, sat at the rear of a walled courtyard with a carefully tended rose garden laid out in a geometric design centered around an empty fountain. Even though it was almost mid-November, a few of the roses were still in bloom, their blossoms shining sweet and pure in the gritty fog.

Kate tried the carved wooden doors in the front of the chapel, but they were locked tight. She was standing on the cobblestone walk, wondering whether she should go in search of a custodian or return to the coffee house where Charles was waiting for her, when a small nun in a black habit and cowl, hands clasped and head bowed, came striding around the corner of the building and bumped into her.

"Many pardons," she exclaimed, raising her apple-cheeked face. "I'm afraid I wasn't looking where I was going!" She adjusted her gold-rimmed eyeglasses, which had slid down her nose. Her hands were large and capable-looking, rough with ordinary work. "Are you waiting for someone, my dear?" she asked solicitously.

"I should like to know about a wedding that took place here some time ago," Kate said. She paused. "Quite a *long* time ago, I'm afraid, Sister. But perhaps there is a chapel register I might consult."

The wrinkles in the nun's forehead smoothed out, and she smiled. "God has sent you to the right person, Miss—"

"Kelly," Kate said. "Kathryn Kelly."

"And I am Sister Ursula." The nun reached into a pocket of her habit and extracted a key, fastened to her waist by a long ribbon. "I have been mistress of Saint Saviour's chapel for going on twenty-six years now, and one of my responsibilities is keeping the register."

"Twenty-six years," Kate exclaimed, doing a rapid calculation. The wedding, if there had truly been one, was well within that framework. "That's a very long time!"

"Indeed it is." The nun beamed. "I was appointed by dear Mother Agnes—may she rest in eternal peace—when I first came to Saint Saviour's to work in the hospital. I did my novitiate at the mother house in Kent, you see, and arrived directly here, green as a new leaf." She paused and assumed a modest expression. "Mother Agnes's appointment of a sister so young and inexperienced as chapel mistress seemed quite extraordinary to me then, although I suppose I should be more humble. Pride is one of my worst failings."

"I think it was quite a remarkable achievement," Kate replied in an admiring tone. She was about to prompt with another question, but Sister Ursula didn't seem to require any special encouragement to talk.

She went on, in a pious tone, "The Sisters of Mercy believe that each of us has an important gift to give to God, you see, and we are all urged to yield ourselves completely to His service through whatever gifts we have been generously given."

"And your gift is overseeing the chapel?"

"Exactly, God be thanked. He has placed me precisely where I can serve Him best." Sister Ursula gave a delighted laugh. "Isn't that quite miraculous?" She inserted her key in the lock and the heavy door swung silently open. Inside, the air was chill and faintly sweet with the scent of incense and old leather-bound hymnals. The Gothic arch of the ceiling seemed to reach toward the heavens, and the stained glass windows on both sides of the nave shone like jewels set into the stone wall.

"It is a lovely chapel," Kate said, genuinely impressed.

"The Sisters were the first order established after the Reformation," Sister Ursula said, lowering her voice, "and we have a long tradition of service within the Anglican Church. But for all that we are quite ecumenical here in Osnaburgh Street. The dear lady who founded our hospital and built this chapel in 1872, God bless her sweet and loving spirit, was quite insistent upon our serving *all* the people. Saint Saviour's receives the sick of every denomination, and we never interfere in the practice of their religion."

Kate made an effort to turn the flow of the nun's words in the direction of her inquiry. "The wedding I wanted to ask about—the bride was Roman Catholic, I understand."

"Well, then, there you are." Sister Ursula turned down her mouth. "You see? Even the Popish are welcome here. Reverend Mother even permits them to have their priests, if they insist."

The Popish? Kate caught the barely disguised dislike in Sister Ursula's tone. She knew the English anti-Catholic sentiments well enough, for she herself had been raised Roman Catholic. Perhaps Annie's secret marriage posed a threat to her husband's family because *she* was Catholic.

The moment the thought came to Kate, though, she knew it had to be wrong. A family might not be happy to receive a Catholic daughter-in-law—Charles's mother had certainly put up a fuss, even though Kate was not a practicing Catholic. But if the couple were determined, the parents usually accepted the marriage and put the best face on it. It might have been different a century before, but in this modern day, surely no father would so fear a Catholic connection that he would have his son's wife committed to a lunatic asylum or countenance the murders of five women to keep the marriage a secret. Unless the family's rank and prestige were so delicately balanced that—

"The register is in the alcove," Sister Ursula said, closing the door and pocketing the key. "What year did the wedding take place?"

"It was 1885, I believe," Kate said. She felt a great, heavy sense of anticipation, almost of foreboding, settle like a mantle over her. Miraculously, she had followed the trail of clues this far, from Bloomsbury to the East End to Cleveland Street and Saint Saviour's, and at each station along the journey she had learned something new, had been given some new revelation. What would she learn from the register? Nothing at all? Or everything—the date of the marriage, the names of the witnesses, the name of the bridegroom. And if she were to learn the bridegroom's name, what would that reveal about the terrible crimes of Jack the Ripper? Which of the ancient families of England would destroy lives to keep their name and reputation inviolate?

A moment later, she was standing in front of a large, heavy book, open on a table. The gold-bordered ivory pages were ruled into lines and columns, each numbered and filled with names and dates, the ink fading to sepia. Reverently, Sister Ursula turned the pages. "'Eighty-nine,'" she murmured. "'Eighty-eight.'" She paused. "'Eighty-six—ah, here we are, 'eighty-five. What was the date, my dear?"

"Early in the year, I believe," Kate said. "Certainly prior to April. The ceremony was witnessed by my cousin, Mary Kelly. The bride's name was Annie Crook. I don't know the name of the bridegroom." The name of

213

the bridegroom, it now seemed to Kate, almost certainly held the key to this whole tragic thread of events, from the secret marriage to the murders.

Sister Ursula ran her finger down the column. "Annie Crook, Annie—" She stopped. "This should be it, I suppose, on March fifteenth. Annie Elizabeth? Oh, yes, here is your cousin's name, as witness, only here she signs herself Marie Jeannette Kelly. The other witness, I see, was a man by the name of Walter Sickert. The groom's brother, I suppose, or his father." Her dreamy smile held more than a little envy, Kate thought. "It makes me happy to see the names of a wedding party in our register and think of the joy they felt as the vows were exchanged. So much delight in the small compass of a wedding ring! I always pray that the happiness of their wedding day shall last forever, and be shared by all those who know and love them."

Forever! Kate thought. If her two informants were to be believed, poor Annie's tragic happiness had lasted only a short while, and had led to such indescribable villainy that it still echoed across the kingdom.

With these thoughts swirling in her mind, Kate gazed at the register. They were here, the four names, the final, ultimate evidence of the marriage. The name of Annie Elizabeth Crook, written in a poorly formed cursive script. Marie Jeannette Kelly, awkwardly printed and badly blotted—Mary Kelly, styled in the French manner. Walter Sickert, elegantly decorated with a pair of artistic flourishes.

And the bridegroom's name? The name of the man whose secret and ill-conceived marriage had been prologue to such an unholy course of events? Kate bent closer, trying to make it out, for it was almost illegible.

And then it came clear, and she felt an almost sickening sense of disappointment. Sickert, it was—A.V. Sickert—the same name that Mrs. O'Reilly had given her an hour earlier. The bridegroom had borrowed his friend's name, not only for his everyday doings in Cleveland Street, but for his wedding as well.

She turned away from the register, and Sister Ursula closed it with a gentle reverence. "I hope," she said, "that you've learned what you came to know."

"Yes, thank you," Kate said, with a slight smile. But there was nothing to smile about. She was no closer to the one truth she had come to learn. The name of Annie Elizabeth Crook's husband was still a mystery.

28

"Lady Randy is sure to have a clever magazine, for she is so clever, brilliant, keen of wit. She is highly educated, observing, and has as varied a knowledge of the world and society as it is possible for a woman to have... Lady Randy's acquaintance is limited only by the confines of the earth."

Town Topics
1899

JENNIE CHURCHILL SAT at the desk in the library at Sibley House, reading the kind note that Manfred Raeburn had sent through Winston, complimenting the story Beryl Bardwell had written for the first volume of *The Anglo Saxon Review*—and commending her great skill in choosing contributors. She read it with a slight smile, thinking how good it was to have Manfred's able services. He was such a dear boy, and so competent. He seemed to know just what she wanted almost before she knew it herself. If only he weren't so nervous—he positively made her nervous, as well. And it would be nice if he and Winston could get along better. She did not understand the animosity between them, but as long as it did not rise to the level of discomfort, she supposed they could all live with it.

Jennie laid Manfred's note aside to give to Kate, and began to leaf through the manuscripts he had sent for her review. There was a poem—rather a gloomy thing, Jennie thought—from Algernon Swinburne, and a twenty-five-page story from Henry James, written in his usual indeterminate style, as well as five letters from the Duke of Devonshire. If these early submissions were any indication of the quality of the work that was to appear in *The Review, Maggie* (as Jenny still thought of it in her own mind) ought to be a stunning success, a work of quality and substance.

Manfred had also sent several recent press clippings with the manuscripts. One, from *Town Topics*, was highly positive about her efforts, but the others were the usual carping criticisms that were aimed at any new thing— especially a new thing that was thought of by a woman. One critic wrote that it was "presumptuous" to think that a mere woman could bear so significant an editorial burden. Another thought that while Lady Randolph was "splendidly fit" to handle the editorial side of *The Review*, her management skills would be proven sadly lacking. Jennie bridled at both these criticisms, but she did not take them personally. They were the sort of thing that small-minded men wrote about large-minded women. In fact, criticisms and oppositions such as these only strengthened Jennie's commitment to dear *Maggie*, and her resolve to make the magazine the very best in the entire world.

But neither the manuscripts nor the press clippings could hold her attention. Instead, she found herself drawn to the passionate, pleading note she had received from George, less than an hour ago, hand-delivered by a messenger. It lay beside her on the desk now, carefully typed, as if George did not trust himself to write for fear that his emotions might overpower his hand. She took it up to read it for the third time.

My dearest, darling Jennie—

I respect your wish not to see me, sweetheart, just as I respect your every wish and desire. But I *must* plead my case & try to persuade you to reconsider.

By now, Lord Charles has most likely told you what happened, but I need to be sure that you understand that I never intended to spy on you. When I discovered that you were going to Cleveland Street, I fell into the disgraceful misapprehension that you were going to visit a lover. I cannot explain how this wrong idea came into my head, except to say that I was seized by a jealousy so intense that it blotted out all reason. I left your house and rushed to Cleveland Street. I found a place where I could watch, and after you came out and got into your carriage, I went up the stairs and came on the same appalling sight that must have greeted you—a man, dead, with a knife in his back.

You can imagine my shock and horror, dear Jennie. Not that I thought that *you* had committed the deed! No, never in my wildest imaginings could I think *that!* But I was nearly overcome by the fearful apprehension that you might have been seen by others, and I have scarcely been able to sleep a wink since—especially because I did not know where you were and could not assure you of my undying love and support!

I know how intolerably I behaved last night, and I can only beg you to think of my anguish in the past few days, knowing that you are in trouble and finding myself powerless to help. Forgive me, my own precious Jennie, and take me back into your heart and your arms, for the thought of life without you is appallingly hateful. Neither of us can ever be free of the other, my dear. I remain, eternally, devotedly,

Your own George

Should she, would she, forgive him and take him back? Jennie's sigh was a mixture of frustration and perplexity and she threw down the note with an impatient gesture. Since she had known George, her life had not been her own. He had pursued her, written to her, sent gifts and flowers, and embarrassed her with his attentions. But whatever his jealousies, she knew that George could not have killed Finch. The man had been newly dead when she found him, and George had been with her since the evening before. Anyway, George would never have stabbed Finch in the back. If he had raced to Cleveland Street before her to confront the man, he would have insisted on having satisfaction, however illegal dueling might be. As far as the Finch affair was concerned, there was, in Jennie's opinion, not a very great deal to forgive except for a moment's impetuosity.

But that wasn't the entire question, was it? Jennie sat back in her chair, frowning. Forgiving George was one thing, but taking him back was quite another. If she were going to break off the relationship, now was the best time to do it, when she could justify her decision by citing his jealousy. And there was certainly enough good reason to break it off. None of her friends thought the connection a suitable one, and even the Prince (who, God knew, had had enough unsuitable liaisons of his own!) had taken it upon himself to warn her that she risked social censure if she continued to be seen in public with a young man the age of her son. Already the invitations to country-house weekends were beginning to taper off, as people understood that an invitation to Lady Randolph meant as well an invitation to her young lieutenant. Randolph's family were clearly distressed at the thought of her being connected with a man with no fortune of his own. And even Winston, who had supported her so wholeheartedly in other family crises, had made a point of stating the obvious: that whatever George's merits, the ability to support a wife was not among them. "We must frankly face the fact that we are poor, Mama," he had written. "If you marry a young man with no prospects, who cannot help you to pay that seventeen-thousand-pound note, you are both likely to be dragged down by the debt." And of course, her connection with George held the very real possibility of social embarrassment for Winston, whose political career was in that vulnerable period of incubation. From that point of view, he was right to point this out.

But it was exactly this attitude on the part of her family and her so-called friends that made Jennie angry—angry enough, at this moment, to toss her pen onto the desk and begin pacing up and down in front of the sofa where she had rejected George the night before. Her spirit recoiled from the idea that she must choose a husband from the ranks of the men who could afford to marry a lady of her standing. Even more, she was repelled by the thought that Society believed it could dictate to her what she might or might not choose to do.

The gall of Daisy Warwick, of all people, advising her to look for more suitable lovers of her own age, as if her heart could be subject to her intellect! The audacity of the Prince, kind-hearted and well-meaning as he was, to write to her that a liaison with George would be both mischievous and foolish, and that it would cost her the royal friendship! Couldn't they see, these "frightfully concerned" friends of hers, that their very opposition propelled her in a direction exactly opposite to their wishes? Couldn't Winston, who was so much like her, understand that to contradict his mother was to ensure that she would become even more fixed in her resolve?

For Jennie Churchill knew herself well enough to know that she was compelled by contraries, and that when her will was opposed, her will grew diabolically strong. It had happened when she first met Randolph, so many years ago at the Cowes regatta, when she was scarcely nineteen. When he proposed after only three days' acquaintance, her mother had positively put down her foot, and the Duke and Duchess of Marlborough had adamantly refused their permission, even going so far as to threaten to cut off Randolph's allowance. But of course, these refusals had accomplished the opposite purpose, hardening Jennie's resolve to have the man she loved, whatever the opposition and whatever the cost. The same thing had happened a good many other times since, whenever she wanted to do something or go somewhere or become someone, and was denied. At these times, something inside her rose up ferociously to defend her right to make a fool of herself, if that was what it amounted to. But it was *her* right, and she *would* have it, and that was all there was to say about it!

And in that spirit—knowing that she was very likely

making a blunder from which she might never recover, knowing that she was acting out of willfulness rather than wisdom and that her action should certainly have strong negative consequences for Winston and Jack—Jennie sailed back to the desk, shoulders straight, chin high, and picked up her pen to write:

Dear foolish, impetuous George,

Of course you are forgiven, from the bottom of my heart. You write so passionately and with such force that I can deny you nothing. Only wait a little while, until Lord Charles has ended this ugly business, and I promise you that all shall be right between us.

God bless you, my love, my own,
from your loving Jennie

29

"Letter from Colonel J.P. Brabazon to Winston Spencer Churchill upon the successful conclusion of Winston's suit for slander against A.C. Bruce-Pryce; 9 March, 1896:

My dear Boy:
I cannot tell you what intense pleasure your telegram gave to me & what a very great relief it was also… For one cannot touch pitch without soiling one's hands however clean they may have originally been and the world is so ill natured & suspicious that there would always have been found some ill-natured sneak or perhaps some d—d good natured friend to hem & ha! & wink over it—perhaps in years to come, when everyone even yourself had forgotten all about the disagreeable incident…

Ever my dear boy Yrs,
J.P. Brabazon"

CARRYING A SMALL bag containing a clean shirt and his shaving things, Winston turned out of Great

Cumberland Road and headed in the direction of Paddington Station, which was so near that there was no sense going to the bother of a cab. He was on his way to Bath to address a gathering of the Primrose League sponsored by a Party man named H.D. Skrine, a one-night stay only, but no less important for that. It was his maiden effort for the Tories—officially, that is, for he had already made several other informal speeches, to see what response there might be to his entry into the political arena. Ordinarily, the event should have brought him great joy in the anticipation, but what had happened the night before had changed all that. And even though he tried to push the memory of what his mother had told him out of his mind, it kept rearing up like a savage dog, to chew away at him.

It was too damn bad she couldn't have saved the news until he'd delivered his address at Bath, Winston thought, resentment mixing with his fear and sadness. As it was, it would be bloody hard to keep his mind on his speech. And so much was riding on this showing of his! Oliver Borthwick at the *Morning Post* was sending a reporter, which meant that the small and relatively unimportant local event would receive full coverage. This news—which had thankfully come before his mother told him about the fraudulent accusations against his father, or he could not have properly concentrated on writing his speech—had raised both Winston's sense of anticipation and his level of anxiety, and he had spent a great many hours working out his thoughts. He was especially proud of the combative tone of the piece and sure that one sentence, in particular, would catch the *Post's* attention: "England will gain far more from the rising tide of

Tory Democracy than from the dried-up drainpipe of Radicalism." He repeated this splendid sentence to himself as he strode up Baker Street, thinking how much his father would have appreciated the sound and the sense of this pungent assessment of the Radicals. But the thought of his father brought back the ugly memory of his mother's revelation, and he fell into an even darker despair that still held him in its clutches as he turned off Praed Street into the station.

Paddington was crowded, as usual. It was the terminus from which Society embarked on special trains for royal functions at Windsor and holiday-seekers took second- and third-class carriages for the Cornish coast. It was also an Underground station, having initiated the first service of the Metropolitan Railway, so there was a great deal of City traffic. But for all the crowds and hurly-burly, Winston had no difficulty identifying the top-hatted, frock-coated reporter, a Mr. Reginald Carlson, who had stationed himself under the three-sided clock above Platform One. They were to travel down together, so they consulted the departure board and purchased tickets for Reading, where they would change for Swindon and Bath.

Winston had never been very good at dissembling, but knowing that he had better do his best to impress Carlson, he put on a cheerful face. He had expected that there might be a bit of introductory chitchat with the reporter, but that he should soon be left alone to read through his speech. When they were settled in the cream-and-chocolate railway carriage, however, he discovered that the journalist—who appeared to be a cross between a political reporter and a Society columnist—wanted to talk, and that he had already selected a topic of conversation. They were scarcely out of the station when he broached it.

"I understand," he said, "that your mother means to marry young Cornwallis-West." He leaned forward and tweaked Winston's sleeve. "What d'you think of the match, eh, Churchill? No older than you, is he?"

The question caught Winston completely off his guard. Stammering his surprise, he managed, "Means to marry! Well, sir, you know more than I do, I must say! I saw Lady Randolph just last night, and she never mentioned it. In fact," he went on, rapidly inventing, "I understand that she has a much different romantic interest these days, although of course I am not at liberty to speak of it."

"Not at liberty, eh?" Reginald Carlson said indignantly. "Well, I like that! Lady Randy is the most-talked about lady in this kingdom. Everybody is demanding to know who she means to marry, and when. It'll be quite a story when it breaks." He folded his arms with a hard look. "Here I am, going to all the trouble of covering this little political rally in Bath, giving you a good angle in the news and all that—and you won't even let me in on your mother's marriage plans?"

"Perhaps she doesn't plan to marry at all," Winston said sharply, incensed by this irritating bit of blackmail. "She is fully occupied with her launch of *The Anglo-Saxon Review.* If you want to write of anything concerning my mother, write of that."

"The way I hear it, she is occupied with her launch of yet another Churchill into politics," Carlson replied. "It must be a nerve-wearing bit of business, all those dinner parties and string-pullings and bread-butterings." He broke into a horsy laugh. "But she's done a commendable job, by all accounts, to get you ready for politics. 'Young Randy' is what they're calling you." He gave Winston an arch look. "A chip off the old block, is that what you fancy yourself? Think you can measure up, do you?"

This incredible cheek was enough for Winston, whose temper was beginning to rise. "I believe, sir," he said haughtily, "that I should prefer to go over my speech. Perhaps you shall give me leave to attend to it."

Carlson laughed again, more offensively. "Well, then," he said, "I s'pose I'll just have to read the newspaper." He unfolded a copy of the *Post*. "Did you see this morning's story about the racing scandal at Aldershot?"

Winston had already taken out his speech, but the question caught him short. "The... racing scandal?" he asked. A chill went through him.

"Right. The Fourth Hussars Challenge Cup." Carlson looked over the top of the paper, his eyes glinting. "Wasn't there a similar problem with one of these Challenges when you were with the Fourth at Aldershot? Seems to me I remember reading something about it in Labouchère's rag. Wasn't it a rigged race?" He paused. "And wasn't there something else, too? Something about harassment or bullying or some such? Bruce-Pryce, I believe the man's name was."

Carlson's questions now seemed not just irritating and offensive, but sinister, for he had, intentionally or unintentionally, happened upon one of Winston's guilty secrets. Three years before, he had been implicated in a regimental racing scandal—and then, scarcely a month later, in a much more disgraceful episode involving the bullying of another Aldershot subaltern named Bruce-Pryce, who was in consequence drummed out of the regiment. The elder Bruce-Pryce, blaming Winston for this reprehensible treatment of his son, wrote an angry letter accusing him of acts of gross immorality of the Oscar Wilde type. The War Office had not acted in either the racing or the harassment matters and had thankfully turned a blind eye to the accusations of immorality. Winston had immediately engaged George Lewis, a solicitor who was particularly sought after because of his ability to settle seamy matters out of court, and for often quite astounding sums. Lewis had sued the elder Bruce-Pryce for libel and forced him to pay damages. But it had been a near thing—a *very* near thing—and Winston trembled still to think of it.

Pretending that he hadn't heard Carlson's questions, Winston rattled his papers, settled himself into the window corner, and affected a deep preoccupation with his work. But he could no more keep his mind on it than he could fly to the moon. It wasn't just Carlson's outrageous and disrespectful allegations about his mother that distracted him, or even last night's shocking story about a forged photograph of his father with one of the Ripper victims and his mother's payments to some person named Byrd or Finch or some such, who had got himself murdered—a murder of which she might yet be accused.

No, no. Far worse than these were Carlson's other questions about that desperate business at Aldershot. Oh, God, why had this happened now, when his political prospects seemed so perfectly ripe, so ready for the plucking? If Carlson resurrected any of that shameful conduct of which he'd been charged—rigging a Cup race, harassment, immorality—it would be enough to sink him, on the spot and without a trace. Worse still, it would invite the attention of that *other* man, who by his testimony could destroy Winston's entire life simply by revealing what he alone knew, which was much blacker than any of the black marks yet struck against his record. And now that this man was so intimately involved with his mother's affairs, it seemed to Winston that the risk of betrayal was growing daily. He had to do *something* to silence this possible Judas. But what could he do?

What *could* he do?

30

> "'Fancy living in one of these streets, never seeing anything beautiful, never eating anything savory, never saying anything clever.'"
>
> WINSTON CHURCHILL to Eddy Marsh
> while walking in the slums of Manchester

CHARLES SAT BACK in his coffee-house chair and regarded his wife, thinking how beautiful she looked, her russet hair curled into ringlets by the damp, her eyes and mouth fiercely intent, hands gesturing. As always, he was amazed at Kate's resourcefulness and her powers of concentration. Once she had got onto something, whether it was one of Beryl Bardwell's stories or a problem in the kitchen or one of the criminal matters she occasionally helped him with, she stayed with it to the end. Her tenacity was an extraordinary virtue, although it certainly made her a demanding and difficult companion. Still, he would not trade that strength and intensity for all the delicate pink-and-white loveliness in the world.

Kate paused to take a sip of coffee and he spoke. "So

you were able to verify the fact of the marriage, then?"

"Yes," Kate said, putting down her cup. "Sister Ursula showed me the entry in the register, dated March fifteenth. Mary Kelly and Walter Sickert—the same man who paid her wages when she worked as the little girl's nursemaid—witnessed the ceremony. The bride's full name was there too—Annie Elizabeth Crook." She made a wry face. "But the groom's name is still a mystery. He signed himself A.V. Sickert. And while Mrs. O'Reilly says she knows who he is, she is clearly afraid to tell. I'm certain that we shall get no more out of her."

Charles leaned forward, his attention caught. "A.V. Sickert? You're certain about those initials, Kate?"

"Certain? Of course I'm certain! Why?" She gave him a narrow look. "You're not telling me that Walter Sickert actually has a brother with those initials?"

"No," Charles said. "I mean, yes. Walter has two brothers, but neither of them has those initials."

Kate's eyes widened in surprise. "You know Walter Sickert, then?"

"I do," Charles said. "We met at one of his showings at the Royal Society of British Artists some years ago, and since, several times. We have some mutual acquaintances—including the Princess of Wales." He paused, then added, slowly, "Prince Eddy was a close friend of Walter's, back in the early eighties."

"Mr. Sickert is an artist, then—and a popular one, I take it, if he is a friend of the royal family."

"He's one of the London Impressionists," Charles said, "and quite a man about town. He has an eye for city life, and his work shows a sharp sense of character. He's done a fine series of music hall pictures and some striking portraits, in an *avant-garde* style." He paused, then said slowly, "A few years ago, the Princess asked me to take one of my photographs of Prince Eddy to Walter, so that he could make a portrait for her." He fell silent, recalling Abberline's enigmatic suggestion, at the end of their conversation, that he talk to Walter Sickert. Yes, it was time he saw Sickert.

Kate ate the last of her pastry and blotted her lips with a napkin. "Doesn't it seem a bit odd," she said, "that a man who was friendly with a prince was also a friend to shopgirls like Annie Crook? Walter Sickert paid Mary Kelly's wages when she was Annie Crook's nursemaid." She paused. "And when I asked Mrs. O'Reilly where I might find the child, she said I should ask Mr. Sickert. What is a well-known painter doing in this kind of milieu?"

Lost in thought, Charles didn't answer until Kate put her hand on his arm. "Charles?"

Charles roused himself. "A friend to shopgirls?" he said. "You wouldn't ask that, if you knew the man. Sickert doesn't paint studio subjects, you see, although his talents certainly give him an entrée to Society. He prefers the vitality and variety of streets and pubs and music halls—the low life, one might say." He smiled a little. "Life among the rough and tumble, the real people. I've heard him say how much he loves the world of sawdust and spittoons, for that's where he finds the real energy of life."

"The kind of world he might find in Cleveland Street," Kate said thoughtfully, "or in the East End."

"He certainly frequents the East End," Charles replied. "I saw a painting of his several years ago, at the Dutch Gallery in Brook Street—'The Marylebone Music Hall,' it was called. Quite a remarkable piece of work, humorous and melancholy at the same time. And he had a studio in Cleveland Street at one point, for I visited him there, on Alexandra's errand." He thought for a moment about the way Walter had received the photograph of Eddy, with a sadly reminiscent smile, as if he were remembering gay times he and the young prince had shared. "I was with him once at a tea given by Lady Eden. The tea table was filled with the most exquisite pastries, all beautifully contrived and artful. But Walter went down to the kitchen and brought back a bun. Everyone laughed, but I thought how much like him it was."

Kate was watching him with that determined look in her eye that he knew very well, but when she spoke, her voice was almost gentle. "And where is Mr. Sickert to be found these days, do you suppose?"

"He has a studio quite nearby, actually." Charles pushed back his chair. "In Robert Street, across from Regent's Park."

Kate put down her cup and blotted her lips with a napkin. "If you mean to see him, Charles, I think you should go alone. The two of you are already acquaintances. He might tell you things he would not if I were present."

Charles was grateful for her tact. Curious as she was to get at the truth and determined to uncover it, she was still willing to let him do it in the most effective way.

"Agreed," he said, and stood. "Shall I summon you a cab?"

"Thank you, but no," she said, and gave him a small smile. "I think I shall spend a little time among the real people before I go back to Sibley House—although," she added wryly, "I do not have quite the Romantic view of them that your Mr. Sickert seems to possess."

"'Romantic,'" Charles said, musing. "I don't think that's the right word for it, exactly. A Romantic looks at the dirt and finds it wonderful. Sickert seems to see both the hopefulness and the hopelessness at the same time, and manages to capture both. It's quite a complex view."

"A complex view," Kate said. "I shall have to think about that."

Commercial Street was much as Kate had left it the day before, the massive gray bulk of Christ Church looming like a great shadow over the weary people, the homeless sleeping restlessly on the benches in Itchy Park, the factory girls in their dirty pinafores, the coal peddler with his sooty coat and half-empty barrow, the coal stolen, most like, from the London docks. Close behind the coal peddler came the gloomy rag-and-bone merchant with his cart, headed for Spitalfields Market.

But with Charles's remarks about Walter Sickert in mind, Kate tried to see Commercial Street from another, more "complex" view. She scanned the gray faces, tried to read enigmatic expressions, sought for some new insight. Was there life and energy here? Was there hope in what she had taken for utter hopelessness?

And little by little, she did see something she had not seen before. A small boy called Whistling Billy— scarcely more than ten, she thought—was dancing on the curb across from Spitalfields Market, to the tune of *The Girl I Left Behind Me*, which he played on his own tin whistle. On the pavement before him was a tray of tin whistles for which he was asking tuppence. She bought two, and he gave her a bright smile and a cheerful nod and swung into an energetic hornpipe, his feet a nimble blur. In front of the park was a penny profile-cutter plying his scissors, a frame of specimens tied to a nearby tree and a stout lady posed before him, whose profile he was cutting. Beside him sat a rack of small birdcages filled with bright yellow canaries, all warbling lustily. Across the way was an old man in a coachman's blue greatcoat, playing *The Sultan's Polka* with many flourishes on a concertina, to a gathered crowd of mesmerized listeners. And behind him was Spitalfields Market, with its vast array of stalls and bins, wicker baskets and wooden boxes, cages of cackling hens and crowing cocks, and trays of lettuces and fresh vegetables.

Was this the life and energy that Walter Sickert had admired in the street people? Kate wondered. And now that she looked for evidences of this *elan*—if that's what it was—she saw it everywhere—a dirty kerchief, bright red and fringed, tied gaily around a neck; a shiny yellow feather tucked with a rakish flourish into an old felt hat; a morose horse with a circlet of purple paper flowers hung around his neck. The ragged skirt with a ruffle beneath, the frayed coat topped by a smart velvet hat, the flash of a gaudy brooch, the flair of a silk scarf. And now that she saw it, she thought she understood it for what it was—heroism of a sort, a kind of audacious daring that thumbed its nose at the worst life could offer, an enterprising arrogance that refused to be trod on, even by the worst adversity. Was that what Charles had meant by the phrase "humorous and melancholy at the same time," to describe Sickert's perception of these streets, these people? She thought so, and was glad.

Seen with her new eyes, Duval Street did not look

quite so dismal as it had the day before. The street was still mean and dirty, its cobbles still broken, the buildings still gray with smoke-smudge. But a lace curtain hung in one window and in another was a brave red geranium. A calico cat was curled gracefully on a pile of rags in a spot of sun, and even the filthy alley passageway into Miller's Court held one lovely thing, an iridescent pigeon feather that she bent to retrieve. The child was gone, the dog was gone, but the girl still sat in the doorway, her hands clasped around her ankles, her cheek upon her knee. Her hair was neatly brushed and fastened with a pair of tortoiseshell combs, and she wore a blue shawl around her shoulders. At the sound of Kate's footstep, she looked up.

"Ellie?" Kate asked.

"How do you know my name?" the girl demanded suspiciously. And then, "I suppose Mrs. McCarthy told you."

"No," Kate said. A small wooden keg, empty, stood nearby. She pulled it up and sat down. "I saw your photographs in Mr. Finch's studio. At least, I think it is you."

"He's dead, though, isn't he?" the girl said bitterly. "Somebody killed him."

"He's dead," Kate acknowledged, in a matter-of-fact tone. She paused. "Did you enjoy posing for him?"

Ellie pulled herself up straight, her dark eyes flashing. "Of course I did," she said, and there was a great dignity in her tone. "I mean to be an actress. A *serious* actress. I mean to do Shakespeare."

And with that, she stood—and was transformed. Her voice fell, became hushed, fearful. She began to scrub her hands together as if she were possessed. *"Out, damned spot!"* she whispered. *"Out, I say!"* She stopped scrubbing and began to whimper. *"One: two: why, then 'tis time to do 't."* Then, raising her eyes and her voice, as if calling to some unseen presence: *"Hell is murky!—Fie, my lord, fie! a soldier, and afeard? What need we fear who knows it, when none can call our power to account?"* Then hushed again, plaintive, weeping and half-laughing at the same time: *"Yet who would have thought the old man to have had so much blood in him."*

Kate, amazed at this unexpected performance, burst into spontaneous applause. "Ellie!" she exclaimed, "that's splendid! A perfect Lady Macbeth!"

Ellie shrugged, herself again. "Thank you," she said. She sat down and her voice grew dull. "But I doubt I'll ever get the chance to play her."

Kate couldn't argue with that. Ellie had an extraordinary talent, there was no question about it. But under the circumstances, it was unlikely that she should have a chance at anything but the cheapest of music-hall theater. Perhaps that was what Finch had seemed to offer when he took those photographs—a chance to move into serious theater. Perhaps that was why she sounded so bitter when she spoke of his death.

"I don't know very much about the stage," Kate said at last, "but I have a few friends who do." It was true— she was acquainted with Bram Stoker, who was the manager of Henry Irving's Lyceum. It wasn't impossible that Bram might give Ellie at least a bit part in one of his productions, for he was known to take a great interest in young people just beginning their careers. But it was certainly impossible for Ellie to begin from here.

Ellie gave her a cynical look, saying nothing in response to Kate's remark.

Kate, too, was silent. She could offer Ellie a place to work, a place to find enough quiet to prepare herself for the stage. But would the girl trust her enough to accept what might seem to be a curtailment of her freedoms? Would she accept what might seem to be charity? After a moment, she spoke.

"I have a home in Essex," she said, "and am in need of a servant. If you should like to work for me and save enough to get a start, I shall introduce you to Bram Stoker, who manages the Lyceum."

Ellie stared at her, disbelieving. "You're lying," she said flatly. "You're one of those missionaries who wants to save souls. Well, you're not going to save mine, damn it! It's *my* soul and if I want to go to hell, I'll bloody well do it!"

Kate smiled a little. "I'm not a missionary," she said. "It is true that I lied to you yesterday, but I'm not lying now." From her purse, she took out a piece of paper and wrote her name and the directions to Bishop's Keep. She handed it, with five florins, to Ellie.

"Here is train fare plus a bit more and my address," she said, and stood. "Think about it a little, and then think some more." She paused. *"If it be now, 'tis not to come,"* she said softly. *"If it be not to come, it will be now; if it be not now, yet it will come—the readiness is all."*

Ellie stared up at her, holding the florins as if she were ready to fling them away.

As Kate walked down the narrow alley, a ray of sunlight pierced the gloom. Something glinted at her feet and she bent to pick it up. It was a second pigeon feather, shining and iridescent, as beautiful as the first. She picked it up, retraced her steps, and handed it to Ellie.

"The readiness is all," she said.

31

"Certainly I have borne what I have for some years without a temptation to be embittered or unjust or to see in my own sufferings anything but the necessary consequences of my own actions."

WALTER SICKERT
in a letter to Jacques-Emile Blanche,
1899

THE NEIGHBORHOOD IN which Walter Sickert had settled was not much different from Cleveland Street, except for being livelier, rowdier, and seedier, with a good deal more cart and omnibus traffic. Hampstead Road was lined with cheap restaurants and French laundries and shabby shops, their windows pasted over with advertising placards. Peddlers' carts filled with penny trifles were parked along the curbs. Costers bawled, quacks harangued, and crowds eddied up and down, dressed in bright colors and the extremes of fashion. It was all, Charles thought as he turned the corner into Robert Street, wonderfully bohemian, a fine place for a painter whose inspiration fed on such liveliness and life.

Number 13 was at the Hampstead Road end of the street, in a row of dark-colored brick three-story buildings built flush with the sidewalks, with wrought-iron railings across the first-floor level, and tall, narrow windows at the second and third. Charles consulted the bell panel to the right of the door and found the initials *WRS* beside the words "Third floor front." He went in, climbed the stairs, and stood for a moment outside the door. From inside came the sound of hammering. Charles waited until it stopped, then rapped sharply with his knuckles. In a moment, the door opened.

"I say," the flush-faced man said, "I do hope you haven't been rapping long. If you have, I shouldn't have heard you." His face cleared. "Hullo, it's Charles Sheridan, of all people! Well, come in, man! Glad you've caught me. I'm off to Dieppe again tomorrow."

Walter Sickert's eyes were green, his hair sand-colored, and he wore a close-clipped beard and a drizzle of a golden mustache over his sensitive mouth. His collar was loose and he had rolled up his shirtsleeves for work. He still held the hammer in his hand.

"Off to Dieppe," Charles said. "Well, then, I *am* glad I came today." He looked around at the packing crates and the paintings stacked in wooden racks. "You're giving up your studio?"

"Not giving it up. Florence Pash will be using it while I'm gone. I thought I'd just pack up this lot to get it out of her way." Sickert gestured to a crate. "Sit there, and I'll brew us up a spot of tea." He placed a kettle on a gas burner on a shelf by the window and got down two cracked cups and a china pot. "You've heard, I suppose, that Nellie and I are about to write *finis* to our marriage." He opened a package and poured loose tea into a tea ball and dropped it into the pot.

"I hadn't heard," Charles said, "and I'm sorry."

Sickert seemed to take the failure of his marriage as a small thing. "We haven't lived together for a couple of years. She lost patience with me, is what it amounts to." He gave Charles a wry, self-deprecating grin. "Fidelity isn't one of my better qualities, I'm sorry to say. It is difficult for me to stay attached to one of the fair creatures for any longer than it takes to paint them." He sat down on the crate opposite, pulled one leg over his knee, and folded his arms. "Marriage suits you?"

"It does," Charles said. He returned the grin. "I should say that I have become profoundly attached to my wife."

Sickert laughed. "Well, if one must be married, I suppose that is the kind of marriage to have. Now, what brings you here?"

"A long trail of clues," Charles said.

"That's enigmatic enough. I daresay it was not the Princess who sent you, then." He sounded wistful, and Charles wondered whether he was hoping for a commission. Sickert's shirt was frayed at the cuffs and the sole of his shoe was worn almost through.

"Not this time, I'm sorry to say," Charles replied. "However, Eddy has been much in my mind of late."

Sickert looked away. "Oh, has he?" he remarked idly.

"As I remember it," Charles said, "the two of you were rather close friends in the mid-eighties. Was that the Princess's doing?"

Sickert's chuckle was reminiscent. "She wanted me to introduce him to artistic society, she said—although I don't think she quite fathomed what that might mean. I was recommended" (he gave the word an ironic flavor) "by James Stephen, who was Eddy's tutor when he was getting ready to go up to Cambridge."

"Eddie couldn't have been twenty," Charles said, thinking that Sickert himself, at the time, must have been in his mid-twenties.

"He was just nineteen, and keen for art. Fancied himself a painter. His mother paints, you know," Sickert added. "She saw the impulse to art in him, and wanted to encourage it. I think she also wanted to let him have a view of the world. The court is such an artificial place to grow up."

"You gave him lessons?"

Sickert nodded. "And took him round to meet Whistler, of course—I was apprenticed to him then—and to art viewings. We ran into Oscar Wilde here and there, and Bernard Shaw, who lived at the top of Cleveland Street. Eddy was quite deaf, you know. The trait was passed on to him by his mother. It made him seem slow-witted sometimes, although that wasn't the case at all."

Charles nodded. He hadn't known the young prince well, but he shared the same impression, that Eddy's deafness made him seem unresponsive and dull. The Queen was said to have thought her grandson mentally retarded.

Sickert's smile lightened his face. "Eddy and I had quite a time of it in those days. I had just started a series of music-hall etchings, and he loved to go to the music halls with me. It was a great contrast to life with that wretched old grandmother of his, I suppose. Such an old harridan, she was—at least where Eddy was concerned. Always dictating what he was to do. And he didn't mean to do *any* of it."

"I'm not surprised," Charles said with a smile. "He used a pseudonym when he was with you, I suppose."

"He went about as my brother," Sickert said. "He loved the anonymity, especially in Cleveland Street. That's where I had my studio, at the time. Number 15. The building's been pulled down, though." Sickert paused, then frowned, as if coming back to the present. "I say, you're asking a great many questions, Sheridan. What's all this in aid of?"

Charles let a moment pass. "I saw Frederick Abberline yesterday," he said, "in the line of some investigative work I've been doing. He recommended that I talk with you."

There was a silence, into which the hiss of the kettle intruded itself. Sickert rose from the crate and poured water from the kettle into the china pot. "Freddy Abberline," he said thoughtfully. "Haven't heard from him since James Stephen died. What's he up to these days?"

"He's retired, living in Bournemouth." Hearing Abberline spoken of so familiarly, Charles exploited the opportunity. "He sends his regards, and says to tell you that anything you can do to help me shall be much appreciated." He paused. *"Anything,"* he added, with a significant emphasis.

"Ah," Sickert said. He picked up the teapot and cups. Not looking at Charles, he placed them, with a bowl of sugar cubes, on one of the crates. "Sorry, there's no cream," he said.

"Sugar is fine," Charles said, and waited for Sickert to pour the tea.

"And what is this project I am to help you with?" Sickert asked, handing Charles a cup.

"A friend of mine is being blackmailed. The leverage is a photograph—a forgery, as it turns out—of her

243

husband, with the last of the Ripper victims."

Sickert looked up with a start, his eyes intent. "Who?" Then, "Not Mary Kelly, of course. The husband."

Charles didn't answer. Instead, he said, "You paid Mary Kelly's wages, I understand, when she was nursemaid to Annie's child."

Sickert's cup stopped halfway to his mouth. "Did Freddy tell you that?" The tone was one of surprise, rather than resentment or anger.

"Yes," Charles said—untruthfully, for the information had come through Kate. Then, mixing truth with a lie, he added, "He also told me about the wedding at Saint Saviour's, and Annie's basement flat in Cleveland Street, and the baby."

Sickert's eyes widened. "How the devil did you get *that* out of him?" he exclaimed. "I thought his lips were sealed to eternity, on pain of losing that bloody pension of his!"

Charles said nothing, and after a moment, Sickert put down his cup with a clatter. "Well, then. Since he's told you all that, he must think you're trustworthy. And if he means me to help you, I suppose I must." He became thoughtful. "I owe him that, for what he did for me— and for Stephen too, poor chap. It was all very hard in those days." He looked up. "What do you want to know?"

"The story. From the beginning. I know the general framework, but I need to hear the details."

Sickert sucked in his breath, then let it out again. His voice was tight. "Including the... killings?"

"Yes," Charles said. "Including the killings. Begin with Eddy and Annie, please."

For that, Charles knew now, was the incredible truth

behind the secret marriage—that the bridegroom who had signed Saint Saviour's register as A.V. Sickert, who had dared to marry a Catholic commoner, and who had fathered a child within the sacred bonds of holy matrimony and without the permission of the Queen, was none other than the young Eddy—Prince Albert Victor, the Duke of Clarence and Avondale and next in succession, after the Prince of Wales, to the throne of England and the British Empire.

32

"Jack and Jill went out to kill
For things they couldn't alter
Jack fell down and lost his crown
And left a baby daughter."

A Cleveland Street ditty

"The Sign of the Entered Apprentice
This is part of the ritual of receiving an apprentice
Mason. The Master draws his right hand across his
throat, holding his hand open with the thumb next
to his throat, and then drops it down by his side. The
allusion is to the cutting of the throat which would
be the penalty of revealing Masonic secrets."

WILLIAM MORGAN
Freemasonry Exposed,
1836

THE STORY BEGAN, Sickert said, in Cleveland Street,
where in the autumn and winter of 1883, Eddy,
masquerading as the painter's younger brother, began to

visit the studio at Number 15. He did a little sketching, met other artists, and in general, enjoyed the bohemian life, a marked contrast from his grandmother's straitlaced and ritually formal court. Across the street from the studio was a tobacconist's shop run by Charlotte Horton and a confectioner named James Currier. Annie Crook, who lived a few doors down in the basement of Number 6, was employed in the shop and occasionally came to Sickert's studio to model for him.

Sickert introduced Eddy to Annie and the two young people became friends. While someone from the court might have seen it as an unusual relationship, Sickert did not: Annie was loving and lively, he said, and she bore a strong resemblance to the person Eddy loved most in the world, his mother, Alexandra. For a time, Annie did not know the prince's real identity, and behaved toward him as she would any young man whom she fancied. For Eddy's part, he found Annie's honesty and openness a refreshing change from the pretense and artifice of the court. At some point, he told her his secret, and was delighted when it made no difference between them. She was just as natural and easy with the prince as she was with the boy, and he treasured the time they spent together.

The friendship between Eddy and Annie ripened into love, and she became pregnant. Loving his Annie, Eddy insisted that they be married, although Sickert counseled against it. In fact, according to Sickert, they were married twice: once in an Anglican ceremony and afterward in a Roman Catholic ceremony held in Saint Saviour's Chapel. Annie gave birth on 18 April, 1885, to their daughter Alice Margaret, in the infirmary at the Marylebone Workhouse in Euston Road. She might have borne Alice at Middlesex

Hospital, which was very nearby, but she preferred to seek the greater anonymity of Marylebone.

Sickert paused and added, in an explanatory tone, "Eddy didn't have to marry her, you know. He could have sent her off somewhere with an allowance, and been done with the whole affair. That's the way it's done at court. That's the way his father did it, over and over." His eyes grew sad. "But Eddy loved Annie—that was his great tragedy. He loved Alice, too, and that mean little basement where Annie lived. He told me once that it was their secret trysting place, and should be forever sacred to him. In his romantic naiveté, he believed he could keep the marriage hidden, a special, private thing, safe from the clutches of the Queen." He shook his head. "I tried to tell him how futile it all was, but Eddy had been raised as a Royal. He *would* have it his way, whether or no."

"I don't suppose the marriage was ever valid, legally speaking," Charles said. "The prince was under twenty-five, and he married without the Queen's consent, which the Royal Marriage Act requires. It could have simply been set aside, and there would never have been any question of the child's inheriting."

"That might have been the Crown's view," Sickert said, "although the Church would have held the marriage canonically valid. But that wasn't the problem. The common people and their attitude toward the royal family at that time—*that* was the problem, you see. Eddy's father was constantly the subject of scandal, and the Queen herself was not a great deal liked. She had hidden behind her widow's weeds too long to suit the populace. And there was the Fabian Society, and the socialists, and the anarchists. I don't suppose I'm telling you anything new," he added.

It was all true, Charles thought. In the mid-eighties, it was well known that the Queen lived in deathly fear of revolution—had even been, herself, the target of an assassination. She would have feared that Eddy's marriage to a Catholic commoner, valid or invalid, could bring down the Throne, and with it, the Empire. And well it might, Charles thought, given the popular sentiment against the royal family. But that was another chapter, and they needed to get on with the central narrative.

"What about Mary Kelly?" Charles asked.

"Ah, yes, Mary," Sickert said, and took up the story again.

A friend of Sickert's, a man named Bellord, a partner in a Cleveland Street firm of solicitors, had founded the Providence Row Night Refuge for Women, at Crispin Street and Raven Row. When it became clear that Annie was pregnant and should soon have to stop working, the shop owner, through Sickert, asked Bellord to find a replacement from among the young women who came to the refuge. He chose Mary Kelly, who seemed bright and ambitious, and she was trained to take over Annie's job. But after the child was born, Eddy decided that Annie should have a companion and help with the child, and gave Sickert the money to pay Mary to move into Annie's basement and take care of Alice.

"I wasn't in favor of it," Sickert said. "Mary was young and had no training as a nursemaid. But she was strong-willed, ambitious for better things, always on her dignity." He grinned ruefully. "She didn't think I treated her with enough respect, but she wasn't above leaving the baby in my care when she trotted off to the East End to see her friends. Then back she would come,

Miss High-and-Mighty, to pick up the Little Princess, as she called the child." He made a face. "If it hadn't been for Eddy, I should have told her to shove off. But I loved him, you see, and I felt that this marriage was good for him, that it gave him a genuine love and warmth that he could find nowhere else. And I was fond of Annie—she was a dear, good girl, and utterly faithful to him. Eddy was her whole life."

Charles could not help but be struck by the pathos of the account, but he kept his voice steady. "How long did this arrangement go on?"

The prince's secret marriage was kept from the royal family for a surprisingly long time—perhaps in part because Sickert had taken the little group to France with him a time or two—but could not be hidden forever. The unhappy end came some two years after the birth of Alice Margaret. A gang of ruffians, strangers to the neighborhood, appeared on the corner of Howland Street. They began to quarrel loudly among themselves and then broke into fisticuffs, attracting the attention of neighbors and passersby. While everyone was watching the fight, two coaches that had been waiting in Goodge Place turned the corner into Tottenham and thence into Cleveland Street, stopping outside Annie's basement. Eddy, who was there at the time, was seized and borne off, to be confined to court under the supervision of the Prime Minister, Lord Salisbury. Annie was taken to Guy's Hospital, where she was kept for five months or so and then released as a certified lunatic.

"And she was, by that time," Sickert said bitterly. "The game was up. Gull had done his work, and—"

"Gull?" Charles asked, thinking of what Robert Lees had told Kate. "Sir William Gull?"

"Yes, Gull. Physician-in-Ordinary to the Queen. Eddy's doctor. Doctor as well to the Prince and Princess of Wales." Sickert's mouth twisted. "The great Gull performed some sort of operation on poor Annie's brain, and when he was finished with her, she was partly paralyzed, given to fits, and amnesic. She was infected with syphilis, too, by being injected with tainted blood." His tone was corrosive. "I owe that little piece of intelligence to Bland-Sutton, a surgeon at Middlesex Hospital, who got the gory details straight from Gull himself." He laughed harshly. "You might say that our Annie was the first of the Ripper's victims."

That last remark was extraordinarily tantalizing, but Charles decided to leave it for the moment. "Where is Annie now?"

Sickert shrugged. "Anywhere, everywhere. St Pancras Workhouse, the last time I knew of her, a year or more ago. She doesn't remember me, and she's deeply suspicious of any attempts to help her. I've long ago reconciled to letting her fend for herself."

"And Mary Kelly?"

Mary Kelly, Sickert went on, had been out with Alice on the day Annie disappeared. She was frightened and distraught when she learned from the neighbors what had happened. She left Alice with Sickert and fled back to the East End, to Dorset Street, where a friend of hers, a woman named McCarthy, kept a lodging in Millers Court. Sickert followed Mary there a few days later and warned her to keep quiet, or she might find herself in the hospital, with Annie. But Mary—self-willed, impulsive Mary—had not listened. She began to drink heavily and regularly, and her tongue wagged, and before long she had confided her experiences to three friends, Mary Nichols, Annie Chapman, and Elizabeth Stride. Like Macbeth's witches, they had brewed trouble, concocting a scheme that would bring enough money for a new start in life. They sent Sickert a blackmail letter to be forwarded to "the appropriate persons," threatening to make the whole story public. And not just the story of Eddy's marriage, either, although that was bad enough. They intended to tell about Annie's shameful treatment and reveal who was behind it, unless they were paid for their silence. Ironically, the amount they demanded was pitifully small. To women who sewed sacking or glued a gross of matchboxes for tuppence farthing or sold a night's lovemaking for fourpence, a guinea was a small fortune, ten guineas unimaginable wealth.

Charles was suddenly aware that he had been holding his breath. He let it out. "What did you do with their blackmail demand?"

"What do you think I did? I gave it to Eddy immediately. Annie was lost to him, his marriage was gone, and he was up against it. In despair, he told his father, who told Salisbury and some of his Masonic friends." He poured himself another cup of tea and sat.

His Masonic friends? Charles sat for a moment, lost in thought. Finally he roused himself. "And then what?"

There was another silence. When Sickert spoke, his voice was thin and reedy. "I don't think Eddy's father, or Salisbury either, intended that murder be done."

"But murder was done. By the Ripper."

"Yes. And when the blackmailers were all dead, and another poor soul killed by mistake, he went out of business."

"That would've been Catherine Eddowes?"

"Right. Eddowes didn't even know the other women. Just before she was killed, she was jailed for drunkenness at Bishopsgate. She gave the policeman the name of Mary Kelly, and she had a pawn ticket in that name in her pocket."

"A coincidence, I suppose," Charles said, "but fatal all the same."

"Indeed. When they got Eddowes, they thought they were done—until the newspapers came out and they realized their mistake." Sickert shook his head. "I'll never know why Mary Kelly didn't leave the City— too paralyzed with fear, I suppose. Or perhaps she had turned fatalistic. By that time, she might have thought there was nowhere to run. Anyway, they did her on the Prince of Wales's birthday, as a present to him." He showed his teeth. "Ghoulish, eh?"

Charles was silent. Ghoulish wasn't the word for it. Surely the Prince himself had not ordered this! What kind of deranged mind had imagined such things? Was it Gull's crazed intellect? Or—

"Meanwhile," Sickert went on, "poor, annihilated Annie was wandering the streets like a lost soul. Eddy was utterly heartsick and couldn't keep himself out of trouble. There was that affair with the male brothel—"

"Just down the street from Annie's flat," Charles put in.

"Exactly," Sickert replied. "He *would* come back to the neighborhood every chance he got, poor man. The brothel scandal was quashed pretty as you please, of course, and the one journalist who dared to write of it was bundled off to jail. Eddy was packed off to India out of the way, but once back in England, he fell in with a dissolute crowd that liked to play with boys." Sickert's smile had no mirth. "At The Hundred Guineas, Eddy was known as Victoria."

"Ah," Charles said. The Hundred Guineas was a club where the members assumed women's names and quite often, women's garments.

"It is quite an irony, isn't it?" Sickert cleared his throat. "He was drinking and dissolute—I believe he too was syphilitic—and could no longer be kept under any kind of control. His father thought a wife might rein him in and suggested that he go about getting one, and what did he do?" He smiled dryly. "He proposed to the Princess Helène, another Roman Catholic, which of course sent the Queen into hysterics and brought poor Salisbury to the brink of revolution again—in his imagination, of course."

"From the Crown's point of view, then," Charles said, "it was a good thing that the Prince died when he did." He paused. "Although I've heard..." He let his voice trail off.

"Ah." Sickert looked directly at him. "What have you heard?"

"That he did not die in '92," Charles said softly. "That he is, even now... alive."

It was true. Eddy had become so increasingly irrational and was such an unsuitable heir apparent that news of his demise had clearly come as a relief to the government. In fact, some weeks before the death was announced, Charles had heard that there was a plan afoot to have the prince committed to an asylum, and that after he set a second fire at Sandringham, even his mother had agreed that he must be confined. His reported death and funeral put a stop to the rumors for a time, but soon they were circulating again, and Charles heard it said that Eddy was being held in Balmoral, the royal Scottish residence on the River Dee.

"Even now alive," Sickert repeated musingly. There was a silence, broken only by the rattle of wheels on the pavement below. "Well, then," he said finally, "there it is."

"Yes," Charles said, "but those are only rumors. I wonder whether you have any direct knowledge."

Another silence. "Abberline is a better source on that subject than I." Sickert sounded irritated. "Why can't you get it from him? I've given you everything else you wanted."

"Not quite," Charles said. "The Ripper—you haven't told me who he was." He paused. "Who they were."

Sickert laughed dryly. "They're dead, you know. The whole lot of them. All but the chap who drove the coach. That's where the women were killed—except for Mary. They were lured into the coach with the promise of a fast piece of work at a good price."

This came as no surprise to Charles. It was common for customers to invite prostitutes into their carriages, to be let out some while later, some distance away. "The coachman's name?"

"Netley. John Netley. He used to drive Eddy to Cleveland Street when he came to visit Annie. Since he already knew the secret, he was recruited to take the Ripper—the rippers—into the East End."

"Is Netley still in London?"

"He was five years ago, working as a coachman out of a depot at the Great Central Station, in Marylebone." Sickert scowled. "He tried to run Alice down, you know. Twice. The first time when she was about four. Then again, just before her seventh birthday, in Trafalgar

Square. She had to be taken to the hospital that time. He's a bad character, that one. If he's not dead already, I warrant he won't last much longer."

Charles took a deep breath. "And Gull was the Ripper himself? You're sure of that?"

"Who else could have carved them up so exquisitely besides that old vivisectionist?" Sickert said, in a barbed voice. "But he didn't work alone. And he wasn't the mastermind. Gull had the stomach to be a butcher, but his mind was failing fast. He lacked the wit to think the whole thing through—except for the bloody rituals." Sickert laughed sarcastically. "He could handle those, all right. Oh, yes, he could handle *those*."

"The rituals," Charles said slowly. "You're speaking about the mutilations, I take it."

He had studied the reports of the Coroner's inquests and knew the basic details—and of course he had seen Mary Kelly's body. As he recalled, each of the women (except for Elizabeth Stride, where the Ripper had evidently been interrupted) was mutilated in much the same way: their throats cut from left to right, their abdomens opened to the breastbone, their intestines removed and placed over the shoulder. In the last two killings, organs were missing: Catherine Eddowes' kidney and uterus, Mary Kelly's heart. In the latter killings, as well, rough triangles had been cut in the victims' faces.

"Yes," Sickert said, "I'm speaking of the mutilations." There was a pause, and when he spoke again, his voice held a note of half-veiled surprise. "When you see Abberline, give the fellow my thanks, will you? I must say, it's a relief to talk about it, even ten years later. Get the whole thing off my chest, as it were." He straightened and said in sudden realization, "By Jove, it *is* ten years, isn't it? Ten years, almost exactly. Mary Kelly was murdered on the ninth of November." He gave a harsh laugh. "HRH's birthday. Quite a gift, that, from his fellow Freemasons."

Charles looked up. It was true, then. His suspicions were correct.

"You don't look surprised," Sickert said. "I suppose it had already occurred to you, then."

"Just now, actually," Charles said. Although now that he thought of it, he couldn't understand why it hadn't come to him before.

"I suppose," Sickert said, "I had better explain that angle, although I should have thought Abberline would have done so, since he was the one who found it out and told it to me." He gave Charles a slantwise look. "You are a Freemason?"

"I was once," Charles said, "when I was in the Army. I'm afraid I did not take it very seriously, or rise through the degrees, or pay much attention to the rituals."

"Well, then." Sickert sipped his tea, then put down the cup. "Do you remember hearing anything about a message chalked on a passageway wall at the scene of Catherine Eddowes' murder?"

"Indeed, I witnessed it myself," Charles said. "I was called to photograph the scene, but it was very early in the morning and there was not yet enough light. What I saw was written in a strong, well-shaped hand, and the words were quite clear."

"But you didn't photograph it?"

"Commissioner Warren came, just at sunrise. He sponged the wall himself, fearing that the message might incite a riot. There wasn't an opportunity to photograph it, unfortunately."

"And do you remember what it said?"

"It was so enigmatically worded that I have never forgotten it," Charles said. He quoted: "'The Juwes are the men that will not be blamed for nothing.'"

"And I suppose you took the word *Juwes* to be a misspelling for the word *Jews*, and were not surprised by the commissioner's action."

"Oh, I was surprised," Charles said, "as was everyone there. Several of the detectives, particularly those of the City Police, were nearly livid. The message was the first real clue, the *only* clue ever left by the Ripper. It could have been photographed, then covered with a blanket and the passageway guarded so that it was not seen by the public. No one present could understand why the commissioner did such a thing. It seemed totally incompetent."

"An incompetent policeman, a competent Freemason," Sickert said dryly.

"A Freemason?" Charles asked in surprise, then checked himself. Of course, Warren was a Freemason. Most of the men in positions of authority were Freemasons. In fact, that's how some of them got those positions.

Sickert ticked off Warren's titles. "A District Grand Master, a Past Grand Sojourner of the Supreme Grand Chapter, and member of the Royal Alpha Lodge, of which Eddy himself was the Right Worshipful Master. It was Commissioner Warren's sacred obligation to scrub off that declaration, in order to protect the men who wrote it. They were also Freemasons."

Charles stared at him, the whole thing beginning to make a gruesome sense. So the word "Juwes" didn't refer to Jews, but to Jubel, Jubelo, and Jubelum, the three apprentice Masons who, according to tradition, treacherously murdered their Grand Master and were ritually executed for the crime. Freemasons referred to them collectively as the *Jues*—a deliberate allusion to the Jews who crucified Jesus Christ. And the Ripper's mutilation, the removal of the women's intestines, mirrored the way the three *Jues* were punished for their betrayal, their vitals taken out and thrown over the left shoulder. It had become the symbolic penalty for revealing the secrets of Freemasonry.

"So the mutilation," Charles murmured, "was in effect a secret code, making clear to the initiated who was responsible for the killings."

"Exactly," Sickert said. "And remember that the victim was found in Mitre Square, and that a piece of her apron was cut off and placed directly under the message."

The mitre and the square, Charles thought—the Masons' tools. Mitre Square itself had been named for the Mitre Tavern, where Freemasons had met for two centuries. And the apron—of course! He himself had taken a photograph of Prince Eddy and the Prince of Wales wearing their Masonic regalia: ceremonial aprons made of white lambskin and lined with white silk, meant to symbolize the aprons worn by stonemasons. The clues were so clear, so unmistakably clear, as long as one understood the arcane lore of Freemasonry.

Watching Charles's face, Sickert smiled. "I see that you're getting the picture."

"I am," Charles said. "The women were killed to keep them silent, and mutilated as a—a what? A Masonic joke? A warning?"

Sickert shrugged. "Who knows? The Freemasons are fond of symbolic acts, so it might have been a gesture of tribute to the Master of their lodge. Or perhaps they thought it would silence other persons who might have some scandalous information they thought to turn into ready money. Or perhaps the mastermind behind the crimes was simply engaging in a cruel joke. The man was certainly capable of it. He *was* mad, you know."

"Who?" Charles demanded. *"Who?"*

"Why, don't you know?" Sickert said. His face was twisted. He laughed unpleasantly. "It was Lord Randy, of course."

"Randolph?" Charles whispered, feeling suddenly sick.

"Mad as a hatter," Sickert said. "Mad as the great Gull. The newspapers got that right, at least. It was the work of a warped mind."

For a long moment, Charles could not speak. At last, he said, "Is there any proof?"

"I doubt it. Or if there is, you'll never see it, nor will anyone else. It is buried deep in the bowels of Whitehall. I learned what I know from Eddy's tutor, James Stephen. He was a brilliant man—called to the bar, kept chambers, wrote poetry. He had been treated by the grand and glorious Gull for a head injury, and the two knew one another well. He told me and Abberline, together, what he knew, and then he died." He added, with heavy irony. "It is said that he starved himself to death."

"Starved—" Charles could go no further.

"That's the official report," Sickert said. "It's all a very bad business and best forgotten. There have been times when I've feared for my own life. But Alexandra likes me, because of my affection for Eddy. That's what's kept me alive, I think." He cocked his head, listening.

"Someone's coming up the stairs. Perhaps I should have told you about—"

The door opened, and a young girl of twelve or thirteen burst in, carrying a bunch of violets. She was a pretty thing in a white shirtwaist, blue skirt, and white stockings, with long, dark hair and delicate features in a heart-shaped face.

"Hello, Walter," she said. She spoke loudly, and with an odd rhythm. "I'm not intruding, am I? Should I go away again?"

"No, don't go, Alice," Walter said, also loudly. He motioned to her to come and stand beside him and slipped his arm around her waist. "Lord Charles, I should like you to meet Miss Alice Crook."

Charles stood and took the girl's hand. "Miss Crook," he said gravely. "I am very pleased to meet you."

"You'll have to speak up," Walter said. "She's deaf, you know." He smiled slightly. "Like her father."

33

"'The fact is, we have all been a good deal puzzled because the affair *is* so simple, and yet baffles us altogether.'

'Perhaps it is the very simplicity of the thing which puts you at fault,' said my friend."

Edgar Allan Poe
The Purloined Letter

CHARLES CAUGHT A cab at the corner of Hampstead Road and Euston. He directed the driver to Paddington Station, where he went into the telegraphic office and spent some time carefully composing a telegram to Frederick Abberline, in Bournemouth. That done, he turned up his collar and trudged down Baker Street in the direction of Mayfair and Sibley House. It was late afternoon now, well past teatime, and the day had turned cold. There was a bite in the damp gray air, the presage of winter weather, and the mist blowing up from the river was like needles against his face. He might have caught another cab and saved himself a chill, but he wanted to clear his mind before he arrived at Sibley House and it was time to relate Walter Sickert's incredible story to Kate—and to Jennie.

It had been a strange and eventful day, a day that had dispelled, at least in Charles's mind, much of the mystery that surrounded the most atrocious crimes London had ever known. There were still a great many details he did not know now and perhaps would never know, but the basic outlines seemed clear, even simple. If all that he and Kate had learned were true, the Ripper killings were the result of an unfortunate marriage obliterated by the royal family and a blackmail attempt by a one-time nursemaid and her friends, whose murders had been clothed in a mad Masonic ritual.

But as he trudged along through the gathering twilight, Charles felt no triumph over the secrets that he and Kate had uncovered in the basements and lofts of Cleveland Street or the dirty alleys of the East End. What was to be gained from any of this knowledge? Eddy was either dead or permanently out of reach—and certainly out of the succession, his misdeeds having condemned him to a life of exile and imprisonment. Annie was disabled, her mind destroyed, a wanderer among the outcasts of the City. The men who had done the killing, Sir William Gull and Lord Randolph Churchill, were both dead—Gull (if Lees' story was accurate) having died in a lunatic asylum, Churchill of syphilis, also a maniac, at the end. Only the coachman survived, apparently: questioned, he might be able to fill in some of the missing details, but what of that? Alice's birth record could be found, Lees' story could be checked, the Masonic affiliations could be confirmed—but to what end? There was nothing left to know about the Ripper killings that mattered to anyone, anywhere, except as a matter of forensic curiosity, or to serve some abstract ideal of justice.

Justice! The thought of it set his teeth on edge. There had been no justice anywhere in the whole of this foul business, only fear, and exploitation, and high-level corruption. How high did it reach? To the Prime Minister, certainly, and the Prince. To the Queen? Very likely—the old lady was notorious for her demands to be told each minute detail of government, and neither her son nor the Prime Minister would have dared to keep Eddy's marriage and Mary Kelly's blackmail letter from her. And Sickert was only speculating when he said that the Royals had not sanctioned murder. Charles knew from personal experience how the Prince's instructions were given, with a wink and a nod. And even if the directive had not come from HRH or Salisbury, they could not have escaped the knowledge of the women's deaths. The papers had shrieked the gruesome news— the police reports, the inquest reports, the interrogation of suspects—from the end of August to early November. The Royals might have called off their dogs at any time after the first murder, and they didn't.

Oblivious to the traffic, Charles crossed Oxford Street, splashed to the thigh with gutter filth by a passing brewer's wagon and nearly run down by a motor lorry, whose driver flung curses at him like stones. The fog wrapped around him like a cold, wet shroud, and in spite of the hurrying crowds that brushed past, he felt desperately alone. Yes, he had found it all out, but to what purpose? The knowledge could serve no one, bind no wounds, heal no broken hearts. No justice was possible, no public resolution, no restitution.

But with this thought came another. What about the

children? There was Alice, the Little Princess—except that she wasn't a princess, for her mother was a Catholic commoner and her father no longer a prince. She was only a pretty child with a delicate face and something of her grandmother's look, saved from the gutter by the generosity of her father's friend, not very stable himself, who had taken the responsibility for seeing that she had some sort of decent life. No revelation of her parentage, of her connection to the Ripper killings, could ever change her circumstances or bring anything but unhappiness to her.

And there was Winston. It had been his mother's desperate efforts to silence Finch that had opened up this whole affair. If any word of Randolph's involvement in the heinous murders were to reach the public in her son's lifetime, Winston's political ambitions should be ruined, his life wrecked. As far as Winston—and his brother Jack, too—were concerned, the sooner the Ripper was forgotten, the deeper the secret was buried, the safer their futures. They had nothing to do with the sins of their father. Justice could only destroy them, as surely as it would destroy Alice.

Charles thrust his hands deeper in his pockets and ducked his head into the wind, the air flowing like cold water inside his collar and down his back, the clopping carriages and darting hansoms moving past in the deepening twilight, the gas streetlights, newly lit, emerging like haloed beacons in the gloom. Five minutes later, he had reached Sibley House, and Richards was opening the door and clucking over the wetness of his coat and shoes, and Kate was standing at the library door, her russet hair shining in the light, her hand held out in loving welcome.

"You're wet and cold," she said. "Come in by the fire, my dear."

He did not answer. Instead, he took her by the shoulders and kissed her mouth, then folded her into his arms, warming himself in her warmth, cleansing himself in her fresh, clean scent. It would not be easy to relate to Lady Randolph Churchill the horrors he had heard today, but Kate would be there, and by her very presence would help him to say what needed to be said, only that much and no more. He touched her forehead with his lips, tenderly, thankfully. Kate would always be there, and for that, he was unutterably grateful.

34

"PLEASE CONFIRM JACK RC AND WG STOP CAN
YOU SHED LIGHT ON PRESENT WHEREABOUTS
OF PAV STOP WALTER SENDS REGARDS STOP
SIGNED SHERIDAN"

F RED ABBERLINE READ the enigmatic telegram one more
time. He folded the flimsy yellow paper, pushed it
into the pocket of the woolen shirt he wore under his
mackintosh, and stared out to sea, where the gray of the
sky and the gray of the water met with no perceptible
boundary. He had come down to the pier, as he often
did these days, to be alone, to think, and to remember—
remember things he desperately wished he had never
learned and fervently hoped he might someday forget.

But that was a fool's dream, he thought wearily. What
he had discovered would be with him to the day he died,
an albatross chained around his neck, a leaden weight
on his heart. Worse yet, it was a burden he could not
lighten by speaking of it, except to Sickert, who already
knew the worst of the horror. He could not speak of it to
Sheridan, before whose integrity he felt compromised

and dirty; nor to his wife, Emma, whose only joy in life was the house he had bought her with the coin of his complicity. He could not tell the world that he knew who committed the crimes that had riveted the attention of the entire Empire, the murders that had appeared to baffle even Scotland Yard. He could not tell, because his knowledge was now a state secret, and to reveal it was not merely madness, but treason.

Abberline had joined the Metropolitan Police as an idealistic and naive young lad of nineteen and had risen swiftly through the ranks: to Sergeant in two years and Inspector in ten. He had been a good policeman; more, he had been an honest policeman. This had been a rare and a hard thing, especially after he was assigned to the Whitechapel C.I.D. The division was rotten to its core. Payoffs were routinely accepted as part of the policeman's salary, and corruption was a part of the policeman's world—but not for him. He had risen above the rot even in that Godforsaken part of London, and through the strength of his moral character and reputation he had succeeded in the nearly impossible job of keeping his hands clean for over twenty years.

But a decade ago, he had been pulled, willy-nilly, into a succession of terrible events. He had been captured in their inexorable grip just as he himself had captured hundreds of criminals and delivered them into the swift embrace of justice. Except that it was not justice that had seized him, but the rot. Struggle as he might to keep himself clean—and he *had* struggled, hadn't he?—it had at last gathered him into its filthy embrace and pulled him down.

In the spring of '88, Abberline was transferred from Whitechapel to the West End and instructed to keep an eye on the young Prince Albert Victor, called Eddy, who seemed to be hell-bent on getting himself into as much trouble as possible. Eddy believed him to be a bodyguard, but Abberline was in actuality a spy, paid above his ordinary salary to report directly to Francis Knollys, private secretary to the Prince of Wales. He was to tell Knollys where Eddy went and with whom, and was also directed to be on the lookout for prostitutes who might attempt to approach the young prince. Eddy was to be kept from women, at all costs.

The surveillance duty was not difficult and Emma had happily welcomed the extra money it brought, but it wasn't long before Abberline felt uncomfortable with the work. Eddy was rumored to be incapable of learning, but Abberline found him sweet and simple, and suspected that it was the young man's deafness which made him appear backward. In fact, Abberline saw, the prince's deafness was so severe that it opened him to influence and possible corruption, an easy mark for men who did not have his best interests at heart. Abberline felt increasingly protective toward the prince, who seemed to be driven by some sort of inward despair and anger, and even though he felt himself a Judas each time he made his report to Knollys and collected his additional wage, he comforted himself with the thought that he was doing Eddy a good service by looking out for him.

The duty continued less than six months, however. Knollys abruptly terminated his employment around the middle of August, and Abberline was sent back to Whitechapel. The first of the murders occurred at the end of August, and he was given responsibility for the investigation, to which dozens of detectives were assigned. In the beginning, he had been glad to get back to the routine of police work and the company of his colleagues, and began to systematically pursue the leads his detectives turned up. But then the second murder occurred and he began to sense that something was wrong, that the rot was rising around him. The third and fourth murders, on September 30, convinced him that the ritual mutilations were a kind of secret code and that the vocabulary of the code was Masonic, some of the details of which he had encountered in a book called *Freemasonry Exposed*, written by an American Freemason who had been murdered for his revelations.

Knowing that Freemasons were involved in the murders had not taken him any closer to the actual perpetrators, however. For one thing, he could not imagine a motive. He discovered that Nichols and Chapman and Stride were acquainted, but that didn't mean a great deal—the three women had lived close to one another and frequented the same taverns. But when Mary Kelly was murdered and he began to trace various leads into her past life, a clearer picture began to emerge. As a skilled and experienced investigator, he found out a great deal about Mary Kelly within a few days of her death. He learned that she had once worked for a confectioner in Cleveland Street, then was hired as a nursemaid for a woman named Annie Crook, who had been married in the chapel of Saint Saviours to (it was said) some member of the royal family, a close friend of the painter Walter Sickert. He learned also that Annie Crook had been kidnapped and mistreated, and that Kelly had returned to the East End and gone to drinking and, with three of the other dead women, had resorted to blackmail.

Yes, the details had come quickly, and when he put

them all together, he realized, with mounting horror, that Annie Crook had been married to Prince Eddy and had borne him a daughter, that the women had been killed to silence their tongues, and that the killers were Freemasons, although at that point he could not name the murderers themselves.

But it wouldn't have done him any good to name them, if he could. By the time he had understood the Masonic implications and pieced the rest of the details together, he knew that the rot had swallowed the entire case, and Scotland Yard and Whitehall with it. For his two superior officers, Robert Anderson and Sir Charles Warren, Assistant Commissioner and Commissioner of the Metropolitan Police respectively, were both high-ranking Freemasons and obviously committed to a cover-up. He could point to a half-dozen instances of their mismanagement and interference with the case—not the least of which was Anderson's leaving for an extended holiday in Switzerland the day after Chapman's death; Warren's order to the divisional police surgeon to suppress the details of the mutilations; and Warren's otherwise incomprehensible erasure of the Ripper's chalked message. To top it off, Warren himself resigned as commissioner just hours before Kelly's death, and his failure to notify Abberline of his departure had led to enormous confusion and delay at the crime scene, and the potential loss of evidence. The Home Office followed by illegally removing the inquest from Whitechapel to Shoreditch Town Hall, placing it under the direction of a coroner who aggressively suppressed important evidence. The next day, Abberline was told to turn in his notes and close his investigation. But these events came as no surprise.

He had known since Chapman was killed that the fix was on.

From that time forward, Abberline understood that there was no getting out of the rot. His next significant case came seven months after Kelly's death. It was the Cleveland Street brothel affair, where he was ordered to make sure that the important men—Eddy, Lord Arthur Somerset, and Lord Euston, even the brothel owner—escaped before he closed in on the two minor suspects he was told to arrest. In due time these two unfortunates were allowed to plead to minor charges, served short terms, and disappeared. After that ridiculous debacle, which lost him the respect of the few police officers who still believed in him, he was assigned once again to tag after Eddy, who was rumored to be suffering from syphilis and certainly looked the part. Realizing that the extent of his knowledge about the crimes and the cover-ups put him in danger, Abberline tried to keep his head down—but still, there was a near miss or two, and he began to be afraid.

Then came the shocking news, in February of '92, that Eddy was dead, and Abberline was hit as hard by the blow as if the prince had been his son or his brother. And on the day after this devastation, there came another. He was contacted by Walter Sickert and taken in great secrecy to talk with a man named James Stephen, who had been confined for the past few months to a lunatic asylum in Northampton. Stephen, who was a barrister and poet, as well as Eddy's one-time tutor, long-time friend, and brother Freemason, seemed to Abberline to be perfectly lucid. He had a story to tell and names to name, and he urgently wanted, he said, to set the record straight.

Abberline listened carefully, mentally checking the dates, the details, and the evidence Stephen offered against what he knew as fact from his own investigations. The names Stephen named—Dr. Gull, Lord Randolph, and John Netley—confirmed Abberline's own suspicions, although he had not been able to find any direct incriminating evidence. The story was entirely plausible, entirely possible, and the teller's present condition—he was clearly dying—gave to his tale the added significance of a deathbed confession.

But *was* it the truth? Abberline had to admit that Sickert and Stephen might have concocted it between the two of them, perhaps to cover up their own involvement. Through their relationship to Eddy, they themselves were deeply involved in the case, in one way or another. Had they participated in the murders, as well? Should their names be added to the suspect list? It was possible, but there was no way to know, now. The investigation was ended. The case was closed. The rot had triumphed.

Within a few weeks, Stephen was dead, of self-imposed starvation, according to the official report. By this time, Abberline had heard the rumors that were circulating about Eddy—that he had not died of pneumonia, but of poison; alternatively, that he was not dead at all, but in exile. Both seemed equally plausible to Abberline, given what he knew of the way the marriage had been handled, and what had been done to the women. He continued to give Stephen's story a great deal of careful thought, measuring the names of Gull and Churchill and Netley against the evidence he himself had collected, and concluding, on balance, that Stephen spoke the truth.

Several days after Stephen's death, Abberline went

to see Robert Anderson, who was still the head of his department. He told Anderson that he had written down what he knew and surmised about the Ripper's crimes and had put the document in a safe place, leaving instructions for it to be released to the public if he were to die suddenly. He was not yet fifty, but he was ready to retire, if the department could do without him, and if one or two minor requests were filled, such as the payment of his pension and perhaps a little something extra on account of faithful service. Anderson replied, straight-faced, that the department would be devastated by his loss, but he would see what he could do. The next day, his resignation was handed to him. He signed, and received an envelope containing the first of the payments that still continued to come to him, in cash. Emma found the house of her dreams in Bournemouth, and that was the end of his career as a policeman.

The sky was dark now, and the gaslights on the High Street were winking on. He had missed his tea, but no matter. Emma's sister was visiting and the two of them would never miss him. But his table was waiting at the Dog and Pony and a stein or two of ale would do very well in lieu of tea, with perhaps an eel pie to go with it. Tomorrow morning, when Mr. Peters opened the post office, he would send a telegram to Sheridan. He already knew what it would say.

YES STOP NO STOP REGARDS TO WALTER STOP GOOD LUCK TO YOU. STOP. ABBERLINE

35

"Would that I could discover truth as easily as I can uncover falsehood."

CICERO
De Natura Deorum

THE ROOM WAS so silent that the fall of ash in the fireplace seemed loud and startling. Jennie's face was turned toward the fire, and Charles was sitting in his chair with his head flung back, his eyes closed. Kate sat quietly beside Jennie, watching them both and thinking about the fantastical story Charles had told them. Prince marries commoner, marriage destroyed by Prince's family, blackmailers murdered by half-mad Freemasons, police officials conceal the truth, Prince removed from the succession and imprisoned in secret exile. The whole thing was so riveting, so utterly compelling, that it deserved to be the plot of one of Beryl Bardwell's novels, if nothing else.

But the central question was not whether Sickert's tragic tale held the listener's breathless attention or compelled fear and horror and anger—although it certainly did all

275

of that. What mattered was whether the story was true, and as to that, Kate could not be sure. It seemed almost *too* novelistic a tale to be true, the plot elements too neatly contrived, the details too fully explained. But she had to remind herself that Charles, who got the story straight from Sickert himself, seemed to believe it—and Charles was not easily persuaded. What was more, certain parts of the narrative were authenticated by the fragments of information she herself had gathered from other sources. Still, a great deal of the story could not be confirmed. It depended only upon eyewitness testimony, and most of the witnesses were either dead or deranged. Except for Sickert himself, of course. It was entirely a question of veracity. One either believed him or one did not.

Jennie roused herself. "Thank you, Charles," she said quietly. She sounded sad and resigned. "I suppose I knew, even then, although I should have denied it to Heaven."

Charles opened his eyes. "It can't be proven," he said. "Most of it is merely Sickert's word, and the rest of it— what he says James Stephen said, for example—is merely hearsay. It would be helpful if Abberline had uncovered some corroborating evidence, but if so, I doubt he will tell me. He was a good policeman, but his silence has been bought and paid for."

Jennie sighed heavily. "It is sad to think that Randolph could do such things, although you *must* believe me when I say that it was his illness that drove him. Perhaps it is even sadder to think, though, that the government would go to such lengths to cover up a scandal." She shook her head. "But there have been an untold number of other scandals, all hushed up. I don't suppose we should be terribly surprised by this one."

Kate stood, feeling the need to step away from the story. "It's rather late. Shall we see what's become of dinner?" She was reaching for the bell when the door opened and Richards came in. Winston was behind him, dressed formally, his hat under his arm, as if on his way to a dinner party.

"I'm sorry to barge in," Winston said when he'd been announced, "but I must speak to Lady Randolph. Urgently, I'm afraid."

"Thank you, Richards," Kate said. "You may go."

Sotto voce, Richards replied, "Dinner is just ready, your ladyship. Will Mr. Churchill be staying?"

"Winston," Kate said, "we'll be eating soon. Will you join us?"

"I'm sorry, no," Winston said. He seemed flustered. "I'm on my way to dinner with Lord Balcarres, and I've only a minute. I shan't keep you from your dinner."

Richards withdrew and Winston stood, awkwardly, for a moment. Finally he sat down beside his mother and said, almost in a whisper, "Another letter has come, Mama." He drew an envelope from his pocket. "I came in from Bath in a tearing hurry, caught up the post, and opened your envelope in error." His voice rose. "There's another press clipping—and he says you must give him five hundred pounds or he'll go to the police and tell them that you were at Finch's on the day of the murder!"

"Not now, Winston," Jennie said wearily, waving away the envelope. "Not tonight. It's too much. I just can't bear any more."

"But Mama!" Winston protested. "Something must be done! We can't just hand over—" He stopped and gathered himself up. "I think you should go away. To

277

France, perhaps. Or to India, to visit the Curzons." He turned to Charles and said, in a commanding tone, "Lord Charles, tell her that she *must* go to India, straightaway." His face darkened. "Once she is safely out of harm's way, this person can be... dealt with." The last few words were almost a snarl.

Kate took the envelope out of Winston's fingers and handed it to Charles. "Thank you, Winston," she said quietly. "I believe the situation can be managed without sending your mother on such a long trip—or resorting to violence."

Winston stood, hand on hip. "But what's to be *done?*" he demanded. His jaw jutted and his large round eyes were hard as glass. "If the man is paid, as Finch was, he'll just keep on asking for more. If he isn't—"

"Winston," Jennie interrupted, "why don't you go on and enjoy your dinner. Lord Charles will take care of this matter."

Winston was sputtering. "But—but—"

Charles stood up. "Be a good chap, Winston," he said wearily. "There shall be time later to go into it. You have an engagement, and we are all very tired here."

It was true, Kate thought. She herself was fatigued, and Charles was drawn and pale.

Winston looked from one to the other of them. "Quite right," he said at last, making a visible effort to calm himself. He bent down and kissed his mother's cheek. "I do hope you'll give consideration to my idea of India, Mama. We could go together, for I have decided to return there myself, very quickly. For the polo tournament."

"But I thought you intended on beginning your political efforts!" Jennie exclaimed, startled. "I've been moving heaven and earth to give you your chance. And now you say you're going back to *India*—for a foolish game?"

Winston smiled, but did not make a very good show of it, Kate thought, and his explanation sounded lame. "But it is a very *important* game, Mama, and I owe it to the Fourth to play my part. And the time shall not be lost, of course. I shall take my manuscript with me, and work on it en route." He gave her a smile. "I am booked on the S.S. *Osiris*. Come with me, dearest, and we shall make a fine holiday of it. It is a good way for you to escape from these threats, and from that tiresome George, too. And we shall have *such* fun together."

Is that it? Kate wondered. *Is Winston trying to get Jennie away from George? Does he fear that she will marry him and drag her sons into the social ruin that was sure to follow? Or is there something else behind Winston's precipitous departure? Is he running from something? From someone?*

"You may go if you choose," Jennie said stiffly, "but I cannot. There are things I must do here. For one, I can't possibly leave *Maggie* in Manfred's hands and go off on holiday to India. Capable as he is, he requires my direction."

At the mention of Manfred, Winston's face flushed even redder and his nostrils flared. Kate, watching, remembered the animosity between them. Perhaps George wasn't the only man of whom Winston was jealous.

"I shan't give up trying to persuade you, Mama," he said, obviously attempting to steady himself. "After you have read the note and the clipping, I believe you will see the wisdom of my suggestion. Leaving England may be the only answer." He bowed to Kate and Charles. "Good night."

When he had gone, Jennie shook her head. "What an exhausting boy he is," she said tiredly, "and so ridiculously full of himself. India! After all I have done to help get his political career underway, I cannot believe that he is dashing off to play polo! It is utterly irresponsible of him to be swayed by such schoolboy distractions. What in the world will the Party think?"

But Kate did not believe it was polo that drew Winston to India, so much as something else pushing him. *Something has happened to frighten him,* she thought. Was it the blackmail note, or what he had learned about his father's situation, or something else? But there was no ready answer to the question, and she was too weary to puzzle long over it.

"Richards says dinner is ready," she said. "Perhaps we shall all feel better after we have eaten."

Their conversation during dinner was not sprightly, and Jennie, pleading a headache, retired almost immediately afterward to her room. Kate and Charles returned to the library, where Charles poured himself a whisky, sat down in his chair by the fire, and put his feet up.

After a moment, Kate prompted, "The letter Winston brought—aren't you going to read it, Charles?"

Charles sighed. "Oh, I suppose," he said testily. He took out the envelope, which Winston had already torn open, and pulled out a letter and a newspaper clipping. He read both in silence, then tossed them down on the table beside him.

"After everything that happened today, I'm not in the mood for this kind of thing," he said.

"What does the blackmailer want? Money?"

Charles closed his eyes. "Five hundred pounds," he

said wearily. "The love of money is the root of all evil. Read these, Kate, and see what you make of them."

The newspaper clipping, from an unidentified paper, was terse, to the point, and threatening. Kate was glad that Jennie had not wanted to read it.

POLICE CONTINUE INVESTIGATION

The Metropolitan Police are continuing their investigation into the murder of Thomas Finch, of Number Two Cleveland Street, Fitzrovia. A reliable anonymous informant has offered to aid them in identifying the chief suspect in the crime, a veiled lady seen leaving the murder scene. Further developments are expected shortly.

The note that accompanied the clipping was typewritten, on a half-sheet of thin yellowish paper. "I will trade my silence for five hundred pounds," it said. "Get the money and wait for my instructions." There was no signature.

Kate looked from the note to the clipping and back again, thinking that Jennie really should go to the police. The longer this went on, the more suspicious her visit to Finch's lodgings appeared. On the other hand, if she went to the police, the resulting notoriety would disgrace not only herself but Winston. It was a hopeless dilemma.

She frowned down at the note, thinking that something about it seemed to tug at her memory. The phrasing? She read it again, but nothing came to her. The paper? Perhaps, for it was of a familiar sort that could have been purchased at any stationery shop. The typing was ordinary, too—although from the way the letters were inked, slightly heavier at the bottom, she rather thought that the note had been typed on a down-strike machine. The British seemed to favor them, although she herself much preferred her own Remington up-strike machine, which had come from America.

But still there was *something*. Her frown deepened. Holding the note, she crossed to the desk where Jennie had earlier left a pile of manuscripts and two notes. Jennie had asked her to read one of the notes, which contained a complimentary reference to a short story Beryl Bardwell had written for *Maggie*. Having smiled over it, she had bundled the other materials into a drawer, for the second note (which Jennie surely had not intended to leave in plain sight) was of an embarrassingly private nature and Kate had not wanted the servants to happen on it.

She opened the drawer now, pulled out the papers, and began to leaf through them. When she found what she was looking for, she smoothed it flat and reached for the magnifying glass that was kept in the top drawer. She bent over and studied the note for a moment, then laid the blackmail note beside it and studied them both intently. After a moment, now completely sure of what she was seeing, she straightened.

"Charles," she said urgently, "come here, won't you? I should like to show you something very interesting."

Her words were met with a soft snore. That great detective, Lord Charles Sheridan, was asleep by the fire.

Kate went to him and shook him. "Charles," she said, "come to the desk. There's something you must see!"

Grumbling sleepily, Charles got out of his chair and followed her. But a moment later, he was awake and alert. "By Jove, Kate, I think you've solved it! But why in the world—"

The door opened and Richards said, with a sniff that disapproved of late-night comings and goings and especially of this brash young man, "Mr. Winston Churchill, my lord."

"I'm afraid your mother has gone to bed, Winston," Kate said. "She was very tired."

"It's not my mother I've come to see," Winston replied. "I've come because—" He shifted from one foot to the other, awkwardly. "That is, I've come to tell you—I mean—"

"For God's sake, Winston," Charles said impatiently. "Spit it out, will you? We don't have all night."

Winston bowed his head. "I've come because I know the identity of the extortionist," he said in a tone that sounded almost humble, "and his motive. I was hoping to keep the thing from Mother by getting her away, but I see now how foolish that was, and how... well, *cowardly* of me. I have behaved in a self-centered and entirely dishonorable way, and I confess to being utterly ashamed of myself. I am the guilty party, you see. The culpability lies with me." He brought his heels together, lifted his chin, and squared his shoulders as if he were facing a firing squad. "It's time the ugly truth was brought out into the open—and the sad business brought to a close."

36

"When one is in love one begins by deceiving one's self. And one ends by deceiving others. That is what the world calls a romance."

Oscar Wilde
A Woman of No Importance, 1893

HANDED THE ENVELOPE by a messenger as he came off the cricket field behind the Royal Hospital in Chelsea, Lieutenant Cornwallis-West wiped his face with a towel and went to sit down on a wooden bench. He was still breathing hard from the exertion, but as he held Jennie's lavender-scented note in his hand, he breathed harder, and his heart began to pound at a fearsome rate. It could only be a reply to his plea for forgiveness, and he turned it over in his fingers with a deep trepidation.

What would she say? If she rejected him, he really did not know what he would do. Could there be some other man? Yes, most likely. And probably Winston was urging her to turn him away. Winston certainly didn't like him, nor did Jack, and both of them would give anything if Jennie would abandon her interest in him. Or was she so frightfully confounded by this other business—this gruesome Finch affair—that she could not think which way to go? He already deeply regretted having meddled in the matter, fearing that his efforts had done his cause more harm than good. But couldn't she see that he was the only person on earth who could save her from the mire of that dreadful Cleveland Street affair?

Well, there was nothing to do but read what she had to say. He ripped open the envelope, pulled out the note, and read it swiftly, his heart leaping with a lover's joy as he began to take it all in. Yes, he was forgiven! Yes, she loved him! Yes, a future lay before them, bright with the promise of true love! Now the way lay clear to his proposal, and perhaps in a few months, Lady Randolph would call herself Mrs. George Cornwallis-West, and he would be the husband of the most beautiful woman in the land.

George closed his eyes and held the note against the sweaty front of his cricket shirt, imagining the ecstasy of being married to Jennie. But it was only a moment before the romantic dream of the future began to give way to the practical realities of the present. If Jennie truly intended to lay open the way to a marriage proposal, he would have to speak to his father and mother immediately.

And *that* prospect was enough to bring him down to earth with a thump, for he could easily imagine what his father and mother were going to say to the idea of his marrying Lady Randolph. They had already made their views on the subject quite plain, especially with regard to his obligation to marry for money. No matter how he protested, they were absolutely set on his getting his hands on Mary Golet's fortune in order to ease the family's debts and mortgages. It wasn't enough that they had married his older sister to the Prince of Pless's fortunes and had their eye on the Duke of Westminster for the younger. Now they wanted him to marry money and use it to redeem the dreadful situation they were in.

But he did not intend to marry for money, and they should have to be disabused of that thought and be reconciled to Jennie. And when Ruthin Castle and the Denbighshire holdings came to him, he meant to sell, family sentiment or no. The estate was heavily encumbered, but it should fetch enough—a hundred thousand pounds, perhaps—to take care of him and Jennie. In the meantime, he should have to leave the Guards, for while he loved the freedom and excitement of a Guardsman's life, he could never support a wife, especially such a wife as Jennie, on a Guardsman's pay. Winston had put it to him bluntly, only a few days before: "Love starves on an empty stomach." George could only agree, of course, and if his family would not help to support him and Jennie, he would go to his Bond Street friends and see if they could not point the way toward a few firms that might pay him well for the use of his name on their directors' roster. And he could probably think of something else in the way of business, although he certainly did not have much head for it.

At the thought of Winston, George frowned darkly. He was confident that he could bring his father and even his mother around eventually, but Winston— that peremptory, impertinent, and pugnacious *boy*— was quite another matter. Jennie's son had taken an aggressive dislike to him and seized every possible opportunity to come between him and his mother. In fact, George suspected him of whispering malicious lies to Jennie about his innocent friendships with other women, in a brazen effort to drive them apart. And Jenny, for all her lovely virtues, had one dreadful flaw: she could not say no to her son. Whatever Winston wanted, his mother moved heaven and earth to get for him.

George sat quite still, chewing on the ends of his handsome gold mustache. Yes, it was entirely possible that Winston, with his diabolical scheming and intrigue, would yet step in and snatch his dream away.

37

"The efforts which we make to escape from our destiny only serve to lead us into it."

Ralph Waldo Emerson
Fate

THE OFFICE OF *The Anglo-Saxon Review* was on the fourth floor of a four-story building, and Manfred Raeburn, a pigeon-fancier from his youth, was in the habit of raising the window sash to the top and spreading a handful of grain on the sill for the birds. They, in turn, had learned to expect this generous offering, and came by the dozens to accept it, filling the morning air with the eager whirr of their wings. This morning, Manfred was captured by a particularly handsome gray-green bird with a green bill, pink feet, and a distinctive pattern of iridescent purple on its flight feathers. It reminded him of the pigeons that he and his brother Arthur had raised in the loft they had built behind the barn in Shropshire so long ago, and its soft cooing brought back a surge of memories. Arthur at eight, laughing with delight, his favorite pigeon perched on his hand. Arthur at fourteen, hanging a newly won blue ribbon around the neck of one of his birds. Arthur at nineteen, triumphantly hanging his Hussars sword at his hip. Arthur at twenty, hanging—

Manfred shut his eyes. This was not the way to begin the morning, especially when he had several important things to do. Or perhaps it was, for it was the memory of Arthur, hanging limp from the rafter of the barn, that drove him to do what he had done, what he was doing now. He turned from the window, took off his tweed coat and draped it on the coat rack to the right of the door. Then he poured himself another cup of tea from the pot he had brewed earlier and sat down at his desk, where he took a Turkish cigarette from the leather holder his sister had given him, lit it, and leaned back.

He sat thus for a few moments, smoking and thinking, mentally scanning his scheme for its flaws. Then, finding none—or at least none so substantial that they might scuttle the mission, he reached for a piece of flimsy and turned to insert it into the typewriter that sat at his elbow. Without hesitation, he pushed up his cuffs and set to work with the practiced skill of a journalist who spends a fair portion of his day at the keyboard.

Hunched over the typewriter in his shirtsleeves, a cigarette hanging from his lower lip, his forehead puckered in a frown of concentration, Manfred Raeburn should have seemed to any who entered the office the very picture of a young literary man driven by the dream of making a name for himself: hard-working, diligent, ambitious. In fact, the casual observer, glancing from the gold desk plaque engraved with the words "Managing Editor" to the impressive stack of letters from such writers as Rudyard Kipling, H.G. Wells, and

Henry James, might justifiably conclude that this very young man had already achieved something of success and importance on the London literary scene, and predict that, with the help of Lady Randolph Churchill, he should surely achieve more. Manfred Raeburn, such an observer might remark, should call himself a fortunate young man. A happy and secure young man. A young man who had already climbed halfway up the ladder of success.

But the one person on this earth who knew Manfred Raeburn intimately—his sister Maude—would see in his posture and in his face something else, something that would deeply worry her. In the furrow between his eyes, in the constant nervous chewing of his lower lip, in his close-bitten nails, she might read his desperation, his mounting anger. And knowing all too well what unhappy ghosts haunted his past, she might worry about her brother's present intensity of expression, the tension between his shoulders, the fierceness with which he attacked the typewriter. Apprehensive for his health, she might have tried to lure him away from the office, might have pleaded with him to come to Shropshire for the weekend, might even have attempted to get him to accompany her on a trip to Egypt or America.

But Maude, the only person on earth who knew and loved Manfred, was not here. There were only the cooing pigeons on the sill of the open window, only the shouts and the clatter of vehicles rising up from the street four floors below, only the footstep on the landing and the creak of the door opening—

Manfred looked up from his work, squinting through the cigarette smoke that wreathed around his head. The gentleman standing on the other side of the desk wore a neatly trimmed brown beard, a brown tweed lounge coat, and brown wool waistcoat and exquisitely tailored trousers. His bowler hat was under his arm and he carried a walking stick.

"Good morning, Raeburn," he said.

Startled, Manfred recognized Lord Charles Sheridan. What the devil was he doing here? Some silly errand for Lady Randolph, no doubt. Damned impolite of him to have barged in without even the courtesy of a knock. But Manfred had learned not to reveal his true feelings in such situations. He snatched the cigarette out of his mouth, stood, and said in a deferential tone, "Good morning, m'lord. I'm afraid you've caught me with my nose to the grindstone." He paused. "Is there something I may get for you? There's tea, if you like."

"Thank you, no." Lord Sheridan took the leather chair opposite, crossed one leg over the other, and balanced his bowler on one knee. "Just give me a moment, if you will." He took out his pipe and tobacco and set to work in a leisurely manner, filling his pipe.

Still standing, Manfred watched him, increasingly unsure of himself. What did Sheridan want? Why had he come? He could feel the hostility rising within him and the despair that always came with it when he was in the presence of gentlemen like Lord Sheridan, the painful understanding that he was the wrong sort and that no matter how hard he tried, he could never belong. It had been the same way in the regiment, when he and Arthur had passed all the military tests with flying colors, met or surpassed every requirement, only to fail before the highest hurdle of all, the hurdle of social status. That was why Arthur—

Manfred tightened his jaw. No, none of that now. What did this man *want*?

When Sheridan had finished tamping the tobacco, he lit it and then glanced up, as if suddenly remembering Manfred's presence.

"Oh, sorry," he said. "Do sit down, Raeburn. I want to ask you a few questions."

Manfred resisted the urge to thumb his nose at this manifestation of arrogance and impoliteness. Still standing, he said, in a markedly cooler tone, "Questions? About what?"

Looking past him, out the window, Sheridan pulled on his pipe. "About Tom Finch."

Manfred felt his knees suddenly go weak. "Tom... Finch? I don't believe I know..." He sat down, trying to collect himself, muttering the name several times. Then: "Oh, right," he said, as if he had just remembered. "Tom Finch. He's a photographer, isn't he? When I was over at the *New Review,* he brought some of his work for us to have a look at. Of course, the *New Review* didn't go in for that sort of thing, but I felt he had a certain style—" He knew he was rattling on, and forced himself to stop. "Why do you ask?"

Sheridan did not answer the question. Instead, he uncrossed his legs and put his hat on the floor. Then he took out his wallet and removed two newspaper clippings, placing them in front of him, the edges precisely touching. "Because," he said, "he is dead."

Manfred's stomach lurched. "Dead?" He swallowed. He could not read the clippings upside down, but they looked like—he swallowed again, and said, more loudly. "What do you mean, 'dead'?"

Again, no answer. Again, into the wallet. Without

looking up, Sheridan took out two typewritten notes and laid them on either side of the clippings, just touching, just so, as if they were playing cards.

Manfred's eyes were fixed on the notes. "What," he heard himself asking hollowly, "are... those?"

"They are demand notes received by Lady Randolph in the past few days," Sheridan replied. He reached into the side pocket of his coat. "Tom Finch was in the unsavory business of photographing people— particularly important people whom he caught *flagrante delicto*, as it were, in the midst of unwise acts. He claimed to have such a photograph of Lord Randolph Churchill, with one of the victims of the Ripper killings—a woman named Mary Kelly. He was using it to blackmail Lady Randolph." From his pocket, he took out a Manilla envelope from which he extracted a photograph, placing it above the notes and clippings.

"Blackmail!" Manfred exclaimed, trying not to look at the photograph. His voice was high and thin, and he heard it as if from a great distance. "Why, I call that shocking! Poor Lady Randolph! Why would anyone do such a—"

"At some point," Sheridan continued, in his precise, dry voice, "another party learned of the photograph and felt that he could put it to a better use. Finch, however, had already had a change of heart. He wrote to Lady Randolph to tell her that he would no longer annoy her with his demand letters and to offer her the negatives."

"To offer her—" Manfred heard his voice crack and the words fail.

"Exactly," Sheridan said. "However, before Finch could make good on his intentions, the other party learned of his plans. They fell out, and Finch got the worst of it.

The police found him face-down in his shepherd's pie with a knife between his shoulder blades. His murderer made off with one or more prints of the photograph."

Someone made a choking noise. It might have been Manfred, but he wasn't listening. He was trying to weigh the likelihood that Sheridan was guessing. The man did not sound at all speculative—but where had he come by his information?

"What the other party did not know, however," Sheridan went on, "was that the photograph for which he killed Finch was a forgery, and that the negatives used to construct it were hidden in a photographic studio elsewhere on Cleveland Street."

"A... forgery?" Manfred's words were a whisper, and he scarcely heard them. Involuntarily, his hand had gone across the desk for the photograph. He pulled it back.

Sheridan turned the photo and pushed it toward Manfred. "Exactly. It was a rather clever forgery, you see—clever enough to have deceived Lady Randolph and clever enough to have taken in Finch's killer. However, the negatives have been recovered from Finch's studio, and clearly reveal how he fabricated it."

"I—I—" Manfred's throat was too dry to continue. He seized his cup and swallowed some tea. "I don't see why you—"

"Why I have come to you?" Sheridan asked. With the tip of his finger, he pushed the two typewritten notes across the desk. "Because these notes were typed on that machine at your elbow." He paused and added gently, "And since you are the only occupant of this office, it is logical to assume that you typed them. Wouldn't you agree?"

Manfred turned to stare at the typewriter, as if he had never seen it before. "On *this* machine?" Now he was sure that Sheridan was guessing. There was no possible way he could know—

"Yes." Sheridan took a pencil from the cup on the desk and pointed to a line in one of the notes. "The lowercase *o* is slightly defective. You can see that it is flat at the bottom." He paused. "If you cannot make it out, I shall be glad to offer you my hand-lens."

Manfred found it suddenly very difficult to see the notes on the desk in front of him. He blinked to bring them into focus, but they were still a blur.

Sheridan went on, relentlessly logical. "And if you are inclined to point out that this demonstration proves only that the two notes came from the same machine, consider this." Out came the wallet again, and a third typed note, the commendatory one Manfred had written to Lady Randolph about Beryl Bardwell's short story. "You can see the same flattened *o*," Sheridan said, pointing. "This note has your signature on it." He nodded toward the typewriter. "And if I'm not mistaken, the paper in the machine at the moment is the very same yellow flimsy you used for the second demand note."

There was a long silence, and then Manfred heard himself saying: "But anyone could have come into this room and typed those blackmail notes on this machine." The suggestion sounded thin and unconvincing, even to him.

"But not everyone had a motive," Sheridan said gravely. He rose and turned, just as the door opened and Churchill strode in, a few paces ahead of a police officer in a blue serge uniform.

Without preamble, Churchill said, "I've come to tell

you that I'm awfully sorry for what I did, Raeburn."

Manfred was struck dumb, and the despair washed through him like a bitter flood. They not only knew that he had killed Finch and tried to blackmail Lady Randolph, but they knew why, and their knowledge robbed him of everything. There was nothing left of his plan for revenge, nothing left of his hopes, nothing left of his future. It was gone. All gone. He half turned toward the window, where the bird with the iridescent feathers had come back to peck at the remaining bits of grain. Such a beautiful bird, Arthur's bird, its feathers sleek and glistening—

Sheridan was looking at Churchill. "I want Raeburn to hear the whole thing, Winston," he said. "Everything you told me last night."

Manfred heard Churchill's words through a great roaring in his ears. "Ragging you and your brother was unforgivable of me," he was saying, "and I shall be haunted by my actions for the rest of my life. I want you to know that I am heartily sorry, Raeburn. I could not know that what I and the others did might lead to your brother's suicide, but if it is of any help to you, I have thought of myself with a deep loathing every day since his death. If only I could go back and undo what we—"

"Stop 'im!" the officer cried. " 'Ee's jumpin'!"

Manfred heard that, too. But he had already swung one leg over the windowsill, and the desk was between the three of them and himself. They could not reach him in time. He cast one last glance at the pigeon as it flew up and away, and then he was over the edge and falling free.

38

"Man Dies in Fall from Window

Pigeon-Fancier Suffers Fatal Accident

Mr. Manfred Raeburn, Managing Editor of *The Anglo-Saxon Review*, fell to his death from the fourth-floor window of his office on Thursday morning. According to witnesses, he was intent on feeding pigeons at the window-sill when he lost his balance and fell to the street below. Lady Randolph Churchill, Editor of the *Review*, expressed deep sorrow at his passing. 'He was a talented and capable editor,' she said. 'It will be difficult to replace him.' Mr. Raeburn is survived only by his sister, Miss Maude Raeburn of Queensway, Bayswater."

The Times,
18 November, 1898

KATE KNOCKED AT the door of Maude Raeburn's apartments, which occupied the second floor of a brick building in Bayswater—not a fashionable address, but clean and well-kept. Miss Raeburn herself, wearing a loose caftan dyed in dark greens and purples, opened the door.

"Good afternoon, Lady Charles," she said. She did not seem surprised, nor embarrassed, at the prospect of receiving a visitor in something other than mourning garb.

"I've come to pay my respects," Kate said, "and to tell you how sorry I am about your brother's death."

"Thank you," Miss Raeburn said. "Do come in and have a cup of tea."

She led the way down a hall hung with framed photographs of herself and other women in walking and cycling costumes, posed before various mountains and lakes and pyramids. The small parlor into which they went was crowded with exotic furnishings and souvenirs of foreign countries: a vase of ostrich feathers, an African mask, a stuffed bird in a glass case, a large pottery urn filled with carved walking sticks. There were several shelves full of smaller pieces of pottery with a variety of glazes, and baskets of all shapes and sizes. The air was filled with the exotic scent of some foreign incense.

"I'll be just a moment," Miss Raeburn said, and disappeared. Kate sat on a velvet settee in front of the parlor fire, looking around, and after a few moments, Miss Raeburn returned with a black-lacquered tray. She poured tea out of a red porcelain pot decorated with Oriental designs into small cups without handles. Apart from her exotic garb, she looked much as she had the night she and her brother had dined at Sibley House, but was much more subdued and somber. And now that Kate studied her more closely, she realized that the woman was older than she had thought—in her mid-thirties, perhaps. She was certainly several years older than her brother.

"Lady Randolph asked me to convey her condolences," Kate said, sipping the tea. It had a strange taste but was very pleasant, and the flaky Greek pastries Miss Raeburn offered had a honey-rich flavor. "She wanted to come with me, but under the circumstances—" she hesitated, half-wishing she hadn't begun the sentence.

"I'm sorry for what Mannie did," Miss Raeburn said, "and for any injury he caused Lady Randolph. But there are two sides to the story, you know. Mannie was wrong, but he acted out of a great injury. Forgive me for speaking bluntly," she added, setting the tea tray to one side and settling herself in a large rattan chair. Her voice was matter-of-fact, without inflection. "I'm afraid I don't know how to speak of it other than frankly. It's no good brushing it under the rug, is it?"

"I should like to hear the other side of the story," Kate said. "And perhaps it might help you to speak of it. I understand that you are all alone, now that your brother has died."

"You *are* kind," Miss Raeburn said. She gave Kate a sideways glance. "I admire your novels, you know. I particularly enjoyed the one in which the heroine flies around the world in a balloon. You are quite clever. Adventurous, too. You Americans are always adventurous."

Kate was glad that an answer did not seem required.

"I am something of a writer and adventuress myself," Miss Raeburn went on, gathering speed. "Travel pieces for magazines and newspapers, chiefly. I also give magic lantern lectures for the benefit of women who secretly wish they could abandon their husbands and children and go jaunting off to other countries in the company of adventuresome women." She sat for a moment, the firelight glinting in her light hair, and then said, more slowly and in a different, softer tone, "And yes, I am alone now, entirely alone. My mother has been dead for some years, and my father—he was a farmer in Shropshire—died of grief after Arthur's death."

"Arthur was your brother?"

"Yes. He hanged himself in Father's barn." Kate could hear the bitterness that crept into Maude Raeburn's voice. "After he and Mannie were driven out of the Hussars. That was his dream, you know. Arthur lived for the adventure of soldiering."

"I'm so dreadfully sorry," Kate said quietly. "It must have been awful for you."

Miss Raeburn gave a little nod of acknowledgment. "But life goes on," she said. "At least, it has done for me. Father couldn't bear the disgrace. And Mannie—" She turned her head. "I'm not surprised he chose his own solution."

Kate took a breath. "The men who were there, my husband, Winston Churchill, the policeman—they tried to stop him, but they couldn't reach him in time."

There was another long silence, and then Miss Raeburn said, "Mannie loved Arthur more than anything in his life. They dreamed of a military life together—brother officers gloriously defending the far-flung borders of the Empire." She laughed, sadly. "From the time they were children, that was all they ever talked of. Father tried to tell them that it was nonsense, that farmers' sons could never be officers, but they wouldn't listen. They would saddle Father's draft horses and ride out across the meadow with long, heavy sticks for lances, pretending to be cavalry officers leading their regiment to relieve General Gordon. Then Uncle Oliver died—he was my mother's brother and had made a small fortune as a bicycle manufacturer—and left Arthur and Mannie three hundred a year each. They insisted on using the money to enter Harrow. Father pointed out that a military career was beyond their reach, that the money would be barely enough to keep a horse and pay mess bills, but eventually he gave in. So Harrow it was, and then Sandhurst." Her lips quirked. "Harrow is where they had their first skirmish with the Little Napoleon."

"That was their name for Winston?" Kate asked.

"Oh, not just theirs—everyone's! He was such a bossy, arrogant boy, so impressed with himself. No one liked him, you see, while Arthur and Mannie had any number of friends. I daresay there was more than a bit of jealousy there, and worse at Sandhurst. Arthur was gifted in military strategy, and easily bested Winston on the examination. Mannie was quite a strong horseman, and snatched the riding prize out of the Little Napoleon's fingers."

"I see," Kate said gravely. Knowing how competitive Winston was, how he measured his own worth against the performances of others, she could begin to understand his animosity toward the Raeburn brothers.

Miss Raeburn eyed her. "Are you sure you want to hear any more of this? It's sordid—in its way. Oh, nothing like a crime, I mean," she added. "Just your ordinary gentlemen's bullying and brutality."

"I want to hear it," Kate said. "I want to understand."

Miss Raeburn nodded. "Well, then. Somehow, Arthur and Mannie got into the Fourth Hussars and found themselves at Aldershot. But it was very like belonging to a gentlemen's club. In addition to keeping a batman and groom, they had to pay for coach subscriptions, band subscriptions, theatricals, a wine cellar, even a pack of hounds. Not to speak of their uniforms and kits, which came to something over seven hundred apiece."

Kate gave a smothered exclamation. She had known that it required money to enter the military, but she had no idea how much.

"Indeed," Miss Raeburn said dryly. "It was completely ridiculous, but they couldn't see it. They were so pleased to have been commissioned into the Fourth. Their fellow second-lieutenants weren't at all pleased, however, because of course Arthur and Mannie weren't gentlemen. They were asked, politely at first, to resign their commissions. When they refused, they were bullied and badgered. They never went to sleep in a dry bed, their possessions were smashed and pilfered, and they were flogged and held head-down in a horse trough, where Arthur nearly drowned. The end came when they returned from exercises one day to find their bags packed and loaded onto a cart. Mannie tried to convince Arthur to stay and brave it out, but he was a sensitive young man, and was completely broken. He resigned his commission that day. Two days later, he was dead."

"But what about the commandant?" Kate exclaimed. "What about the upper levels of command? Didn't anybody see what was going on? Couldn't they *stop* it?"

"Why?" Miss Raeburn asked, with a toss of her head. "The ideal of the 'brotherhood of officers' exists at all levels. If a man isn't of the right sort, he doesn't belong, and the sooner he realizes that and gets out, the better."

Her lips had an ironic twist. "Perhaps that is hard for you to understand, being an American."

"Perhaps," Kate said. She frowned. "You didn't mention Winston Churchill. Was he involved in the bullying?"

"There were four or five others, but he was the ringleader," Miss Raeburn said shortly. "The worst and cruelest of the snobs."

Kate was not surprised at Maude Raeburn's opinion. But she felt she had to say something in Winston's defense. "I think," she said, "that young Mr. Churchill's military service has changed him."

"Do you? I don't. I believe that he is using the Army as a platform for a political career—a career which he can scarcely finance, any more than my brothers could finance their cavalry commissions. And I certainly didn't find anything in his military reporting to suggest that Mr. Churchill is anything but manifestly ambitious for himself and willing to sacrifice others to gain his own ends." Miss Raeburn fell silent for a moment, staring at the fire. "God help England if he should succeed in his ambitions. Can you imagine the consequences if that young man should be called to serve with the Cabinet, or as Prime Minister?" She shuddered.

After that, there was hardly anything more to say. A few moments later, Kate murmured her goodbyes and left. As she walked down the street toward Bayswater Road to hail a cab, she reflected on the course of events, the terrible chain of causality that had led from a boy's jealousy at Harrow and Sandhurst, to a young man's bullying at Aldershot, to a suicide in Shropshire, thence to a murder in Cleveland Street and finally to another suicide in Fleet Street. Arthur Raeburn had died by his own hand. Manfred Raeburn, bent on avenging his brother, had killed Tom Finch to obtain the photograph he intended to use to destroy Winston's political ambitions. And now Manfred was dead. Was that the final conclusion? Had they arrived at the end of the terrible trail?

39

"The comfortable estate of widowhood is the only hope that keeps up a wife's spirits."

JOHN GAY
The Beggar's Opera
1728

SARAH PRATT STOOD beside Mr. Hodge in the morning room, her hands clasped and her head bowed, as he began his recital to her ladyship. The tragic story seemed to go on endlessly, from Dick Pratt's first astonishing appearance at the kitchen door, to his demands for food, drink, and clothing, and finally, to his sudden, shocking death.

"He *drowned*?" Lady Charles asked, in a horrified tone.

"He was attempting to cross the Stour by walking across the lock gates," Mr. Hodge said with a disapproving frown. "It was a very foolish thing to do, for the man was so apparently inebriated that he could scarcely stand, much less balance himself. This is according to one of his drinking partners," he added. "Once in the water, I fear he was doomed. He was encumbered by Lord Charles's riding boots, which he obtained from this house by extortion."

Her ladyship shook her head. "What an irony," she said sadly.

Sarah Pratt was not sure what iron had to do with it since the boots were made of leather, but it did seem to her to be eminently just that Pratt's greed for drink *and fine boots* should have sunk him. She had been enormously relieved when she discovered that Pratt had indeed died by drowning (rather than rat poison) and that the constable had come to escort her to the jail so that she could identify the mortal remains. Still, her relief had been colored by her consciousness of her own dreadful guilt, and she could not feel easy until she confessed her thefts to Mr. Hodge, who had been quite stern with her, as he should. And to her ladyship as well, with a true remorse for her theft.

But Lady Charles, having now heard the entire story, was not stern. She turned to Sarah with a sympathetic look. "I am so sorry, Mrs. Pratt, that you have lost your husband."

"Oh, please don't be sorry, your ladyship!" Sarah burst out. " 'Ee was a bad man an' got wot 'ee deserved." She could not say how glad she was to have been returned to the comfortable estate of widowhood, but she could say something else. She twisted her hands, her voice breaking. "I'm so dreadf'lly sorry to've took wot didn't b'long t' me, on 'is account. It wuz wrong o' me, very wrong!"

"Yes, it was wrong, Mrs. Pratt," Mr. Hodge said firmly. "And it was wrong to lie to your employer about your situation. I think, under the circumstances—"

Sarah was never to know exactly what Mr. Hodge

thought because Lady Charles interrupted him, in a gentler tone. "I think, under the circumstances, that Mrs. Pratt's earlier marital condition should best be forgotten. And it is no great crime to give food and drink and clothing to the poor and needy—in fact, I recall the vicar exhorting us to exactly that endeavor not two Sundays ago." She smiled. "But I do hope that in future, Mrs. Pratt, you will not hide your light under a bushel, as it were. When you offer gifts of food from our kitchen, please make Mr. Hodge aware of your good works."

"Oh, yer ladyship, yes, yer ladyship," Sarah cried eagerly. "Oh, I *will*, yer ladyship, I—"

"Thank you, Sarah," Lady Charles said. She turned to Mr. Hodge. "With regard to our kitchen staff—"

"I'm afraid I have bad news, m'lady," Mr. Hodge said. He cleared his throat, not looking at Sarah. "Mary Plumm has given her notice. In fact, she has already left."

"My goodness," Lady Charles said, with some surprise. "She didn't last long."

"I think," Mr. Hodge said carefully, "that on balance she was not an entirely suitable person for the position. She was—" he cleared his throat again. "I am sorry to say, m'lady, that she was quite impertinent to me, when I had occasion to remonstrate with her about walking out late last night with one of the stableboys. And while Mrs. Pratt herself showed great forbearance with the young person, I hardly think that she was a helpful addition to the kitchen staff."

Sarah could not have said how grateful she was to Mr. Hodge for keeping to himself the whole circumstance of Mary Plumm's explosive departure. She did not want her ladyship to know that she had allowed herself to be manipulated by a mere kitchen maid, and that she had given in to the girl's blackmail. With a warm look at Mr. Hodge, she said, "It don't matter if it takes a week or two t' find another maid. I kin do th' work by myself." The fact was that she had been doing it herself for the past week, with a heavy dose of Mary Plumm's insolence to boot.

"Your cooperation is commendable, Mrs. Pratt," Lady Charles said, "but I should like to offer an alternative. I have just received a post from a young lady I met in London. Her name is Ellie. To be quite honest, she has ambitions for the stage and might not be with us long, but she strikes me as a willing worker. And if she has another trade besides acting, she might find life a bit easier. Will you give her a chance?"

On an earlier day, Sarah Pratt might have expressed her dismay at being asked to teach an aspiring actress how to make potato crulles and strain the soup. But today she was so full of gratitude toward her employer and Mr. Hodge that she bobbed her head and exclaimed, "O' course, yer ladyship! A chance she shall have! I'll do my best t' see that she learns an' does a good job an'—"

"Thank you, Mrs. Pratt," Lady Charles said, smiling. "And thank you, as well, for the loan of your clothing. It was very kind of you to allow Lady Randolph and me to make off with your best hat in the rain. It served us well. By way of thanks, Lady Randolph has sent you this, from her very own wardrobe." And with that, her ladyship produced a fancy cardboard hatbox, with the words "Paquin's Distinctive Parisian Millinery."

Distinctive Parisian millinery! Sarah could scarcely draw her breath. She took the box with trepidation, lifted the lid, and peeked at the marvel of pink tulle and silk roses inside. "Oh, yer ladyship," she breathed, "it's beautiful! I'll wear it t' chapel on Sunday, I will." Then she felt a surge of disappointment, remembering Dick Pratt, scarcely cold in his grave. "Oh, but I can't. It's too gay fer a widow."

The corners of Lady Charles's mouth quirked. "Put it away for a time, then. Since your husband was absent for a *very* long while, I don't think you should be expected to observe an extended period of mourning."

One more peek, and Sarah closed the lid. "Yes, yer ladyship," she said somberly, but inside, her heart was singing.

"Very well, Mrs. Pratt," Lady Charles said. "You may go, and I shall send Ellie to you directly."

Still whispering her thanks, Sarah took her box and departed.

Authors' Notes

"In endeavouring to sift a mystery like this, one cannot afford to throw aside any theory, however extravagant, without careful examination, because the truth might, after all, lie in the most unlikely one."

Pall Mall Gazette
December 1888

Bill Albert writes about the Whitechapel murders:

Writing an historical mystery is not the easiest task in the world. Writing a mystery that contains an unsolved historic mystery is even more difficult, especially if the writers intend to explore a possible solution. And when that historic mystery is the infamous serial murders of Jack the Ripper—about which dozens of books and many hundreds of articles have been written—that difficulty is further compounded.

Susan and I have not attempted to "prove" a particular theory of the Whitechapel murders of 1888. However, Ripperologists (as students of the Ripper killings playfully style themselves) will immediately recognize that our approach to the solution of these murders is not original with us. It is based on a group of related theories advanced over the last twenty-five years by five British writers:

Paul Bonner, Elwyn Jones, and John Lloyd of the BBC, in their research for the 1973 television docudrama, *Jack the Ripper,* uncovered the existence of Joseph Sickert, the son of Walter Sickert, who repeated the stories about the killings that he said his father had told him. The BBC research is documented in the book, *The Ripper File,* published in 1973.

Stephen Knight, writing in 1976, presents a compelling case against a group of Masonic murderers, including Sir William Gull, who acted on behalf of the Crown to conceal Prince Eddy's marriage to a Roman Catholic commoner. This is the story, essentially, that Walter Sickert tells Charles in Chapter Thirty-Two. Knight also argues for a massive cover-up at the highest levels of the police and the government, and includes information about the clairvoyant Robert Lees, whom Kate and Jennie meet in Chapter Twenty.

Melvyn Fairclough, author of *The Ripper and the Royals,* proposes that the leader of the Ripper gang of Freemasons was Lord Randolph Churchill. The most persuasive evidence he offers for this accusation is a letter from Detective Inspector Frederick Abberline to G.J. Goschen, Chancellor of the Exchequer, naming Churchill and Gull as co-conspirators. Like Knight and the BBC researchers, Fairclough also relies on the recollections of Joseph Sickert.

We have treated these true-crime works as historical references and have endeavored to make our fiction consistent with the facts the authors compile and present.

Having said that we do not offer an original solution; however, I also have to say that as theories go, the Masonic conspiracy theory seems to us highly plausible, especially given the symbolic nature of the mutilations, which is itself powerful evidence for Masonic involvement. The chief argument against the theory—that a gang of "gentlemen Jacks" could not have successfully pulled off the crimes under the noses of the police—is countered by evidence that Chief Commissioner Warren and Assistant Commissioner Anderson (both advanced Freemasons) were involved in a cover-up that began and ended in the Cabinet. Other arguments (that Gull was incapacitated at the time by a stroke and that Walter Sickert and J.K. Stephen were themselves members of the Ripper gang) can either be rebutted or do not substantially contradict the basic theory. What is more, no one has ever satisfactorily explained how a single lunatic Jack could possess (all at once) the motivation to commit the killings, the skill and medical knowledge needed to perform what amounted to surgical operations under primitive field conditions, the foresight to organize the murders, and the physical strength to transport four corpses from unidentified murder sites to the places where they were discovered. The question of why the killings stopped so abruptly after the murder of Mary Kelly is also troubling, if one is arguing for a serial killer without a rational motive. Altogether, it seems to us that the Masonic conspiracy theory has a great deal going for it.

But we are novelists, not detectives or true-crime writers. Among the dozens of possible approaches to the solution of the Ripper crime, we adopted the one that fitted most neatly into our main story line. For us, the primary attraction of the Masonic conspiracy theory—especially as it is presented by Melvyn Fairclough—was that it proposed Randolph Churchill as one of the Rippers. It provided a stage upon which we could confront our characters—Jennie and Winston Churchill—with a frightening threat to the Churchill family reputation, and see how they might act to protect themselves and each other.

Susan Albert writes about Jennie and Winston Churchill:

Jennie Churchill is one of the most interesting women of her time. She was the daughter of an American stock speculator, the wife of a renegade aristocrat, and the mother (and chief cheerleader) of one of Britain's most remarkable and controversial political figures. She was probably the lover of the Prince of Wales, certainly the long-time lover of a handsome Hungarian count (Count Charles Kinsky), and the beloved of too many men to count.

Apart from these relationships, however, Jennie defined herself by doing, after the age of forty-five, things that other women did not do at all. She started a literary magazine (1898); obtained, funded, and outfitted an internationally sponsored hospital ship to serve men wounded in the Boer War (the *Maine*, 1899); wrote a memoir and several plays (1907-1910); and developed an Elizabethan theme park in the middle of London (1911), complete with a jousting tourney and full-size replica of one of Drake's famous galleons. Yes, she did indeed marry young George (1900), but the romantic marriage could not survive her fiscal extravagances and her husband's emotional extravaganzas.

In his memoir, George wrote that he "found it a bit thick" to have to pay for a barouche that Randolph Churchill had purchased nearly twenty years before, while Jennie confided sadly to her sister that she hated having to endure George's passionate affairs with actresses. They divorced in 1913, and George immediately married his current actress. In 1918, Jennie was married again, to Montague Porch, who was even younger than George. In 1921, she forgot Robert Lees' caution about watching her step, put on a pair of new Italian shoes, and fell down a stair, breaking her left leg. Gangrene set in, and the doctor amputated the leg above the knee. Two weeks later, on June 29, 1921, her femoral artery ruptured and Jennie Jerome Churchill died. To Lord Crewe, Winston wrote: "The England in which you met her is a long way off now, & we do not see its like today. I feel a very great sense of deprivation."

Winston Churchill is often seen through the heroic lens of his actions during the Second World War, and people of our generation feel a particular affection for his courageous leadership in the face of the German threat. In this book, however, we were interested in an earlier Winston: the arrogant, ambitious, and opportunistic young man who had far more enemies than friends and whose impatience to get ahead created one furor after another. As an officer in training at Aldershot, Winston had a disgraceful record of pranksterism, race-fixing, and hazing. (Our fictional story about the bullying of Arthur and Manfred Raeburn is modeled on a similar incident that took place in 1896. The Bruce-Pryce affair ended in a lawsuit, rather than a suicide, however.) In India and Egypt, Winston made enemies by criticizing the military judgments of his senior officers in his newspaper dispatches and in *The Malakand Field Force* and *The River War*. (Winston took Charles's advice and changed the title.) In South Africa, during an escape from a Boer War prison camp, he used his brother prisoners shamefully. Through all his early years as a soldier, he was accused of being a medal hunter and a "glory hound" and of exploiting his Army experiences to launch and finance a political career.

Churchill was elected to Parliament as a Conservative, but that alliance didn't last long. In 1904, amid a great hoopla and hubbub, he crossed the floor to join the Liberals, and when they came into power a short time later, he was invited to join the Colonial Office. At the time, he was writing a biography of his adored father, Randolph, which Winston's own biographer calls "one of the most systematic whitewashings that any biographer ever attempted." In 1910, he was named Home Secretary, a Cabinet position that gave him access to the police files on the Ripper and would have allowed him to remove any evidence that incriminated his father in the Whitechapel murders. Through the late 1920s and 1930s, Winston and his wife Clementine were often visited at the family home of Chartwell by a famous British Impressionist who taught Winston to paint.

The artist's name was Walter Sickert.

References

Here are a few books that we found helpful in creating *Death at Whitechapel*. Other background works may be found in the references to earlier books in this series. If you have comments or questions, you may write to Bill and Susan Albert, PO Drawer M, Bertram TX 78605, or E-mail us at china@tstar.net. You might also wish to visit our website, http://www.mysterypartners.com.

The British Journal Photographic Almanac & Photographer's Daily Companion. London: Henry Greenwood, 1896 & 1897.

Cannadine, David. *The Decline and Fall of the British Aristocracy.* New Haven: Yale University Press, 1990

Churchill, Peregrine and Mitchell, Julian. *Jennie: Lady Randolph Churchill. A Portrait with Letters.* Glasgow: William Collins Sons & Co., 1974.

Churchill, Winston S. *Frontiers and Wars* (The Malakand Field Force, The River War, London to Ladysmith, Ian Hamilton's March). New York: Konecky and Konecky, 1962.

Churchill, Randolph S. *Winston S. Churchill Volume I Companion Part 1 (1874-1896) and 2 (1896-1900).* London:

William Heinemann Ltd., 1967.

Fairclough, Melvyn. *The Ripper and the Royals*. London: Gerald Duckworth & Co. Ltd., 1991.

Jones, Edgar. *The Penguin Guide to the Railways of Britain*. Harmondsworth, England: Penguin Books Ltd., 1981.

Jones, Elwyn and Lloyd, John. *The Ripper File*. London: Futura Publications Ltd., 1975.

Knight, Stephen. *Jack the Ripper—the Final Solution*. New York: David McKay Company, Inc., 1976.

Manchester, William. *Winston Spencer Churchill: The Last Lion*. New York: Dell Publishing Group, 1989.

Martin, Ralph G. *Jennie: The Life of Lady Randolph Churchill*. Englewood Cliffs, N.J.: Prentice-Hall, Inc., 1972.

Morgan, Ted. *Churchill: Young Man in a Hurry 1874-1915*. New York: Simon & Shuster, Inc., 1982.

Sutton, Denys. *Walter Sickert: A Biography*. London: Michael Joseph, 1976.

Wilson, Colin & Odell, Robin. *Jack the Ripper: Summing up and Verdict*. London: Corgi Books, 1988.

For more information, media enquiries and review copies
please contact > marketing@oldcastlebooks.com